WIXLEY WOOD

WIXLEY WOOD

Paul Knibbs

The Book Guild Ltd
Sussex, England

This book is a work of fiction. The characters and situations in this story are imaginary. No resemblance is intended between these characters and any real persons, either living or dead.

The Book Guild Ltd
25 High Street,
Lewes, Sussex

First published 1998

Set in Baskerville
Typesetting by Acorn Bookwork, Salisbury, Wiltshire

Printed in Great Britain by
Anthony Rowe Ltd, Chippenham, Wiltshire

A catalogue record for this book is
available from the British Library

ISBN 1 85776 208 8

For Ken

Prologue

May

Early morning sunlight filtered through the ancient grove of Wixley Wood, outlining a small, watchful herd of deer.

In the near distance, beyond the silence of the wood and across the meadows lush with new grass, the man in the chequered shirt bent forward and pressed his eye to the clear lens of the theodolite, and the variety of trees loomed large beneath the pale blue sky.

A light breeze ruffled the man's hair as he made his adjustments and noted his findings on a small notepad, before he gathered up the tripod and returned to the small van. The van was inconspicuous, which was just how the man wanted it, and as he stopped briefly to pour himself a mug of hot tea from a large thermos, he managed to appear like any other sightseer or holidaymaker pausing to enjoy the sights and sounds of the countryside.

It was another hour before the man could be seen again, this time on the opposite side of the grand, sweeping wood.

The man straightened up from the tall instrument and made a second table of calculations, which he compared with those he had taken earlier and, satisfied with his conclusions, he returned to his vehicle and within minutes was gone, disappearing along the winding country lanes, and leaving no trace that he had ever been. Deep within the wood, beneath the wide canopies of oak and sycamore, the small group of roe-deer, the young fawns gambolling at their mothers' sides, continued with their quiet rambling through the peaceful, sunlit glades.

Chapter 1

June

Alan De Angelis climbed out of the sunburst-red BMW and crossed the narrow road before pausing to contemplate the small cottage.

The wooden gate to the front of the short pathway was old and hanging by one loose hinge, the paint flaky and shot through with woodworm. The small garden had long been overgrown, and weeds had broken through the gaps between the neatly laid flagstones which formed the pathway. The small two-bedroomed cottage itself looked older than its years, its curtainless windows giving it an eerie quality.

'Lots of work to do,' Alan muttered to himself before pushing the gate open and walking up the path to the front door.

He pushed his key into the lock and opened the door, allowing the musty, stale air from within the cottage to assault his nostrils. Leaving the door open, he walked through the bare hallway and into the small kitchen, where the back door was situated. He inserted a large, cumbersome key into the ancient-looking lock and turned it, having to use more force than he thought would be necessary.

Then Alan pulled the door open and stepped out into the rear garden.

The front garden was a landscaped paradise compared to the veritable jungle at the rear of the cottage. The grass stood a foot high in places, the long winding pathway all but disappearing beneath its onslaught, and the hedges were unpruned and neglected. Alan walked down the path, between the five tall Scots pines which towered above the unruly, almost wild garden, until he reached the lower far end. The pond was dry and surrounded by nettles, and what had once been a waterfall had collapsed into disrepair.

Alan turned and surveyed his new property. The cottage

looked even worse from this side than it did from the front, he thought, as he passed a critical eye over the red tiled roof, which was partly covered with bright green moss.

The lower wooden fence which surrounded the eighty-foot-long garden was old and broken and in places had fallen to the ground, leaving wide gaps through which many a nocturnal animal had made its passage, beating itself a path through the tall, thick grass.

Alan walked slowly back up the garden and, upon re-entering the old cottage, began making his way from room to room, opening the windows as he went. The winding staircase creaked beneath his tread. He opened the side window in the east-facing front bedroom and leaned out, resting his elbows on the weather-beaten sill.

The view was quite wonderful, which was one of the reasons why he had bought the old, run-down cottage in the first place. His view to the River Wix was uninterrupted; there was only a hundred yards between it and the cottage, which was the last in the lane. Beyond the river he could see the sunlit tower of St Mary's Church rising between the cluster of chestnut trees which fought for space in the small churchyard. Looking to his left Alan could see the rooftops at the centre of the village and the tops of the tall sycamore trees that adorned the village green, the lush grass presenting itself to his view in one or two places, peeping in return from between the row of cottages on the far side of the river.

Alan walked out of the small room and crossed the landing leading to the larger west-facing bedroom. Leaning out of this window Alan commanded a view across his own back garden and over the rolling green pastures beyond. To his left, Poachers Hill sat large and serene, the single lane which ran like a vein down its side showing itself fleetingly between the trees and hedgerows that guided its path. Alan took a deep breath of the clean, fresh air, sucking it down into his lungs and then holding it there, savouring its flavour. He looked for all the world like a man at peace.

The first rays of warming sunlight, heralding another bright

June day, filtered through the leafy branches atop the tall oaks of Wixley Wood and passed over the two figures emerging into the open field. The taller of the two, a silk cravat knotted smartly at the throat, reached into the fob pocket of his immaculately tailored scarlet waistcoat and produced a gold hunter.

It was a magnificent timepiece. The lid depicted an English hunting scene, and the face was of flawless ivory.

'Four-thirty,' murmured Fox.

The canine snapped the watch closed and lifted his brush from the lush grass, wet from the early morning dew, before turning towards the slender figure hovering at his elbow.

'A good night's work, I think.'

'Not bad,' sniffed Weasel, from the folds of the camel-hair coat and the long white scarf which hung to his navel, and he peered from beneath the peak of his flat cap in the direction from which they had come.

Fox followed his companion's gaze. 'I think you'll find we were not followed,' he muttered, matter-of-factly.

'Better safe than sorry,' Weasel replied. 'Anyway, I think we should lay off Cobden's chickens for a while,' he continued, as he fingered the two lifeless hens which protruded from his pocket. 'He'll be onto us soon!'

'Perhaps,' Fox replied, non-committally. Fox lifted one of the dead hens from Weasel's pocket and held it up towards the brightening sky and judged it weight appreciatively. 'Three pounds and mine, I think, old man.' Fox flashed his companion a triumphant smile, revealing a long row of pearl white teeth.

'Mine's younger,' Weasel countered, winking up at his partner. 'Anyway, it's time I got on. I'll see you tonight.' He turned to go.

'Perhaps not,' Fox answered. 'Things to do, old boy.'

'Such as?' Weasel demanded, stopping and looking back.

'Affairs of the heart, don't you know.' Fox grinned mischievously, his brush twitching at the tip.

'Oh, I see.' Now it was Weasel's turn to grin. 'Getting laid, are you?'

Fox cocked a lofty eyebrow. 'Certainly not,' he said, turning away and setting out across the field. 'Merely dinner.'

'Who with?' Weasel called.

'With whom!' Fox corrected him. 'Cheerio.'

'Tonight, Foxy,' Weasel cupped his paws to his mouth.

'I said perhaps.' Fox's jaunty stride did not break as he disappeared across the gently rolling field.

'Oh, come on puss.' Jennifer Cobden pouted as she began to realise that no matter how many times she paraded the ball of string in front of Twinkle, there was going to be no moving the ginger tom from the sun-drenched kitchen step.

'You're hopeless!' Jennifer abruptly abandoned her attempts at enticing Twinkle from his lethargy and, after pocketing the small ball of string, she set out across the cobbled farmyard towards the sound of her father working beyond the barn.

'Twinkle's hopeless,' she declared as she approached her father, who was bent over the door to the henhouse. 'All he does is sleep all day,' she said, shielding her eyes from the bright sun as she looked up at her father. Douglas Cobden laid aside the claw hammer he had been using on the henhouse and scooped his daughter up in his arms and placed her on his broad shoulders.

'Well, I expect he's been up all night,' he said, as he broke into a trot across the yard, which sent his daughter's blonde ringlets bouncing around her face.

'Horsey rides,' the seven-year-old squealed delightedly, clinging onto her father's thick black hair. 'I can see for miles from up here, Daddy.'

'I'll bet you can,' replied her father, as he came up short of the kitchen step. 'Now then,' said Douglas darkly, looking down at the sleeping cat. 'What's wrong with you, sleepyhead?' he demanded.

Stretched out across the red brick step, Twinkle, the ginger tom, did not so much as twitch. Douglas was not sure whether the cat was asleep or just choosing to ignore him. Jennifer, however, was more certain.

'See,' she said haughtily, 'I told you so!'

'Well,' her father slitted his eyes at Twinkle in mock anger, 'we shall have to do something about that, shan't we!'

'Oh no you won't!' came a warning from the kitchen window, causing Douglas to turn towards it.

Leaning through the window, a wisp of loose hair hanging across her forehead and a smudge of flour on the end of her nose, Mary Cobden finished drying her hands on a tea towel and admonished her husband again.

'Now you two, leave Twinkle alone and come and have your elevenses,' she ordered, before disappearing back into the kitchen.

'Tea and bickies,' said Douglas, lowering his daughter to the ground. 'Come on,' he said, and he stepped over the sleeping cat and entered the comparative gloom of the kitchen.

The kitchen was large and spartan and dominated by a large wooden table which was scrubbed clean and surrounded by four wooden chairs.

The three of them sat at the table and Mary dipped a digestive biscuit into her tea before speaking.

'How's the chicken run?' she asked, looking up at her husband.

'Almost done,' he replied.

'How many did it get this time?'

'Only two.'

'Poor chickens,' Jennifer chimed in.

'Poor bloody fox when I get hold of it,' muttered Douglas, sipping tea from a huge white enamel mug. 'I'll sit up tonight,' he continued, looking automatically at the shotgun which hung above the hallway door.

The gun was a Purdey, his pride and joy, with his name engraved in the butt. He had saved long and hard as a young man to have it and he had learned to be a fine shot.

'Can't keep losing birds to this pest.' He swallowed another mouthful of tea.

'I'll make you a flask later,' said his wife.

Outside on the step Twinkle opened one eye and stretched. A very sweet child, he thought, but I'll be damned if I'm playing chase the stringball in this heat. He opened both eyes and blinked up at the bright yellow sun. Far too hot for that, he concluded.

Twinkle sauntered nonchalantly across the yard and jumped up onto the flint wall which surrounded it, and contemplated the chicken run with a sardonic eye. Well, should be some action tonight, he thought, looking out towards Wixley Wood shimmering on the horizon.

The hot summer day drew to a close and Douglas lowered his bulk into the old, threadbare armchair and crossed his legs at the ankle. With the broken shotgun resting across his lap and the flask of hot tea by his side, he settled himself for what he knew could be a long night.

The barn was large, with a hayloft above and room below for his machinery and animals in the wintertime, and the floor was covered with a scattering of old straw. The window offered him a wide view across the yard to the chicken run, and beyond to Wixley Wood.

The sun, now a glowing orange ball, sat just above the wood and was sinking slowly behind the trees.

'Dusk shortly, my friend.' Douglas patted the stock of the shotgun and, lifting the weapon to his eyes, squinted through the empty barrels, scanning first to the open fields and then traversing the weapon so that his sights came to rest on the henhouse. He had shepherded the fowls into the henhouse fifteen minutes before taking up his vantage point in the barn and all was now quiet, the birds settled for the night. Douglas lowered the weapon and leaned back in the chair.

The silence in the barn was complete, broken only once as Douglas pushed two fresh cartridges into the open mouths of the shotgun's twin barrels.

Fox leant his weight against his silver-tipped cane and peered around the edge of the flint wall. The farmhouse was dark and silent, and the yard deserted.

'Seems quiet,' he whispered.

'Let's have a look then,' said Weasel. Weasel edged past his partner and through the gate dividing the wall, and ran silently across to the gate of the chicken run. Moments later he was back. 'Easy,' he whispered.

'Splendid,' said Fox, and the pair hurried quickly and quietly across the yard. Weasel hunched over the hasp on the gate and lifted the face of the small padlock toward the moonlight.

Standing at his shoulder, Fox cast a wary eye around the farmyard, every sense attuned to the nocturnal sounds.

Weasel drew a bent pin from between his teeth and inserted it into the keyhole, and felt delicately for the padlock's mechanism. He paused to allow a heavy cloud to pass across the white face of the moon before placing a second pin into the keyhole and, after giving it a sharp turn of his wrist, he emitted a quiet grunt of satisfaction as, with an almost inaudible click, the tumblers gave up the unequal struggle and the lock fell open.

Weasel pushed the gate open a fraction and eased his agile frame through the gap before stepping toward the henhouse, wrapped silent and still in the darkness. Fox, his senses as taut as a bowstring, followed his companion through the opening before slowly pushing the gate closed.

Fox hurried across the dry earthen floor to where Weasel was already lifting the latch on the henhouse door, and the two crept into the dark interior, their eyes rapidly becoming accustomed to the gloom.

Weasel drew his lips back over his sharp white teeth as the pungent odour of the roosting chickens flared his nostrils.

'Two each,' whispered Fox, the words catching in his throat, and he stepped forward towards the first line of peacefully sleeping hens.

The kill was over in seconds, the cracking of the expertly wrung necks of the four dead hens the only sound to break the silence.

Fox's wide canine grin flashed through the gloom and was answered by the equally frenzied leer of his companion. Fox fought the atavistic urge to carry on the slaughter, physically shaking off the inherent bloodlust in his soul, and he laid a restraining paw on Weasel's narrow shoulder.

'That will do, old boy.' The words snatched at his throat, the desire to carry on the kill still within him.

Weasel's breathing was short and sharp, like that of a man who had just run a marathon, and his whole body quivered with the tension of the moment.

'You're right.' Weasel gathered himself with a deep breath, and pushed two dead hens into the deep pockets of his coat.

Fox led the way to the henhouse door, his kill dangling between his claws, and the pair slipped out into the spacious chicken run. The two of them stood a moment to allow their eyes to readjust to the moonlight before stepping towards the gate, and all hell broke loose.

A flurry of feathers suddenly erupted from the deep recess of Weasel's pocket and then skittered across the earthen floor, its head swinging unnaturally on its broken neck. Weasel jumped sideways at the reincarnation of the supposedly dead hen, lost his footing on the slimy excrement left by the birds earlier in the day, and came to rest almost upside down with his face pressed against the chicken wire.

Fox raced across the run, wildly grasping for the erratically scampering hen, which managed to evade his every desperate lunge with a short, spasmodic leap, its wings flapping maniacally and its sightless eyes causing it to bounce repeatedly against the side of the henhouse.

The sudden commotion in the chicken run caused a cacophony of outraged and panic-stricken cries from within the henhouse as the awakening birds mistakenly assumed that their attack was yet to come.

'I'm covered in chicken shit!' Weasel cursed, holding his arms away from himself as he stood looking down at his spattered coat.

'Never mind that!' said Fox as he made another pass at the manic hen. 'Help me here with this bloody thing.'

'Forget it!' Weasel's tone was sharp. 'We've got company, Foxy.'

Fox stopped short, the hen cartwheeling theatrically between his legs, and looked toward the imposing farmhouse standing silently across the yard.

'No lights,' he whispered. The house was still enveloped in darkness.

'Not the house, the barn!' Weasel was already making for the gate.

Standing silhouetted in the doorway of the barn Fox saw Douglas Cobden closing the breech on what was obviously a loaded shotgun.

'Time to call it a day, I think, old boy.'

'Bloody right.' Weasel was already through the gate.

Fox sped across the run and through the open gate, leaving the fallen hen flapping insanely against the wire mesh.

The flask was half empty and a host of cigarette stubs littered the floor around Douglas's feet. Twice already he had leaned forward and craned his neck towards the window, a trick of the light deceiving him. The tiny scurry of the mice in the barn had kept his senses sharp, but now his eyelids were becoming heavy and he had to ruefully admit that he was not as young as he had used to be.

Reaching down to refill his cup from the king-size flask, Douglas missed the sudden movement just beyond the chicken run, so that by the time he had resumed his watch the figure had gone, disappearing into the dark night.

Douglas peered through the window as far as it would allow and, satisfied all was quiet, lifted himself from the chair and walked quietly across to the bucket at the rear of the cattle stall.

Drinking another cup of tea had brought his attention to his bladder and he relieved himself noisily into the bucket.

'Time to pump ship,' he muttered to himself, wondering from where he had got the phrase, as he had never set foot on a ship in his life.

Douglas adjusted his clothing and peered through the dark at a horse collar hanging from an overhead beam. The leather was old, dry and cracked, and the stitching was broken through. Douglas ran a finger along its rough surface.

Long time since I've used that, he thought, thinking back to the shires he used to show annually. A light smile touched his lips as he recalled the year he had won; the cup stood even now in the house, on the timber mantelpiece above the inglenook.

First prize, thought Douglas, remembering with a warm pride the applause which had followed the judges' decision. He had given it up after that, deciding that one win was enough, although the prize money had been useful.

Douglas's reverie was broken by the sudden shrieking of a dozen panic-stricken hens. 'That's it!' he said aloud, cursing himself for having allowed his attention to wander. Douglas ran back to the window and looked sharply in the direction of the chicken run. 'A fox,' he shouted, 'and a bloody weasel as well!' He could scarcely believe his eyes. Douglas snatched up the Purdey and opened the door of the barn, snapping the gun closed as he brought it to the shoulder.

The fox was still worrying a hen but the weasel had become alarmed by his sudden appearance and was already bolting. Now the fox saw him also and, equally alarmed, started running toward the hole it had dug beneath the wire gate.

'I've got you,' Douglas muttered under his breath as he brought his sights to bear on the streamlined canine, the fox illuminated by the light of the moon. Douglas squeezed the trigger and the muzzle flash lit up the night, the recoil thudding into his shoulder.

From the chicken run the fox yelped and stumbled, tripping sideways as the force of the buckshot tore into its coat. Douglas peered over the sights, bright spots dancing before his eyes, and he blinked rapidly to clear his vision from the echoes of the muzzle flash.

The fox was up and running, fast and agile, quartering close to the ground.

'Too high,' Douglas cursed, training his sights on the fleeing fox a second time. The light from the moon disappeared abruptly as a huge dark cloud rolled across its face. 'Bugger,' Douglas swore as the ground towards him was swallowed up in the darkness. Douglas fired the second barrel, the flash from the explosion again lighting up the night, allowing him to see for an instant the fox tumble from atop the farmyard wall. 'Got you, you bastard!' Douglas raced towards the wall, ramming two fresh cartridges into the smoking barrels of the shotgun as he ran.

Behind him the lights in the farmhouse came on as Mary, roused by the gunfire, came running down the stairs in her blue dressing gown and out onto the steps to stand illuminated by the kitchen light.

Douglas reached the spot where the fox had vanished and pointed his weapon over the wall.

'Blast,' Douglas swore under this breath. Neither the fox nor the weasel were to be seen and he knew he would not see them again in this light.

'Did you get him, love?' Mary called from the kitchen door, her words carrying quickly through the night air, still and silent again after its thunderous interruption.

'Yes, but he got away. Still, he won't be back again in a hurry!' Douglas replied, his gaze still searching the open field beyond the wall. Oh no, Douglas thought, turning and heading back towards the barn, he won't be back again in a hurry!

Beyond the fields and under the cover of darkness Fox pushed a claw through the hole in his waistcoat and proffered it for Weasel's inspection.

'And here too,' he said, finding another rent in his attire, 'and another, three, by golly!' Fox's eyes had grown wider at each discovery.

'Never mind, Foxy,' Weasel sympathised, 'you can get it repaired.'

'Easy for you to say. I notice you have no holes.' Fox looked down at Weasel's coat.

'No holes,' Weasel wrinkled his nose, 'just a lot of chicken shit.'

'How awful for you,' Fox said, with heavy sarcasm.

'Never mind,' Weasel repeated. 'We've got three hens. That's good enough.'

'Hmmm.' Fox was far from happy, his attention still focused on his waistcoat. 'I could have been killed!' he wailed.

The idea was not a happy one, Weasel had to admit. 'I know, I know. Don't worry, you're in one piece.'

'I think we'll give Cobden's place a miss for a while,' Fox decided, smoothing his waistcoat as best he could.

'That's what I said last night!' Weasel arched an eyebrow at his companion.

'Yes, well, perhaps you were right.' Fox avoided Weasel's accusing glare.

'Perhaps!' Weasel turned and walked into the dark wood. 'No perhaps about it!'

Fox followed his companion's path, unable to stop fingering the holes in his coat.

Alan opened the kitchen door and allowed the fresh morning air to harry the stale night out of the cottage. The sun was already high in the sky and its brightening rays had long since chased the shadows from the rear of the cottage. Alan leaned against the door frame and sipped at a large mug of hot coffee, and revelled in the tranquillity of the balmy Sunday morning.

'Good morning,' a frail female voice called from across the unkempt lawns.

Alan straightened up and looked in the direction of the greeting. Beyond the broken fence stood the short and fragile figure of a woman in the winter of her years, her grey hair scraped back into a tidy bun and a pair of horn-rimmed glasses perched on her old lined face.

'Good morning,' Alan replied, stepping forward and making his way along the overgrown footpath.

'New neighbour?' the old lady asked, smiling and shielding her eyes from the bright yellow sun with an ancient, wrinkled palm.

'I'm afraid so.' Alan grinned as he approached his new neighbour.

'Oh good.' The old lady smiled, revealing what was obviously an old set of false teeth. 'It will be nice to have somebody next door again.'

Alan inclined his head, accepting the compliment. 'I've a lot of work to do' He looked around the garden.

'Oh yes.' The old lady nodded her agreement. 'But it used to look very nice so I'm sure you can get it back up to scratch.'

'Well, I shall certainly try, Mrs ...?' Alan looked questioningly at the senior citizen.

'Mrs Buxton. How do you do.'

'How do you do, Mrs Buxton.' Alan smiled politely. 'My name is Alan.'

'Do you have a wife?'

'Oh no, I'm single.' Alan grinned widely, knowing what was coming next.

'Well, there are some nice girls in the village,' Mrs Buxton said, confirming Alan's guess. 'A handsome young man like you should be able to find a wife.'

Alan's smile became broader. 'We shall have to see,' he replied. 'It's a little early yet.'

'Yes, well, don't take too long or they will all be taken,' Mrs Buxton warned. 'I must go. Watch out for Tom Dixon.'

Alan gave the pensioner's retreating back a puzzled look. 'Tom Dixon?' he muttered to himself. 'Who the hell is Tom Dixon?'

Alan strolled back between the overgrown hedges and into the cottage, a light frown still furrowing his brow. He donned a pair of black sunglasses before going down the front garden and along Busjibber Lane, and into the village centre. The village was quiet and peaceful, the only sound the gentle clip-clop of a chestnut mare carrying its rider through the picturesque hamlet. Alan smiled up at the rider as the horse drew level and received in return a dazzling smile of porcelain white teeth and full, cherry-red lips.

Mrs Buxton was right, Alan thought. There are some nice girls around. He bought a copy of his usual Sunday newspaper and walked leisurely back along the lane, the newspaper folded beneath his arm. Across the village green the doors of the Three Pheasants public house opened, and the landlord stepped out into the brilliant sunshine and waved a greeting.

'Morning,' Alan called, his words suddenly drowned by the loud ringing of the bells of the nearby church. He paused on the old stone bridge and admired the clear running waters of the Wix before ambling back along Busjibber Lane.

Jennifer skipped light-footed through the buttercups, her blonde hair bouncing about her shoulders and her white socks falling around her ankles.

Mary shielded her eyes from the blazing sun and sat on one of the smaller boulders which marked Dixon's Point, and watched her daughter, her powder-blue dress bright against the deep green of the rolling meadow, stoop to pick one of the shining yellow buttercups and then hold it delicately beneath her upturned chin.

Jennifer came racing back and thrust her chin into her mother's face. 'Do I like butter?' she asked, her small pink tongue poking innocently from between her lips.

'Oh yes, lots and lots.' Mary smiled, and then Jennifer conducted the same experiment on her mother, Mary dutifully lifting her chin to accept the yellow glow.

'So do you, Mummy,' Jennifer declared, before turning and racing off again, the small wicker basket she carried swinging wildly from her forearm.

Mary picked up her own larger basket and followed her daughter across the field, the turf soft and springy beneath her tread. 'Don't go too far,' she called as Jennifer disappeared into the cool shade of Wixley Wood.

Jennifer followed one of the wide winding tracks between the towering oaks and the tall, narrow elms, stooping periodically to pick woodland flowers that caught her eye, until her small basket was brimming with radiant colours.

Mary strolled leisurely along behind, enjoying the calm shadows and gentle cooing of the collared doves high in the broad canopy of leafy branches.

'There's lots here, Mummy,' Jennifer called to her from along the earthen track. 'In here,' she pointed.

Mary looked over to the small sunlit clearing, its sweet grass embellished with bright blooms.

'Oh yes, that's what we're looking for,' she said.

'I'm going to look for some more flowers,' Jennifer declared, looking up at her mother.

'Don't go too far,' Mary warned.

'I won't,' and Jennifer romped away through the clearing and into the trees. She walked between the thin saplings which competed for sunlight against the taller mature trees until she emerged into another peaceful haven, this one alive with bright petals and a host of vivid butterflies dancing lightly on the warm air. She walked around the edge of the hot, sun-soaked glade, picking at the variety of fragrant blooms and laying them neatly in her basket, engrossed in the brilliant hues and tints and oblivious to the pair of eyes hidden in the shade that watched her every innocent move.

Douglas drifted lazily down the leafy tree-lined lane that wound its gentle way down Poachers Hill, enjoying the birdsong and the warmth of the sun on his bare forearms, and Piper, his cocker spaniel, skirmished ahead. At the foot of the hill he could see the blue ribbon of the River Wix meandering through the hamlet of Little Wixley, and the peal of the church bells carried clearly across the peaceful summer's morning.

Douglas emerged from the bottom of the hill into Busjibber Lane, which lay at the edge of the village, and made his way between the rows of small neat cottages and over the stonework bridge which spanned the river.

The bridge was old, with the moss of centuries clinging to its sides, and Douglas paused to admire a pair of snowy-white swans gliding gracefully on the clear running waters below, before walking on and turning into the village centre.

The village basked in the heat of the June morning. The sun was at its zenith, sending long shafts of sunlight lancing through the broad-leafed branches of the sycamore trees which surrounded the village green. It all added to the tranquil setting and Douglas revelled in it. There were few occasions he enjoyed as much as a Sunday lunchtime pint in his local tavern, Sunday being the only day of the week on which he could afford to do so, and he rarely missed it. Douglas walked across the neatly cropped green and checked his wristwatch against the clock above the flint-built village hall before entering the lounge of the Three Pheasants.

'Morning all,' Douglas greeted the usual collection of regulars who sat the length of the mahogany bar. A chorus of hellos welcomed him as he lowered his bulk onto a bar stool. Behind the bar the landlord selected a sparkling clean pint mug.

'Guinness, Douglas?' Mortimer asked, tugging routinely at the white beard which hung to his breastbone.

'That will do nicely, thank you,' Douglas replied.

The lounge was large and spacious and a grand pair of open leaded windows allowed fresh air to pass freely from one end of the room to the other, affording some respite from the stifling summer heat. The room was dominated by a long and heavy roughly cut oak table, and a series of medium-sized prints, all of them eulogising the country life, decorated the walls, together with an occasional randomly placed item of bygone years, a warming pan or a bellows. Brightly polished horse brasses adorned the walls either side of the large fireplace and above it hung Mortimer's pride and joy, an ancient but fully operational man-trap. Mortimer always maintained that the fearsome-looking contraption had belonged to his great-grandfather. However, all the regulars believed he had probably bought it at some obscure antiques shop and only displayed it so as to frighten little old ladies.

Douglas paid for his drink and rolled a cigarette before taking a long draught of the cool, dark beer.

'Now then,' he began, 'listen to this,' and he related to the assembled company his encounter the night before with the fox and the weasel. By the time he had finished his tale all of those sitting at the bar were looking at him as if he had just sprouted a second head.

'A fox?' Mortimer was the first to break the silence that had followed Douglas's account of the previous night's drama. 'And a weasel? Working together?' The landlord's tone betrayed his doubt.

'Yes, and in my henhouse, no less.' Douglas took another mouthful of beer.

At the end of the bar old Max drew his pipe from his mouth, crinkled his left eye mischievously and adopted a crafty voice. 'You didn't happen to have seen Tom Dixon while you were about it, I suppose?'

The assembled regulars promptly collapsed into gales of laughter.

'All right, all right.' Douglas held up a hand towards them. 'You can laugh.'

'We will, Douglas,' Mortimer guffawed, 'we will.'

'I know what I saw.' Douglas defended himself above the howls of laughter. 'A fox and a weasel, I tell you, working in tandem.'

'I believe you. I've seen them as well,' a voice cried from the middle of the room. The laughter stopped abruptly as all heads turned towards the speaker.

Standing alone with a half-pint of lager in his hand stood a tall, gangly young man dressed in a loose-fitting paisley-patterned shirt and a pair of faded blue jeans with holes in the knees. The young man ran his fingers through the unruly shoulder-length brown hair he wore and pushed his thick spectacles back up onto the bridge of his nose before continuing.

'I saw them a few days ago, on my father's estate.' The youth smiled around the room, revealing two enormous front teeth.

Douglas eyed the youth curiously. He had never seen him before. He felt sure he would have remembered if he had.

The young man walked across the room and stood next to Douglas. Douglas shifted on his stool. The youth was standing far too close for comfort.

'It was probably your chickens the weasel was carrying,' the youth said, causing small droplets of spittle to spray from his permanently moist lips and into Douglas's face.

Douglas ran a large calloused palm down his cheeks and leaned away from the broadly smiling young man. 'You're probably right,' he replied, frowning. Douglas did not know who this man was but he was convinced he was not someone to be encouraged.

'Your father's estate, you say?' Mortimer came to Douglas's rescue.

'Oh yes,' the man replied. 'My name is Dembury, Timothy Dembury, but my friends call me Rico because my middle name is Richard, you see.'

'Dembury?' Mortimer asked. 'Would that be Lord Dembury?'

'Yes, I'm his son. I'm a student at university. I'm on vacation at the moment,' Timothy Dembury continued, beaming his wide, wet smile around the room. 'And I know I saw the fox and the weasel.'

'There you are,' Douglas said, turning to the others, 'a witness.'

Timothy smiled. 'I would be glad to testify to it in open court.'

'I don't think that will be necessary,' Douglas murmured, rolling his eyes again at Mortimer.

'Oh no, really.' Timothy would not be put off. 'I wouldn't mind at all.' He finished his lager and placed the glass on the bar. 'Well, it's been nice meeting you,' he said, offering his hand. Douglas felt obliged to accept the offered hand, instantly regretting that he had done so. Timothy had a handshake that made Douglas feel as if he had just taken hold of a lump of cold, clammy dough.

'*Ciao, amigo*,' said Timothy, turning and walking out of the door.

Douglas leaned his weight against the bar and took a deep breath before blowing slowly through puffed-out cheeks. 'What was that?' he asked, of no one in particular.

'That, my friend,' Max said quietly, 'was the aristocratic and intellectual cream of society's youth.' Loud snorts of derision accompanied Max's sarcastic observation.

'I've met his father, actually,' Mortimer observed. 'He seems like a decent chap.'

'Can't say the same for his son,' Douglas said. 'Hope to God he doesn't come back.'

'Tell you what,' said Max, relighting his pipe. 'Lay that mantrap inside the door just in case he does.' The resounding laughter echoed out of the pub and could be heard halfway through the village.

Leaning nonchalantly against the bark of the tall, stately oak which towered over the other trees in the wood and afforded him ample cover from the girl's view, Fox watched with interest as the golden-haired child went about her business of picking wild flowers in the sunlit clearing.

She was a very pretty child, Fox thought, admiring the way her powder-blue dress and white ankle socks added another splash of colour to the numerous shades of red and yellow which decorated the grass in the clearing. Fox straightened up from the wide tree and crept quietly between the thin trunks of the silver birches which surrounded the small clearing, and settled himself behind a low holly bush.

His stealthy tread had not disturbed the young girl. She still had her back toward him. The wicker basket swung from her left forearm as she stooped to pick a betony, its bright maroon petals in full bloom. Fox felt confident that he would not frighten the child, and so he stood upright and peeked over the top of the bush.

Almost immediately the girl, as if warned by some sixth sense that she was under close scrutiny, turned and looked him directly in the eyes.

Fox ducked down beneath the dark green holly and hurried back to the cover of the oak tree. He had not meant to alarm the child, having been merely curious, but he realised as he looked back from behind the tree that not only was the child not frightened, she was actually coming towards him, her clear piping voice carrying to him through the trees. Fox watched closely as the child squatted down on the ground and placed her basket to one side before holding out both hands towards him.

'It's all right, Mr Fox, I'll not hurt you,' she called in her clear voice.

Fox raised both his eyebrows in surprise. There's a turn-up for the books, he thought wryly, and I was worried about frightening you.

The girl lifted a small folded napkin from the wicker basket and opened it to reveal several thinly cut ham sandwiches. 'Would you like some, Mr Fox?' she asked, offering half a sandwich to him.

Fox stood quite still, totally unsure of what to do. He did not want to venture any closer in case he did frighten her, nor did he wish to appear rude by merely ignoring her invitation and walking away into the wood.

Before he had decided on what course of action to take, the child made up his mind for him. 'I'll leave it there for you,' she said, laying the half-sandwich on the ground before shuffling backwards on her bottom until she was four or five feet further back.

Fox, deciding that to be the perfect arrangement, walked slowly forward from behind the tree and sat down opposite the child before picking up the sandwich and taking a large bite.

'Nice, isn't it?' said the child, tucking heartily into her half of the sandwich. Fox had to agree. Smoked ham made a very pleasant change from roast chicken. 'You look very smart in your red waistcoat,' the child continued, causing Fox to blush furiously, ' and I like your silver cane.'

The child took another bite of her sandwich before speaking again. 'My name is Jenny Cobden,' she said, and Fox almost choked on his lunch.

'Cobden!' he croaked over a piece of ham stuck fast in his gullet.

'Don't wolf your food, Mr Fox,' Jennifer admonished him. 'You'll get indigestion,' she said, using her mother's oft repeated warning.

Quite so, my dear, thought Fox, swallowing hard and wondering whether the girl was aware of his identity.

'You're not the naughty fox who's been pinching my daddy's chickens, are you?' Jennifer asked, looking sternly at him.

Oh, dear Lord, Fox thought despairingly, looking away to hide his embarrassment.

'I hope not,' Jennifer continued, 'or I won't be able to be your friend.'

Fox thought that this was probably a prudent time to leave, and so he bowed politely to Jennifer and murmured his thanks before turning and heading back into the wood.

'I'll be here next week if you want another ham sandwich,' Jennifer called after him. 'See you next week, Mr Fox.'

Fox, already some distance away, was not so sure that that would be such a good idea.

That evening the centre of the table at Violets Farm was decorated with a large bowl filled to the brim with the freshly cut flowers Jennifer had gathered earlier in the day, the array of colours standing out brightly in the large kitchen, and Douglas tucked a vivid red campion behind his daughter's ear as she spoke.

'And Mr Fox carries a stick with a silver top on it,' Jennifer gushed, before rapidly devouring another fish finger, 'and he really liked his ham sandwich and I said I would give him another one next week.'

Douglas smiled indulgently at his daughter as a third fish finger disappeared into her mouth. 'Slow down, slow down,' he said gently. 'I hope this isn't the Mr Fox who's been pinching my chickens,' he smiled.

Jennifer adopted a serious look and shook her blonde curls sternly. 'That's a different, naughty fox,' she assured her father, switching to a vigorous nod.

'Well, that's all right then.' Douglas smiled sideways at his wife as Mary placed a huge steaming plate of meat and potatoes on the spotless white tablecloth in front of him.

'Now you stop all this talking,' Mary said as she sat down at her own place, 'and get on with your dinner.'

'Can we go to the woods again next week please?' Jennifer ignored her mother's instruction.

'We'll see. Now eat up.'

Chapter 2

July

The window in the fifth-storey office was open, allowing the hot summer afternoon to move freely around the room. The fat man in the expensive suit stuck a podgy finger on the Ordnance Survey map, his concentration oblivious to the sounds of the traffic motoring through the crowded London streets below.

'And this one?' he demanded.

'Little Wixley,' the other man replied. He ran his hand through his sandy brown hair thoughtfully. 'I don't think that one can be spared.'

'Why not?'

'We would be pushing our luck, quite frankly.'

'Pushing our luck?'

'Yes. If the route goes north of Wixley it will have to run a further fifteen miles. We wouldn't get away with it.'

The fat man tapped the map with his finger. 'Very well,' he decided. 'We shall have to ...' and his words tailed off, the sentence lost in the sudden commotion of gunshots and ringing alarm bells from the street.

The two men exchanged surprised glances and then hurried to the window. On the opposite side of the street a man wearing a clown's mask and brandishing an automatic pistol raced out of a Barclays Bank. The sports bag he carried swung wildly from his arm as he sprinted along the pavement, and he used it to shove aside an onlooker before disappearing into a side street.

'A real-life robbery, it would seem,' the fat man observed as the first police sirens began to wail in the distance.

'Let's hope no one was hurt,' the other man replied.

The crowd began to gather in front of the bank as the first police car screeched to a stop.

'Anyway, where were we?' The fat man turned from the

window and bent over the map.

'Little Wixley.'

'Ah yes, Little Wixley.'

Fox sat on an old tree stump which sported an assortment of vivid fungi and lifted the gold hunter from his waistcoat. 'She's late!' he murmured, snapping the watch closed and peering again in the direction of the quiet sunlit clearing.

As if on cue, Jennifer appeared from between the trees, her blonde curls shining like a halo above her face. Fox suddenly felt unsure as to whether or not he had made the correct decision. Meeting a human child in broad daylight was unheard of and anything could happen.

Fox sat quietly watching as Jennifer perched herself on a fallen log in the centre of the bright clearing and began laying her picnic on a white linen handkerchief she had spread on her lap.

'Mr Fox?' she called, looking towards the trees, her young voice carrying clearly through the noonday.

This is madness! Fox thought. What am I thinking of?

'Mr Fox?' Jennifer called again. 'I've got some more ham sandwiches.'

Fox's whiskers twitched and he ran a dry, rasping tongue across his teeth as his stomach got the better of his common sense. 'I'm sold,' he muttered, appalled at how low a price he could be bought for. Fox jumped down from the stump and trotted quickly through the trees and paused at the edge of the scented glade.

'Hello, Mr Fox.' Jennifer smiled and waved. Fox strolled casually forward and rested his weight on his cane. 'I'm glad you came, Mr Fox,' Jennifer said. 'Mummy gave me an extra ham sandwich especially for you.'

Fox inclined his head and accepted the offered sandwich. 'Thank you, Jennifer,' he said, ' and thank your mother for me.'

Jennifer took a bite from a large, ripe tomato before continuing. 'I told my daddy that it wasn't you who had been pinching his chickens.' She paused to wipe tomato juice from her chin. 'I told him it was a different, naughty fox.'

I'm off the hook, Fox thought gleefully as he savoured the lean ham.

'Do you like your ham sandwich?' Jennifer asked. 'My mummy cooked it herself.'

'Quite excellent,' Fox replied, dabbing at his stiff white whiskers with his silk cravat.

'When I go to school tomorrow I'm going to draw a picture of you,' Jennifer said, between mouthfuls of tomato.

Fame at last, Fox thought, smiling indulgently at the child.

'I shall have to take my crayons to colour you in properly though.'

Fox pricked his ears in the direction of the trees as Mary Cobden approached through the wood. 'Time I was off, my dear.' Fox bowed his head and turned to leave.

'I'll show you my picture next weekend,' Jennifer called to his retreating back.

'I'll look forward to it,' Fox whispered, before being swallowed up by the cool shadows.

'Jennifer?' Mary called from the trees.

'Over here,' Jennifer replied, gathering up her basket. Mary stepped from the shade and sat beside her daughter on the dry log and kicked off her shoes. 'I gave Mr Fox his sandwich.' Jennifer looked up at her mother. 'He said thank you very much.'

'Where is he now?' Mary asked, rubbing her toes in the sweet grass.

'He had to go home. It's his bedtime.'

'Oh, I see.' Mary smiled.

'He has to have an afternoon nap.'

'That's a good idea. I wish I was a fox.'

'You couldn't be a fox. You would have to be a vixen,' Jennifer said, nodding her blonde curls sagely.

'Oh yes, a vixen.' Mary shook her head wonderingly. 'Are you going to help me pick some flowers then?' she asked, slipping her feet into her shoes.

'Yes, I've got some already.' Jennifer took her mother's hand and they strolled back through the trees, vying with each other as to which one of them would fill their basket with the most blooms.

St Mary's Church was old. Built by the Saxons and later improved upon by the Norman conquerors, it stood as a testament to the long history of Little Wixley.

The Reverend Alwyn Jones walked long the churchyard's straight, narrow path, taking delight in the bright blooms which bordered the stone slabs. The collection of chestnut trees which fringed the peaceful church stood tall and calm, luxuriating in the bright afternoon sunlight, and Alwyn paused at the heavy door of the church and stood a moment to admire their beauty.

Alwyn was a young man, not yet thirty two years of age and as yet unmarried. He was not a confirmed bachelor, however, it was just that Mrs Right had not yet presented herself. He struck a slim figure of five-and-a-half feet, yet the slender build beneath the cassock belied an inner strength.

He had taken up holy orders at a young age after having been appalled at the horrors of Bluff Cove and Tumble Down Mountain, his career with the Welsh Guards cut brutally short. He still carried, and always would, a long vicious scar which ran the length of his left thigh.

Alwyn had won the Military Medal at the same time as he had earned the wound, running forward through the hell of the raining artillery shells to successfully rescue a wounded comrade. He had come to in a clean, crisp bed on board a hospital ship, convinced that he had discovered the path his life should take from then on, and he had since dedicated his life to the God he had been brought up to believe in as a small boy in the valleys, and to the well-being of his fellow man.

Alwyn turned and walked up the short flight of steps which had become worn and bow-shaped with the passing of centuries of worshipping feet, and entered the ancient church. Inside it was cool to offer a sanctuary from the heat of the sun. Alwyn seated himself on a pew in the front row and began going over the sermon he had prepared for the following day. He had barely started before the door opened behind him, allowing a broad shaft of sunlight to illuminate the dusty air. He rose from his seat and turned, his hands clasped gently before him, as a tall, muscular young man entered the church.

'Good afternoon.' Alwyn smiled in greeting.

'Good afternoon.' The man smiled in return. 'I'm not disturbing you, am I?' he enquired politely.

'Oh no, not at all, I was just brushing up on tomorrow's sermon,' Alwyn replied. He had not met his visitor before and so he waited patiently for the man to introduce himself.

A long silence ensued as the man, obviously feeling uncomfortable, fastened his eyes upon a stained-glass window. Alwyn decided the onus rested upon himself and so he took a step forward and offered his hand. 'Alwyn Jones,' he introduced himself, his soft Welsh tones blending perfectly with his surroundings.

'Alan De Angelis,' the man smiled, clasping Alwyn's hand in a strong manly grip.

'I don't believe I have seen you in church before?' Alwyn enquired.

'Oh, I've only been in the village a short time, I'm afraid,' Alan explained.

'Where are you living, if I may ask?'

Alan pulled a face. 'I've bought that old cottage in Busjibber Lane,' he said modestly.

'Oh, I know the one. That's splendid. I've thought for a long time that it could be lovely, given a little care and attention.'

'A lot of care and attention,' Alan laughed.

'Well, yes, I suppose so.' Alwyn joined in the laughter. 'What brings you in today? Can I be of help in any way?' he asked, after the laughter had subsided.

'No, nothing special. I hadn't had a look inside, that's all. It's very nice.'

'Yes, it needs some work done, however,' Alwyn observed, passing a lightly critical eye over the roof. 'It's always the roof where a church is concerned, I'm afraid.'

'Does seem to be, it's true.' Alan nodded soberly, joining Alwyn in his contemplation of the roof. 'Well, I'll be off. Nice meeting you.'

'And you,' Alwyn returned the compliment.

Alan walked back down the aisle between the low wooden pews and, feeling that Alwyn's eyes were boring into his back, felt obliged to make a small donation to the fund for repairs to the church roof. Alan opened his wallet and dropped a crisp fifty-pound note into the slot on the top of the locked wooden box which sat on a pine table just inside the nave, before pulling the ornate door open and stepping out into the brilliant sunshine.

Alwyn had not watched Alan leave but had instead returned to his sermon and had therefore missed the donation Alan had made to the fund. If he were ever to discover who had left the money, he would have been mortified that he had not said thank you at the time.

Fox walked quickly through the shady wood with a buoyant smile playing on his lips. He found that he was enjoying the company of the child and was looking forward to their weekly meeting with enthusiasm. He jumped up onto his customary position on the oak stump and passed a careful eye around the open glade. Only the urgent business of the labouring bees and the haphazard fluttering of the multitude of radiant butterflies disturbed the sunny peace.

Jennifer appeared in the clearing, her yellow dress nipped in at the waist, and Fox's long mouth broke into a wide smile of pearl-white teeth.

Fox bounded forward with an almost indecent haste as Jennifer settled herself on the dry and cracked log. 'Good morning, my dear.' Fox glowed as he sat at Jennifer's plimsolled feet.

'Hello, Mr Fox.' Jennifer's smile was as broad as Fox's. Fox bowed his head in greeting and allowed Jennifer to caress his head with her small, gentle palm.

Fox and Jennifer sat in the hot rays of the dazzling July sun, enjoying their ham sandwiches and the pleasure of their secret company.

'This is the picture I drew of you, Mr Fox,' Jennifer declared, producing a large sheet of paper from her basket and holding it up for Fox's perusal.

Fox contemplated the crayon drawing with a mixture of interest and puzzlement. He thought the ears were a little large, but that was easily compensated for by the magnificent brush which rose even above his head. His cane and watch chain were remarkably accurate for one so young, but what bewildered him the most was the fact that Jennifer had coloured him blue.

'It's very good, my dear,' Fox complimented Jennifer's artwork, not wishing to mention the reason for the puzzled frown upon his brow.

'I coloured you in blue,' Jennifer began, and Fox looked up with interest, 'because all the other Mr Foxes are red and you're special,' and Fox beamed, his ego in full flow. 'And besides,' Jennifer continued, 'I didn't have any red crayons,' and Fox's pride burst like a punctured balloon.

'Oh well,' he muttered, a little crestfallen, 'never mind, eh.'

'Miss Tibble, my teacher, said you are the most handsome fox in the whole world,' and Fox recovered a little of his usual aplomb, reflecting that Miss Tibble must indeed have very good taste.

'And Miss Tibble must be right because she knows everything,' Jennifer insisted, nodding her certain belief.

'I'm sure she does.' Fox smiled indulgently at the seven-year-old. He finished his lunch and dabbed his white whiskers delicately on his silk cravat. 'That was quite splendid, my dear, thank you.' He smiled his gratitude and cocked an ear towards the sound of Mary Cobden approaching through the sheltering trees. 'Time I was off, my dear.' Fox turned to leave.

'Bye, bye, Mr Fox,' Jennifer called as Fox blended with the cool shadows. 'See you next week.'

Fox vanished into the deep wood and Jennifer collected her basket and skipped towards the sound of her mother's voice.

Fox watched from the cover of a bed of green ferns until Jennifer and her mother had departed before making off at a brisk pace in the opposite direction. He penetrated deep into the heart of the wood until he found what he was looking for, a small patch of sunlight which had managed to break through the canopy of leaves and rest on an upturned tree stump.

Fox nestled himself beneath the overhanging roots of the stump and rested his head on his paws. Within moments his breathing was slow and regular, and he drifted into a deep sleep.

He woke to the setting sun and stretched and yawned before taking his time to smoke a Monte Cristo.

The wood was coming alive to the sounds of the night, and Fox watched with lazy interest the haphazard antics of a moth before moving off at a gentle trot through the trees.

Fox threaded his way between the thick trunks, sidestepping the brambles and avoiding their sharp thorns, until he emerged onto a narrow beaten track. The track was dark and quiet and Fox padded along it, his sharp eyes penetrating the night with ease, until he approached a narrowing of the track and, without warning, came face to face with the wood's most powerful resident.

He stopped ten feet from the other night-time traveller and felt the hairs rise at the nape of his neck. Although the two of them were not enemies, nor were they friends. Fox inclined his head in recognition. 'Good evening, Badger,' he said softly.

Along the dry earthen track Badger stood like a rock, his large muscular body tense and still. 'Evening,' he replied evenly, eyeing Fox from over his spectacles.

'Splendid night,' Fox offered, and he fingered the weighted silver tip of his cane.

Badger's heavy black eyebrows knitted into a tight frown and the muscles rippled across his broad shoulders. 'Perhaps,' he answered, his voice almost a whisper.

Fox touched the silver tip to his brow and stepped to one side, and the old brock ambled past, his huge paws thudding into the ground. Fox lit a cheroot and watched Badger vanish into the wood. 'Discretion being the better part of valour,' he muttered to himself.

Fox carried on along the track until the trees began to thin, and then he paused at the edge of the wood. A nightjar flew overhead on wings that cracked like a whip, and Fox passed a keen eye across the open fields. The moon was in its last quarter and offered little in the way of light. He trotted quickly out of the treeline and across the dark fields. Rabbits scampered quickly out of his path and disappeared into their burrows, and Fox covered the ground towards the small copse without interruption.

He topped a rise in the rolling ground and stopped in his tracks. Beyond the copse, laid out in even lines, stood row upon row of neat tents and marquees of all shapes and sizes.

'Oh no!' Fox cursed. 'Not another bloody country fayre!'

The country fayre, spread out across the flat, freshly mown grass, basked in the broad glowing beams of sunlight and the lazy but interested strolling of the country folk.

Douglas stood with the broken Purdey resting in the crook of his elbow, awaiting his turn in the penultimate round of the clay-pigeon shooting competition, and shielded his eyes from the glare of the sun with the palm of his hand as Mortimer's shotgun resounded through the sultry afternoon.

Douglas watched intently as the 'gamecock' rocketed out of the thin collection of silver birch trees, the bright red face of the clay taunting the gun, and sighed inwardly as Mortimer plucked it out of the azure sky with a deft skill he knew he would find it hard to match. Two further clays fell in rapid succession to Mortimer's gun, disintegrating in an exploding shower of red chips before Mortimer missed the 'bolting rabbit', the fast black clay reaching safety as it ducked beneath his aim.

'Ten points missed,' Douglas thought, mentally adding up the landlord's score. Mortimer's gun echoed a further four times, each time successfully, before he rested the broken gun and ambled out of the hide.

'Very good, Mortimer,' Douglas complimented his friend.

'Missed the "rabbit" again!' Mortimer shook his white beard in disgust as the next gun took up his position in the hide, a tall, powerful man wearing a white short-sleeved shirt.

'This chap is pretty good.' Douglas nodded in the direction of the hide. 'Do you know him?'

'Can't say as I do,' Mortimer replied. 'Anyway, I'm off for a cup of tea. Good luck.'

Douglas nodded. 'See you later.'

Mortimer strolled across the short springy grass and bought a small tea and a bap filled with meat from the hog roast before moving on to view the carefully crafted sticks in the next stall.

'About time you had one of those,' a light voice whispered in his ear, as he fingered a stout walking stick with a handle carved into the shape of a leaping trout.

'Hello, Susan.' Mortimer smiled without looking around, and his correct guess was answered by a burst of tinkling laughter. 'How are you, young lady?' Mortimer replaced the decorative cane and turned to face his tormentor.

'Not too bad.' Susan smiled, giving Mortimer's beard a light-hearted tug.

'Fingers! My girl,' Mortimer grinned, 'you're not too big to go across my knee.'

'Promises, promises!' Susan giggled.

'I hope you're supporting your uncle Douglas in the clay shoot?' Mortimer nodded in the direction of the range.

Susan looked from behind her sunglasses as Douglas took up position in the hide. 'I will if he gets into the final,' Susan decided. 'I want to watch the falconry display first.'

'I'll probably see you there,' Mortimer said, dropping the empty cup into a black plastic dustbin and nodding farewell.

Susan stood at the side of the roped arena as the peregrine falcon arrowed down from the cloudless blue sky, its streamlined shape slicing through the hot open air like a sharpened blade, and the hushed crowd gasped as the bird's razored talons snatched for the high arcing lure. The falconer yanked the small feathered lure back with a practised arm and the peregrine shot over the heads of the watching crowd, its yellow eye glaring malevolently. Again the falconer swung the lure about his head in a slow circle, whistling and calling to the soaring hunter, and again the ruthless killer lanced down from the sky.

The crowding people held their breath as the peregrine folded its aquiline wings and its legs dropped forward like the undercarriage of a sleek spitfire. The falconer released the line and the lure hung momentarily in the bright afternoon sky before the peregrine's claws snatched it away. Exultant and amazed cries broke from the dry throats of the gathered throng and the falcon dropped lightly to the ground and tore at the lure with a cruel, curved beak.

The falconer gathered up the glossy bird as a ripple of applause passed through the admiring crowd, and Susan strolled her way through the collection of neatly spaced stalls towards the sound of the echoing shotguns. She stepped up beside Mortimer at the edge of the wide range.

'Who's winning?' she asked.

'This is the final; between Douglas and that man over there.' Mortimer indicated with a nod of his head the tall young man wearing the white short-sleeved shirt who stood observing as Douglas reduced another clay to tiny fragments.

'Good shot, Uncle Doug,' Susan called, and Douglas gave her a cheery smile as he reloaded the Purdey.

Susan looked out of the corner of her eye at the man in the white shirt which radiated against the dusky Mediterranean hue of his skin, to discover that she was already the subject of his appraisal. Susan felt her cheeks redden behind her sunglasses and she returned her attention to her uncle as he shot another clay out of the sky.

'Who is the other guy?' she asked casually, without looking away from Douglas.

'No idea.' Mortimer shrugged. 'I think I've seen him around once or twice but I don't...Oh, shot!...I don't know who he is.'

Douglas stepped from the hide, dropping two more spent cartridges onto the growing red heap and made his way over as the young man took up position and closed his gun with a steely determination.

'Nice shooting,' Mortimer said.

'This chap will have to do well to top it,' Douglas agreed.

'What was your score?' Susan asked, as the challenger reduced his first clay to shattered debris.

'Thirty-nine. I missed one of the double targets and a "rabbit".'

'What's the maximum you can get?'

'Fifty points. A "rabbit" is worth ten.'

'What's a "rabbit"?'

'That's one now.' Douglas pointed as the black clay suddenly erupted from the sparse copse and bounced rapidly and irregularly across the uneven ground.

The heavy gun thudded into the young man's shoulder and the clay received the full impact of his aim, exploding in a hail of black shards. Susan watched with interest as the man reloaded his gun with an easy, almost casual manner.

'He hasn't missed yet,' she observed, as the man downed a gliding pair of low clays in rapid succession. 'Didn't you win last year?' She turned to her uncle.

'Only just,' Douglas replied modestly. 'Pipped Mortimer here by one point.'

Mortimer stroked his beard thoughtfully. 'You might lose your crown today, my friend,' he muttered as another clay fell to the challenger's gun.

The black shiny clay of the 'bolting rabbit' suddenly shot from cover for a second time, bouncing at speed across the ground and the darkly tanned man squeezed the trigger, but the clay raced for safety, disappearing beyond a grassy mound.

'That's a ray of sunshine,' Douglas remarked as the younger man ejected the two smoking cartridges.

Mortimer nodded. 'Evens things up a little.'

'How many has he got left?' Susan asked.

'Three,' Douglas replied, 'and he has got to get all of them to win.'

A pair of high clays soared out above the field and the challenger pulled them both to earth with an almost professional ease.

'One more,' Mortimer commented with a resigned air.

'Not over yet,' Douglas muttered.

The final red clay glided fast and low, hugging the contours of the field and the gun plucked it from its graceful travel.

'Oh well.' Douglas's wide shoulders slumped in defeat. 'Can't win them all.'

'Never mind, Uncle Doug.' Susan patted his arm consolingly.

'And it was a close-run thing,' Mortimer observed. 'It was almost yours.'

The young man stepped out of the hide with the broken gun resting in his arm and made his way across. 'My commiserations,' he began. 'That was a good fight.' The man held out a large tanned hand.

'Absolutely.' Douglas accepted the firm grip. 'You shot very well.'

'Thanks very much.' The man smiled, revealing a row of even white teeth.

The marshal walked forward, his brown trilby in tune with his tweed jacket, and offered his hand. 'Congratulations, sir.' He smiled. 'Some fine shooting. Would you two gentlemen like to come forward and collect your trophies?'

The three men crossed the grass to a long trestle-table adorned with a crisp white sheet and a pair of silver cups, one larger than the other, which shone beneath the sun. Douglas accepted his prize with a small bow to the polite applause.

Alan De Angelis lifted his briefly above his head and pocketed the small cheque with a modest smile.

Not bad, Susan thought as she watched Alan receive his prize. Must remember that.

Fox lay in his bed with the soft, thick quilt pulled up over his head, trying desperately to block out the noise of the shotguns echoing above his home. 'Infernal din!' he cursed, pulling the quilt down abruptly and climbing out of the bed. 'How is a chap supposed to get any sleep?' he muttered under his breath as he padded through to the small kitchen.

He poured himself a large mug of coffee from the percolator and sat at the kitchen table before lighting a thin cheroot. The cigar tasted stale and the coffee bitter. 'Why did they have to pick my home for their damnable fayre!' Fox lamented, cursing his luck as the guns continued their relentless pounding.

'For God's sake, stop that bloody racket!' Fox roared, slamming the mug down furiously onto the wooden table. He pricked both his ears towards the ceiling as an eerie silence followed his outraged bellow. ‘At last,’ he muttered, dropping the cheroot into the half-empty mug.

Fox fluffed up his pillows and snuggled down beneath the quilt with a contented sigh.

‘Oh, Foxy,’ Vixen whispered, running her tongue along his stiff whiskers.

‘You must be joking.’ Fox rolled over, turning his back to the sleepy-eyed vixen, and within moments he was snoring loudly.

Susan Hamilton sat at the bar in the lounge of the Three Pheasants and passed a casual eye around the room. Dressed in a white blouse and a pair of white jeans which complemented her long auburn hair perfectly, she exuded confidence. She had no qualms about sitting in a pub on her own. As far as she was concerned, those days were long gone and she was quite capable of looking after herself.

She was also very aware of her own sexual allure. She was only twenty three and was possessed of a perfect hour-glass figure, although she sometimes wished her ample breasts were a little smaller.

Susan sipped at the Diet Coke and looked out of the open windows at the dusk beginning to fall across the quiet village. She enjoyed the tranquil peace of the village on a Sunday. She had been raised in Little Wixley and she had no longings for life in the city.

What she did have a longing for, however, was a man. Village life could be a little unproductive with regard to men. Most of those in the village of her age she had known since childhood, and she really wanted somebody different.

Susan looked out of the corner of her eye at the man standing at the far end of the bar opposite the door. She had seen him at the fayre and once or twice in the village during the past month, quite often nursing a pint of bitter in the pub of an evening, but they had never spoken. She did not know his surname but had heard Mortimer address him as Alan. She also knew that he had recently moved into the village, having bought one of the old cottages in Busjibber Lane.

Susan looked around the room affecting a bored poise whilst actually passing a critical eye over the man. He was tall and well-built, with a mass of dark curls bursting over the open collar of the snowy-white shirt he wore, the short sleeves revealing two strong, muscular arms. Susan allowed her gaze to glide surreptitiously down the man's trim body, taking in the wide black belt which was looped through a pair of tight blue jeans.

Before she had completed her perusal of the man, the door to the lounge opened and Timothy Dembury walked in, his lank brown hair tied back in a long ponytail.

'Yo, Horny Hamilton,' he cried as he spotted Susan across the room. 'What's happening, babe?' he called, walking across the room and pulling up a stool beside her.

Oh no! Susan thought despairingly, not this gibbering idiot again!

She had met Timothy in the White Horse public house at the other end of the village during his last vacation, when he had spent the entire evening refusing to take no for an answer.

'How's it going, doll?' Timothy asked, leering at Susan through his thick spectacles.

Susan looked around the room, wondering whether it would be best to ignore him or to make a break for the door whilst she still had the chance.

'What will it be?' Mortimer asked from behind the bar, giving Timothy a look of withering contempt. For Mortimer the joke was wearing a bit thin and he was becoming heartily sick and tired of this tedious squirt.

'Half a lager, bearded fellow,' Timothy squeaked, his wet rubber lips breaking into a wide grin.

Once more! Mortimer thought murderously. Just once more!

'Now then, horny Hamilton.' Timothy returned his attention to Susan. 'When am I going to have the pleasure of your company?'

Not again! Susan thought. Not again, please!

From his position at the end of the bar Alan De Angelis looked out of the corner of his eye at Timothy.

'How about tomorrow night, Susie?' Timothy was asking.

This is it, Alan thought. Now or never. Alan finished his pint and looked across at Timothy, feeling that he didn't have butterflies in his stomach so much as a squadron of Sopwith Camels.

'She can't go out with you tomorrow night, mate.' he called, standing to his full height so that he towered over Timothy.

'Why is this?' Timothy's smile did not waver.

'Because she's coming out to dinner with me, that's why.' Alan smiled in return. 'I'll pick you up at eight, Susan. See you tomorrow,' he said, before turning on his heel. He paused at the door and looked back. 'You do like Italian?'

'Yes,' Susan replied, before realising that she had now accepted his invitation.

'Fine, see you at eight.' Alan turned and walked out into the warm evening air, leaving behind him a thoroughly crestfallen Timothy and a flustered Susan desperately trying to recover her composure.

Alan walked leisurely along the road until he turned the corner into Busjibber Lane and out of sight of the pub before leaping three feet into the air and whooping like a Cheyenne brave. He walked the last hundred yards to his cottage with a light spring in his step and a smile on his face as bright as the rising moon.

A kingfisher darted along the reeded banks of the Wix, flitting between the long shadows cast by the evening sun, and Fox scooped a pawful of clear fresh water to his lips.

'Much better,' he said, before dabbing his whiskers dry on his silk cravat. In the heart of the wood an old elm had collapsed and died, its bole coming to rest on the far bank, and Fox used the fallen tree as a bridge across the river.

In a hidden cove at a bend in the river, Otter was grilling a trout over a smoky wood fire, and Fox raised the silver tip of his cane in salute before easing his way between the dry, broken branches at the end of the tapering bole. Fox sprang down from the tree and loped at an easy pace through the wood until he emerged into the twilight fields.

A tawny owl watched Fox with unblinking eyes as he in turn watched Jennifer far in the distance at Violets Farm, throwing a ball for Piper to chase.

'Now there's a game I have never played,' Fox murmured contemplatively, and then he trotted across the fields towards the farm. He topped the rise at Dixon's Point and rested his weight against the boulder before striking a match against the bare rock and holding the flame to the end of a Monte Cristo.

'Very peaceful,' he commented, and the ground erupted at his feet.

Fox leapt up onto the boulder in alarm, the end of his cigar almost bitten through, and a mound of brown soil sprang from the grass, followed by Mole's snout and his thick spectacles.

'Moley!' Fox protested. 'You frightened me almost to death.'

Mole smeared a layer of dirt from each lens before peering through the smudged glasses at his accuser. 'Sorry, Fox,' he apologised. 'I didn't know you were there. Had to come up though. Bumped into something, you see.' Mole reached into the mound of earth and proffered a round ball of lead for Fox's perusal. 'What do you make of that?' he enquired.

Fox jumped down from the boulder and took the slightly misshapen lump of blue-black lead into his own paws before passing a knowing eye over it. 'Musket ball,' he nodded sagely.

'Musket ball!' Mole scoffed. 'Ask a silly question,' and he disappeared back into the network of tunnels.

Fox dropped the lump of lead onto the mound of soil. 'It is a musket ball,' he muttered. 'Ask Tom Dixon if you don't believe me.'

Alan dropped a gear and turned the wheel with an easy confidence, and the BMW negotiated the bend with a smooth, untroubled grace. Sitting beside him, dressed in a cream summer dress nipped in at the waist, Susan feigned complete indifference whilst secretly admiring the manner with which Alan handled the powerful saloon.

The car sped over the crest of Poachers Hill, the golden evening sunlight sending sparks rebounding off its bright red bodywork, and Susan felt as if she were taking part in a television commercial. Alan had left the roof down and the warm evening air blew Susan's lustrous auburn hair back so that it tumbled and bounced, wild and unchecked, like the free-flying mane of Pegasus.

Alan depressed the accelerator and the car shot away, cruising out through the hedgerowed patchwork of English fields and meadows. 'This is a lovely part of the world,' he observed, his view of it shielded by a pair of fashionable black sunglasses.

'I love it,' Susan replied. 'I wouldn't want to live anywhere else, I don't think.'

'Have you always lived here?'

'All my life.' She paused. 'What brings you here?'

'Apart from you, you mean?' Alan smiled, and he felt a warm glow when Susan returned a lopsided grin. 'This is the sort of place I have been looking for,' he continued. 'Quiet and scenic.'

'What do you do, workwise?'

'I rob banks.' Alan smiled again.

'That's what I thought.' Susan nodded sagely. 'It's written all over you.'

'Good grief, I hope not. I'm supposed to be in hiding.' And they laughed together for the first time.

The restaurant was small without being cramped, and radiated a cosy, intimate atmosphere. The wine was white and chilled to perfection; Alan made the choice after Susan had coyly explained that the red always gave her an awful migraine.

'Veal!' she had gasped with exaggerated outrage when Alan declared his choice. A long discussion had ensued, with Susan maintaining that the animals were cruelly treated, whilst Alan insisted that they were bred for the purpose. Alan conceded with gentlemanly grace only after Susan had called him a horrible, heartless man and declared her intention never to speak to him again unless he relented. He had settled instead for the lobster, wondering wryly if this would invoke another slap on the wrist as he was certainly of the opinion that lobsters suffered a far worse fate than calves.

The evening went well. She laughed at his sallies in all the right places, and he paid her his undivided attention, replenishing her glass when it was only half empty and enquiring as to the standard of her salmon. By the end of the evening Alan was in such a mood of gaiety that he treated himself to a large cigar; and they had sipped at their complimentary *digestifs*, his a small brandy and hers a peppermint liqueur.

Now the red BMW sat parked outside Susan's flat, the engine quietly purring. Alan watched from behind the wheel, the taste of Susan's warm moist lips still tingling on his as she waved goodnight from her front door.

The car glided slowly away and Alan breathed deeply, savouring the lingering perfumed air. It was ten minutes before he arrived home. It was two hours before he managed to get to sleep. He was woken by one of those sudden electrical storms that the long hot summers always bring. The thunder rumbled and crashed and the lightning lit up the bedroom, and a horse was being galloped through Busjibber Lane.

The fat man in the expensive suit pulled the venetian blinds closed against the dazzling evening sunlight.

'Surely,' he said, 'this would be a relief to the local populace.'

'A relief?' The tall man peered over the top of his spectacles.

'Why, of course.' The fat man returned to his chair. 'No noise, pollution, accidents even.' He waved an expressive hand. 'All things of the past.'

'I am not so sure that some of the residents of these small villages feel the same way. Little Wixley, for example–'

'Little Wixley,' the fat man interrupted with a condescending smile, 'is the only bone of contention, and then only a small bone. You can't make an omelette without breaking some eggs.'

The tall man studied his fingernails, his brow creased into a frown. 'Some omelette,' he muttered.

The fat man lifted a Havana from a silver cigar box and crackled it to his ear. 'This is progress, you do understand?'

'I do understand that what you are proposing may not be illegal...'

'It's not.'

'...but it is morally bankrupt.'

The fat man held a gold lighter to his cigar and inhaled deeply before slowly blowing out a thin stream of blue smoke. He fixed his cold blue eyes on the other man.

'A seven-year-old was killed in Fuldon last year. There have been three other accidents there in the last six years. It is a black spot. There is nothing morally bankrupt, as you put it, about putting a stop to that.'

The memorial to the fallen of Little Wixley stood at the corner of the village green, its granite column engraved with the names of those who had made the ultimate sacrifice in the Great War.

The name Cobden followed that of Appleby and was followed in turn by another twenty two names, all in alphabetical order, a testimony to the first day of the Battle of the Somme, when Little Wixley had lost a generation. Two further names had been added beneath the inscription *1939–1945.* When, on 10 May 1940, the German armies had hurtled across their Western frontiers, the first name had been added. The second much later at Tobruk.

There would have been a third but for the tenacity of a young subaltern in the Queen's Hussars. Victory is an intoxicating drug and, as the SS Obersturmführer had smashed his way though France, he had allowed his victories to inflate his already arrogant ego. He had felt sure that the delay in his advance was nothing more than a trifling irritant. He had not taken into account the youthful idealism and daredevil bravado of a nineteen-year-old British lieutenant by the name of Dembury.

The subsequent citation, printed in *The Times*, told of how Lieutenant Dembury, armed only with two grenades and a Webley revolver, had destroyed a German tank, thereby closing the road and stopping the enemy advance in its tracks, and allowing his own unit much needed time in which to regroup.

The lieutenant had lost two fingers from his left hand in the exchange and was rewarded for his efforts with the Military Cross. *The Times* did not relate how the Obersturmführer had been the third to fall to Lieutenant Dembury's revolver.

Douglas Cobden walked past the memorial and nodded a greeting to the grandfather he had never known, before entering the Three Pheasants.

Max sat in the corner, as much a part of the furniture as anything else, and gave Piper a friendly pat as the spaniel sat at his feet.

'Some storm last night,' Douglas opened.

'Oh yes.' Max nodded. 'I should think Tom Dixon was out.'

Douglas smiled ruefully. 'Apart from that, it's been splendid weather.'

Max had to agree. 'You'll begin with the harvesting shortly if this sunshine keeps up.'

The fields were ripening early. Mile upon mile of golden corn splashed with red blotches of blooming poppies rippling gently in the heat. 'And then the ploughing,' Douglas added as he made short work of his Guinness.

Neither man was wrong. Before the week was out, the countryside echoed to the roar of the harvesters, the huge machines cutting wide swathes through the level fields of corn and throwing up great clouds of dust and chaff, until the land was left with only the straw stacks left behind by the pick-up balers. The silage pits steadily filled, food enough for the dairy herds during the lean winter months, and the fields that only a week before had been burnished yellow with corn turned to a rich brown as the ploughshares tilled the soil.

Douglas and Mary shared a bottle of wine as they sat in matching camp chairs in the small garden at the rear of the farmhouse, and the end of another long day brought a peaceful calm as the sun dissolved into a scarlet and pale blue sunset.

'We might even show a profit this year,' Douglas was saying. 'Make a change, wouldn't it?'

'We made a profit last year,' Mary gently reminded him.

'Not much of a one.'

'You've never made a loss.'

Douglas gave his wife a rueful smile. 'You'll never be rich, married to a farmer, Miss Hamilton.' He smiled as he used Mary's maiden name.

‘I never thought I would.’ Mary returned the smile.

‘That’s something, I suppose.’ Douglas chuckled. ‘At least I know you didn’t marry me for my money.’

Mary stood up and pushed a hand between the buttons of Douglas’s chequered shirt and tugged at the hairs on his chest. ‘Bring that bottle with you and I’ll show you why I married you,’ and she ran her tongue over her lips and arched a playful eyebrow at him before disappearing into the house.

Douglas drained his glass and grabbed the bottle by its neck before following his wife. ‘Shameless strumpet I’m married to,’ he muttered, and then he grinned rakishly. ‘Lucky old me.’

Alan De Angelis checked his appearance in the mirror for the tenth time in as many minutes before realising that he was feeling nervous. He immediately vowed not to look into the mirror again and to calm down, which he attempted to do by sitting in the armchair beside the fireplace and taking two deep breaths.

The knock at the front door caused him to almost leap out of the chair and he had to force himself to walk at a casual pace along the hallway.

Alan adopted a masculine pose as he eased the door open, lifting his chin and thrusting his chest out a fraction, and Mrs Buxton smiled up at him.

‘Ah...Mrs Buxton?’ Alan almost spluttered.

‘Who were you expecting?’ Mrs Buxton asked craftily.

Alan avoided the question, suspecting that the old woman probably knew more than she was letting on. ‘What can I do for you?’ he asked instead.

Mrs Buxton held a teacup forward. ‘I hope I’m not being any trouble, but I wondered if I could ask you for a cup of sugar?’

‘Of course,’ Alan replied, and he hurried through to the kitchen. He poured sugar into the cup, thinking that the last thing the old woman wanted was sugar. ‘Nosey old bat,’ he muttered under his breath.

Alan returned to the door to find Mrs Buxton in conversation with Susan. Mrs Buxton’s old lined face broke into a wide toothy smile. 'You're going to see the castle then?' she said, leadingly. Alan nodded weakly, feeling that he was far from in control of the situation, and wished fervently that the old woman would go away. 'I hope you enjoy it,' Mrs Buxton said, and with a smile for Susan she ambled off along the garden path.

Alan let out an inaudible sigh of relief and turned his attention to Susan, and all his feelings of nervousness returned. Susan looked stunning, and the smile she gave him caused his knees to weaken.

'Well,' Alan said, totally tongue-tied.

'Ready?' Susan asked, sensing his discomfort.

'You're the boss.' Alan smiled. 'Lead on.'

The two of them followed the course of the Wix, talking about everything and nothing, while the sun warmed their backs and the natural world beyond the village buzzed around them.

The slopes of the valley widened until they gradually petered out into high level ground, and Susan pointed to a tree-covered hill which rose out of the ground in the middle of the broadening plain.

'Wixley Castle is on that hill,' she said. Alan looked hard at the steep sides of the hill, searching vainly for anything breaking the skyline which might vaguely resemble a castle turret or battlement.

'Can't see much,' he remarked, shielding his eyes with his hand.

'You'll see,' Susan assured him and she took his hand and they walked together along the narrow road that skirted the hill. The sign in the carpark at the bottom of the hill proclaimed Wixley Castle to have been built by the Normans around AD 1079 as a strategic strong point commanding the only exit from the Wixley Gap.

Alan looked up the hillside, a look of puzzlement etched onto his features. 'I still can't see a castle,' he muttered confusedly.

The gravel path that crunched beneath their feet gave way to a flight of wooden steps, and the trees fell away to reveal the flat top of the hill.

'There you are,' Susan said.

Alan peered around the hilltop at what remained of Wixley Castle. The gateway had all but disappeared, its one remaining wall reaching sixty feet into the sky, as if proclaiming its past glory and defying all the world to bring it down. The curtain walls which ringed the hilltop had crumbled, having failed the test of time, and now stood only a few feet high. In the centre of the flat plateau the motte had vanished completely, only the man-made mound of earth which had been overrun with trees remained to show that it had ever been.

Alan completed his perusal of the depleted castle and looked at Susan. 'Is that it?' he asked incredulously.

'What do you mean, "is that it"?' Susan replied, her voice unsure.

Alan decided that it would probably be imprudent to mention that what he considered to be a sparse collection of ruins was not really worth an hour's walk.

'No suits of armour?' he mocked lightly.

'Very funny,' Susan chided him. 'This is part of our history. We are rather proud of it. Come on.' She took his hand. 'I'll show you around.'

The next fifteen minutes seemed like the longest of Alan's life, and he struggled manfully to keep a look of interest on his face.

'What do you think?' Susan asked after the tour was complete.

'You can feel the history,' Alan replied, thinking that diplomacy and tact was called for. 'It was a good idea. Thank you for showing me.'

Susan's smile was all the reward Alan needed, and he considered the passionate kiss that followed to be a bonus.

The hot afternoon sun filtered away as the dusk fell slowly and gently through the late summer evening, and a barn owl made a low hunting pass on silent wings over the warm farmland. Alan and Susan walked hand in hand beneath the full branches of the beech trees which flanked the clear, sparkling waters of the Wix.

'De Angelis is an unusual surname,' Susan observed as she watched the owl disappear across the quiet meadows.

'My grandfather was French,' Alan replied, ducking beneath a low branch. 'It means "of angels". He came over during the war, flew a Spitfire with the Free French.'

'Of angels, that's lovely.' Susan smiled.

'It's starting to get cold.' Alan changed the subject. 'Let's start heading back.'

'How did you make your money, if you don't mind my asking?' Susan looked up at Alan as they quickened their pace along the river bank.

'On the stock exchange,' Alan replied. 'Started at eighteen, made my fortune by the time I was thirty and now I'm retired.'

'All right for some.' Susan smiled again.

'It was hard work, not physically, but mentally. Long hours.'

'But worth it, retired at thirty.'

'Oh yes, worth it.'

'What are your plans now?'

'Settle down, I suppose. I don't really know.'

'Here in Wixley?'

'Why not?'

The pair walked on in silence, following the course of the winding river until they passed over the stone bridge and into Busjibber Lane.

'Coffee?' Alan asked, as casually as he could.

'Yes, okay,' Susan replied, equally casually, and Alan led the way into the small cottage.

August

Alwyn sat in the study looking out over the well-maintained lawns at the rear of the vicarage with a slight frown creasing his brow. He could not prevent a pair of grey squirrels from making off with the nuts which he left out for the local birdlife. No matter which method he attempted, the dedicated and inventive squirrels managed to defeat him.

Alwyn watched with grudging admiration as the two sneak thieves displayed an almost human intelligence as they foiled his latest brainwave. He had suspended the tubular wire basket which held the nuts from the end of a thin strip of wire that he had nailed to the edge of the bird table, but even as he sat back to see how it fared, he had a niggling feeling that it was doomed to failure, and now he sighed with exasperation as the squirrels hung upon it as lightly as they would a supple branch.

Alwyn opened the heavy leaded window and clapped his hands. The pair of raiders dropped to the grass and scampered away across the sunny lawns and into the sanctuary of a mature sycamore.

'Grease!' Alwyn said with determination.

The squirrel twins sat side by side on a sturdy bough looking between the green drooping leaves of the sycamore at Alwyn smearing grease onto the post which supported the bird table.

'Not the old "grease the post" trick,' muttered the first twin, his soft American drawl betraying his heritage.

'Sure does look like it,' his younger brother by one minute nodded his stetson in agreement.

'Like taking candy from a baby,' they both said as one, before collapsing into a fit of giggles.

The twins watched with open amusement as Alwyn completed the task and then looked up at the tall sycamore. 'Beat that!' they heard him call, his voice full of confidence and certainty.

'I do believe he means us,' the younger twin observed, his mid-western accent bubbling with wry amusement as they watched Alwyn make his way back to the potting shed at the bottom of the garden.

'I guess we could beat our own record here,' the elder twin ventured, and the twins had taken their first nut before Alwyn had emerged from the wooden shed.

The cottage had reverberated to the sound of the hammer and the saw for a month and now stood proudly showing off its new, refurbished exterior as the powerful redolence of fresh paint and new carpets mingled within.

The windows all boasted new frames and the stairs no longer creaked. Both the front and the back of the cottage sported a new door, the front protected by a gabled porch from which hung a pair of wicker baskets, each overflowing with radiant blooms.

A new gate, arched and elaborate, took pride of place between the natural-looking picket fence and the lawn, which, now trim and tidy, was decorated with a tall statue of a slender Aphrodite, an urn of water balanced precariously on her narrow shoulder.

Susan walked leisurely up the short path and around the side of the cottage, passing through the wrought-iron gate which Alan had erected in the passageway, to find him sitting bare-chested on the wooden bench he had bought the week before but had still not decided where to place.

'No slacking,' she said, stooping to accept his kiss.

'No nagging.' Alan smiled, pulling Susan down so that she sat upon his lap.

'Not a lot more to do,' Susan observed, looking around the long garden.

Alan had cut the grass back, beginning with a scythe and later a mower, and had pruned the hedges into neat ornaments. The old broken fence had been torn out and replaced by a taller lattice-work which acted as a windbreak as well as affording some privacy.

Only the far end of the garden, two feet lower and comprising the decrepit pond where the nettles and weeds were still predominant, required attention.

'I should have it all done within a fortnight,' Alan replied. 'It's been a long process.'

Susan ran her fingers through the tight curls which spread the width of Alan's chest and kissed him lightly on his forehead. 'It's one o'clock, let's go down to the pub. I'll buy you a nice cold beer.'

'Can't argue with that.' Alan smiled, pulling on a white short-sleeved shirt.

The two of them walked hand in hand along Busjibber lane, pausing briefly on the old stone bridge to throw a few slices of bread to the pair of pure-white swans which were threading their way through the bulrushes with their brood of fluffy grey cygnets, before strolling on, across the sunny green and into the shady seclusion of the Three Pheasants.

Douglas smiled broadly as they entered. 'Morning, young lady.'

'Morning, Uncle Doug.' Susan put her arms around Douglas's neck and kissed him lightly on the cheek.

'Why don't I get one of those?' Mortimer interjected from behind the bar, a mischievous smile playing at the corner of his mouth.

'Because something might leap out of that enormous beard and eat me whole.' Susan smiled in return, and the assembled male company sat the length of the bar laughed indulgently.

Susan paid for the drinks, which resulted in Alan accepting ribald comments from the others as to how they all wished they could find a woman with such tendencies, before Douglas took Alan's attention.

'You're a strong-looking man,' Douglas began. 'Do you think you are up to lifting a table clear off the ground, a heavy table, mind you?' Alan became aware of the silence that had descended on the room as Douglas asked his question. 'There are free drinks for you and me this lunchtime if we can.'

'What table are you talking about?' Alan asked, puzzled.

All eyes turned towards the large and imposing table which held the dominant place in the room.

'That's the one.' Mortimer indicated with a nod of his head.

Surrounded by a collection of low chairs, the long and heavy oak table stood commanding and scornful, like a barbarian king holding sway over a savage court, defying any to dare challenge its supremacy.

Alan passed a wary eye over its rough surface. The table was thick, at least three inches, closer to four, he thought, paying the table a grudging respect, and it was obvious why the challenge it offered was not one to be taken lightly. Alan was no judge of weight but at twelve feet long and with a surface three feet wide, the table was going to be mighty heavy.

'Have you ever tried before?' he asked, dragging his eyes away from the table.

'Only once,' Douglas replied, 'years ago, when I was your age. Never lifted it then, and never seen it lifted either.'

'Has anybody ever lifted it?' Alan turned to Mortimer.

'Only once.' Mortimer looked fondly at the table. 'Two

firemen lifted it once about twenty years ago. Only time it's ever been done.'

Alan walked across to the table and ran a finger along its surface. 'I should think lots try, eh?'

'About a hundred times a year,' Mortimer replied with a wry smile, and a chorus of chuckles rippled along the bar.

'You can do it.' Susan smiled encouragingly.

'Easy for you to say,' Alan murmured. He was far from sure that he could. The table looked awesome.

'What do you say?' Douglas asked, and Alan felt as if the eyes of the whole world were upon him.

Alan walked slowly down the length of the table and dropped to his haunches at its far end, his eyes narrow, his lips pursed into a thin line. A long silence fell on the room as he weighed the odds. He was beginning to feel that he had little choice. Susan had not taken her eyes from him. In fact, no one had. His long pause to contemplate his chances had drawn the attention of everybody in the room.

Alan decided that a decision was needed before he began to appear too daunted by the prospect of failure, so he rose abruptly to his full height and looked Douglas square in the eye. 'Let's give it a go then.'

Douglas, with a tight smile, took up his position at the far end of the table. Both men dropped to their knees and positioned themselves beneath the ends of the long table, their broad backs pressed up against the underside. They adjusted their positions, placing their feet firmly beneath themselves and bunching their fists so that they dug into the carpet.

'Ready?' Douglas squinted sideways at Alan, his tongue darting across his top lip.

Alan tested his position one last time before replying, 'Yeah, ready.'

'On three then,' Douglas commanded. 'One, two, heave,' and both men flexed their muscles, the cotton of their shirts stretching across their broad backs and over the bulging muscles in their shoulders.

Alan was the first to relax. 'Heavier than it looks,' he breathed. The stout legs still stood embedded deep in the carpet. He adjusted his position, burrowing his back into the underside of the table and his right knee into the carpet.

'All right?'

'On three.' Douglas nodded.

The two men drew a deep breath and heaved, and the veins at their temples swelled with the exertion, their faces turning dark red with hot pulsing blood.

Douglas snorted loudly, the breath shooting through his nostrils as the effort became too much, and Alan did the same. Both men stepped out from beneath the table and stretched their tightened muscles, flinging their arms above their heads and arching their backs.

'Too much for you?' Mortimer eyed both men, his right hand stroking his beard thoughtfully.

'We're not beaten yet,' Douglas replied, sucking down a great lungful of air. The two men looked at each other across the long imperious table, and each read in the other's eyes that tenacious spark of a man hell-bent on victory, and they nodded at each other in complete unison and then ducked beneath the table again.

'This time,' Alan said.

'On three,' and the two men braced themselves and then forced all the power of their muscles upwards into the hard unyielding oak. A long row of sweat broke out across Alan's brow, his teeth clamped tight, and still the table did not move.

Two enormous damp patches had appeared beneath Douglas's armpits, staining his shirt, and still the table remained glued to the floor.

And then, with a sharp, creaking protest, the table began to relinquish its grip on the carpet.

The two men strained against the dead weight, the solid wood digging into their backs and creasing deep furrows across their shoulders.

And then a simultaneous roar broke from their taut throats as the table gave up its hold on the floor and rose an inch above the carpet, its old wood groaning its defiance.

The room erupted into spontaneous applause and Susan fell to her knees and pushed a flat beer mat through the space between the carpet and each of the four raised legs. 'That's it!' she yelled exultantly, and the two men eased their efforts and the table fell to the ground with a heavy thump. Alan and Douglas breathed a relieved sigh together as the enormous weight was lifted from their shoulders, and then eased themselves out from beneath the defeated table.

The applause had become deafening and Mortimer was already pouring the pair their first free drinks. Susan looked at Alan with wide, adoring eyes as the two men clasped each other's hands and congratulated themselves, and then Alan, his mood triumphant, lifted his pint from the bar and threw a long and powerful arm around Susan's waist and pulled her to his chest before pressing his lips to hers in a fierce, masculine kiss, and Susan melted against him, her cry of outrage dying on his lips.

'My reward,' Alan said, smiling broadly as Susan recovered her breath, and she punched him playfully on the firm muscles across his chest.

Douglas raised his glass in a toast to himself. 'I've waited a long time for this,' and he took a long swallow of the beer.

Across the room, sitting alone in a corner, Timothy Dembury looked at Alan with eyes that dripped venom.

Twinkle sat in the shadow of the barn, shielded from the direct heat of the sun by its high wooden roof, with a look of utter contempt on his face.

'They may as well give me a bell to ring,' he muttered angrily. Twinkle had been banned from the house the previous afternoon and was now forced to take his meals in the barn, something which made him wonder how many further indignities would be heaped upon him before this thing was over.

Twinkle had fleas.

There was only one thing about farm life that Mary Cobden could not abide, and that was fleas. Not the smells. Not the long hours. Not the muck nor the weather. Only the fleas. And Twinkle had fleas.

Twinkle knew exactly what that meant. Mary Cobden had one method of dealing with fleas. Twinkle would find himself up to his whiskers in a bath of warm, soapy water, and the repercussions of an episode like that could last for days, perhaps weeks!

He had suffered two baths last year, he could well remember. Douglas had chased him all over the farmyard without success until Twinkle had fallen for an old trick: a plate baited with steaks of tuna. He had barely settled himself to enjoy the feast before the trap had been sprung, and he had still been wrapped in the net when they had lowered him into the bath. Twinkle shuddered at the thought. Still, he nodded to himself, he had learnt his lesson. He would not fall for that one again.

Across the yard Douglas was leaning on the sill of the open kitchen window, looking at the ginger tom. 'A plate of tuna,' he said over his shoulder to his wife. 'That's what caught him last time.'

'And he knows it,' Mary replied.

'It's worth a try, though.'

Twinkle watched with detached amusement as Douglas crossed the yard, a plate brimming with fish in his hands and a cheery smile on his face. 'Puss, puss,' Douglas called. Twinkle snorted derisively. 'Puss, puss, my paw!'

Douglas placed the plate just outside the door of the barn and disappeared inside. Twinkle watched and waited with all the patience peculiar to his species. The sun beat down upon the yard. Only the flies moved beneath its relentless heat. Twinkle yawned. He could keep this up longer than any human. A swift skimmed the cobbles before vanishing over the flint wall. Twinkle flicked a nonchalant paw at a gnat, and Douglas peeped around the door frame.

Twinkle raised a triumphant eyebrow as Douglas leaned against the wall of the barn and gave him a challenging look.

'I see,' Douglas said softly.

Twinkle turned and flicked his tail disdainfully before sauntering away to find himself a place in the sun.

'I do not have fleas!' Fox barked.

'Foxy,' Weasel cocked a frosty eyebrow, 'we all have fleas.'

'Speak for yourself,' Fox said indignantly.

'For God's sake, stop it,' Weasel snapped. 'If you haven't, then you must be the only one of us who hasn't.'

'That, I can assure you, is the case,' Fox replied. He reached into his silver cigar case and selected a Monte Cristo. It was an affected action, as much to do with drawing his mind away from the incessant itching beneath his waistcoat as anything else.

Weasel, of course, was right, and the fact niggled Fox inordinately. Vermin, Fox thought, with an involuntary shudder.

'Something walk over your grave?' Weasel asked craftily. Fox ignored the remark. 'Probably a flea,' Weasel smirked.

Fox almost exploded.

'Calm down, calm down,' Weasel held up a placatory paw. 'I was only joking.'

Fox paced the room, puffing furiously on the cigar. 'I might perhaps have one,' he conceded.

'One!' Weasel laughed aloud.

'Oh, very well,' Fox capitulated. 'If you must know, I'm infested with the damnable things. I probably caught them from you anyway.'

'Now, now,' Weasel consoled him, 'it's not the end of the world.'

'It only feels like it,' Fox moaned.

'You know what to do?' Weasel asked.

Fox nodded. 'Of course.'

'I'll come along.' Weasel got up to leave.

'We're not going now!' Fox almost shouted.

'Why not?'

'It's broad daylight. We'll go once it's dark.'

Weasel sighed helplessly and flopped back onto the settee.

Twinkle opened his eyes a fraction. The sun had turned from dazzling yellow into a glowing red ball that sat just above the horizon, its slow descent making way for the encroaching dusk.

Twinkle lay quite still, his ears pricked, and he caught again the sound of a soft footfall. He leapt up and sprang onto the flint wall just as the net fell onto the spot where had had been lying. He stared balefully at Douglas Cobden, who stood with his fists bunched on his hips.

'I'll get you,' Douglas muttered.

Twinkle dropped down the far side of the wall and loped casually away from the frustrated farmer.

Fox and Weasel stood side by side at the edge of the river bank. 'Looks a bit nippy,' Weasel opined.

'That cannot be helped,' Fox said. He broke two twigs from a nearby bush and offered one to Weasel, and then he held his own twig between his teeth before walking gingerly backwards into the clear waters of the Wix.

Fox blinked rapidly as the fleas raced across his face, away from the rising water that lapped above his silk cravat, and then he dipped his snout beneath the surface and spat out the twig, and the fleas went with it.

'That is that!' he said with finality.

Weasel repeated the performance, coughing and spluttering as he spat out the flea-covered twig. 'Much better,' he said, once he had recovered the bank.

'Now then,' Fox said, turning his thoughts to other matters. 'Something for supper, I think, is in order.'

Weasel nodded. 'Hear, hear to that.'

'Cobden's chickens?' Fox suggested.

'After what happened last time?'

'Oh, I've forgotten about that. I'm not a one to bear a grudge.'

Twinkle spat like a witch and clawed ineffectually at the net.

'It's no good complaining,' Douglas said, as he dipped a finger into the tin bath.

Twinkle screeched and writhed, cursing himself for his foolishness. He had felt sure that Douglas had retired for the night and that he was safe. Safe enough even to take advantage of the plate of tuna. He had sat enjoying the fish, not realising that he was being deliberately put at his ease until it was too late. Douglas had dropped the net on him from the barn gantry.

'Stop struggling,' Douglas ordered as he lowered Twinkle into the soapy water. Twinkle struggled as best he could, ignoring Mary's soft cooing as much as her husband's gruff commands, and Piper, who had thoroughly enjoyed his bath, grinned like a maniac throughout.

It was all over in minutes, the rinsing with clean cold water being the worst part, and Douglas picked the net away from the unhappy cat before letting it race out of the kitchen and into the night.

'That is that,' he said, echoing the words of a fox who, at that moment, was scrutinising his henhouse with hungry eyes.

'It's too dangerous,' Weasel whispered. 'There are some lights on in the house.'

'Something of a challenge, what?' Fox grinned.

'Don't do anything reckless,' Weasel cautioned. 'You remember what happened last time.'

'A case of bad luck, nothing more.'

'And one more case like that may be our last.' Weasel turned from the flint wall, hunching his shoulders into his camel-hair coat. 'Another time, Foxy. Let's go.'

Fox looked longingly at the henhouse. The stink of the chickens was strong in his nostrils, causing his breathing to snatch in his throat.

'Fox!' Weasel hissed.

'All right,' Fox hissed back. 'I can hear you.' Fox prised himself away from the wall and slipped through the gate.

'Foxy.' Weasel's tone was urgent.

Fox paid no attention.

Weasel waited behind the wall, his nerves tense, as Fox raced past the chicken run and headed for the barn.

'Where in the hell is he going?' Weasel mouthed.

Fox jinked out of sight, blending easily with the darkness. Weasel waited for what seemed an eternity before Fox reappeared, moving like a spectre across the cobbles.

'What do you say to that?' Fox asked, as he held the plate of tuna triumphantly beneath Weasel's snout.

Weasel's eyes lit up. 'That makes a change,' he agreed.

The pair devoured the chunks of fish, relishing the juices that trickled down their chins, and Weasel licked the plate clean, his tongue rasping across the china. 'Delicious,' he said.

'First class indeed.' Fox nodded. 'Very nice of them to leave it out for us.'

Chapter 3

September

The fat man in the expensive suit leaned back in the swivel chair and drummed his fingers on the top of the mahogany table. He stared out of the window at the rain falling across the Thames. He lifted the plans from the table and passed a casual eye over them before neatly folding and locking them in his drawer.

He stared again out of the window, deep in thought, before he opened the latest company report. It could not be long before he went under.

'Unless...' he muttered. 'Unless.'

The grey cockerel, a single Plymouth Rock amongst the array of Rhode Island Reds, strutted the length of the flint wall in a haughty fashion, deliberately ignoring the scratchings of the harem of hens that pecked at the cobbles. The proud rooster perched itself on the gatepost and thrust out its breast as it filled its lungs, and its crow rang out into another crisp autumn morning.

Jennifer was scattering handfuls of grain onto the cobbles, and the cockerel flapped clumsily down from the post and joined in the frenzy of feeding. Jennifer swapped the metal pail for a wicker basket and collected a dozen eggs from the henhouse before making her way back across the yard and into the kitchen.

Douglas was seated at the bare wooden table, taking his time over a mug of tea. 'It's lovely out today, isn't it?' he said.

'A nice day for a walk in the woods to see Mr Fox,' Jennifer added as she made room in the refrigerator for the eggs.

Douglas chuckled. 'How is Mr Fox?' he asked.

'I haven't seen him for a while,' Jennifer replied, 'but I'm sure he's all right.'

'What has he been living on if you haven't been feeding him?' Douglas wondered aloud. He knew only too well what the fox in the area was living on, and Jennifer's assurance that it was probably rabbits and mice did nothing to change his opinion. 'My chickens is what Mr Fox is living on,' he stressed, his voice full of frustration.

Jennifer was about to leap to her friend's defence when Mary Cobden came in from the yard. Her ash-blonde hair was cut into a fashionable bob after her previous day's journey into the village and she was also, much to her delight, a few pounds lighter. Douglas was not so sure about the new slimming idea. As much as he liked the new hairstyle, he did not really approve of Mary's insistence that she was too fat. As far as he was concerned she was not fat, merely comfortably plump. He could not abide bony women. Nothing to cuddle up to, he would complain, and he always maintained that it was Mary's buxom and well-rounded figure that had first attracted him. His protests had fallen on deaf ears and he frowned as he contemplated the idea of his wife fading away before his very eyes.

'What are you frowning at?' Mary was looking hard at him.

'Anorexic Annie!' Douglas pulled a face.

'I'm not anorexic,' Mary tutted.

Douglas turned to Jennifer for support. 'Mum's getting skinny,' he said, employing a stage whisper, 'and nobody wants a skinny mum, do they?'

Jennifer pulled a solemn face and gave her head a firm shake. 'A skinny mum is a miserable mum,' she opined with all the conviction of an old sage. Mary heaved a sigh of disbelief. 'And it said on the telly the other night that fat people are happier than thin people.'

Mary emitted a shriek of exasperation at the mention of the word fat, and Douglas decided that a quick exit was probably in order.

Mary's fixed stare propelled him out of the kitchen and he hurried across to the barn, deciding that he would stay out of his wife's way for a good while. Piper came at a trot from the kitchen and Douglas could have sworn that the spaniel was grinning.

Douglas climbed the ladder and his heavy boots thumped on the wooden boards as he made his way across the loft. Twinkle lay curled up on an old blanket and Douglas gave the ginger tom a baleful stare.

'Lazy cat!' he muttered. Twinkle decided to ignore the insult, preferring instead to keep both eyes closed.

Douglas lifted the axe from the corner where it rested and ran a thumb along the blade. Satisfied with the sharpness of the steel, he descended the wooden ladder and made his way around the outside of the barn to the woodshed.

He passed a keen eye over the logs he had gathered during the previous week. They were dry and would make good kindling. He selected a long, heavy log and swung the axe with both hands from above his head so that the blade bit deeply into the wood. Douglas dragged the log clear of the pile and worked the blade free before rolling the sleeves of his chequered shirt up above his elbows. His biceps bulged as he swung the axe again and again in a full swing, the blade arcing through the air from the small of his back and then thudding into the log that lay between his feet.

The thudding was still going on, the wood being systematically reduced to fist-sized logs, when Mary and Jennifer crossed the yard with a tray of sandwiches and three mugs of hot tea.

Douglas let the axe stand in the wood, took a deep breath and ran the back of his hand across his brow. 'What have we got?' he enquired.

'Ham and cheese,' Jennifer told him.

'Together!' Douglas teased her.

Jennifer giggled. 'Not together, silly.'

Douglas perched himself on one of the uncut logs and bit into a thick-cut ham sandwich. 'Delicious,' was his opinion. The ham was home-cooked; Douglas insisted on it.

The early nip in the air had vanished and the day had become glorious, dazzling golden sunlight and azure skies, and the three of them sat in silence, enjoying the autumn warmth.

Across the fields the first tints of brown were beginning to colour the leaves of Wixley Wood, and the skylarks were quieter now.

'The nights will soon be drawing in,' Mary sighed wistfully.

'Will Mr Fox be all right in the wintertime?' Jennifer asked.

'Mr Fox will be fine,' Mary assured her.

Douglas held other opinions. 'Not if I get hold of it first,' he muttered.

Jennifer kept her father's words in her head as she and Mary strolled through Wixley Wood an hour later.

'I must tell Mr Fox not to be friends with any naughty foxes,' she said to her mother.

'Oh?' Mary replied absently.

'Or Daddy might shoot him, like he does with the naughty foxes.'

'That's right.'

Those were not quite the words Jennifer wanted to hear and she raced ahead of her mother and into the clearing. She stood in the centre of the clearing and looked around at the surrounding trees. Fox was nowhere to be seen. She scanned the tree-line a second time and then crossed to the oak stump that Fox usually sat upon. Fox was not behind it and Jennifer's imagination began to get the better of her. Perhaps he had already fallen to another farmer's gun. Perhaps she was never going to see him again. Perhaps her father had already seen him off. Jennifer's eyes were wide and unblinking, like those of a porcelain doll, as she peered slowly around the clearing.

'Hello, old girl,' Fox chirruped as he sprang onto the stump.

Jennifer nearly jumped out of her white ankle socks. 'Mr Fox!' she shouted. 'I thought you were dead!'

'Dead?' Fox squeaked with a mixture of surprise and alarm.

'Well, not really dead.' Jennifer shook her head.

'How dead?' Fox was now utterly confused.

'Daddy says that you will be if you go and take any of his chickens!'

Fox let out a relieved sigh. 'Please assure your father that I will not be going anywhere near his chicken coop,' he lied.

'I already have,' Jennifer told him, 'but I don't think he believes me.'

'I wish he would. I have never been near his chickens,' Fox lied again.

'Cross your heart?'

Fox dutifully crossed his chest with his paw.

'And hope to die?'

'And hope to die,' Fox intoned with as much sincerity as he could muster.

'I believe you,' Jennifer said, and Fox felt suddenly guilty and not a little appalled at how he could stoop so low as to deceive one so young and innocent. However, before he had time to dwell on the matter, Jennifer produced a ham sandwich and Fox's thoughts turned to his stomach.

'Half for you, Mr Fox.' Jennifer divided the sandwich into two pieces. 'And half for me.'

Fox made short work of his half of the sandwich and then picked at his teeth with his tongue before speaking. 'How many chickens does our father have?' he asked casually. 'Just as a matter of interest, of course.'

'Twenty,' Jennifer answered, and Fox's eyes took on a crafty look.

Fox looked equally crafty that night as he and Weasel crouched in the shadow of the flint wall, their eyes fixed on the dark henhouse. 'Twenty plump hens,' Fox whispered, 'ripe for the plucking.'

Weasel slipped beneath the gate and tiptoed across to the chicken run. The padlock was new, large and heavy, but not unfamiliar to him. He crept back to the wall and spoke in hushed tones. 'Piece of cake,' he said, and the pair of them peeped again through the gate.

The silence of the night was suddenly broken as the barn door flew open and Douglas Cobden stood framed in a pool of light with his shotgun at the shoulder. The shotgun echoed through the night, the muzzle flash lighting up the darkness, and Fox and Weasel stood like statues as a piercing shriek went up from across the yard.

Douglas Cobden broke the shotgun and sauntered across the cobbles with a look of satisfaction written all over him, and then he picked up the dead fox by its brush and threw it, with what

Fox thought was a brutal finality, into the dustbin.

Weasel had a throat that felt like sandpaper and Fox's eyes had lost their look of jaunty confidence. The shocked pair slipped back behind the wall.

Weasel was the first to break the silence. 'Did you see that?' he husked.

Fox swallowed hard. 'One could hardly fail to,' he replied.

'That was close, Foxy.'

'A sobering thought, old boy.'

'That was nearly us.'

'Indeed!'

The two of them listened to Douglas closing the kitchen door and then they looked sidelong at each other; and no words were necessary.

If Douglas had looked out of his bedroom window he would have been amazed to see a fox and a weasel racing each other for the sanctuary of Wixley Wood.

Piper trotted across the village green ahead of Douglas, who wore a jacket for the first time. Autumn was well under way. The first leaves were lying on the grass and the days were slowly growing colder. Winter was not far behind.

Douglas entered the Three Pheasants to find a portly gentleman virtually holding court at the bar. Douglas dropped his jacket over a stool and caught Mortimer's attention.

'Guinness, please.' He nodded a welcome.

The fat man in the expensive suit waved an almost regal hand. 'Allow me.' He smiled broadly.

Douglas looked around the bar for somebody to either explain the situation or to make the introductions. Mortimer did the honours.

'Lord Bartholomew,' he began. 'Writing a book about this part of the world.'

'Pleased to meet you.' Douglas accepted the beer with a small nod. 'A book, you say?' he enquired politely.

Lord Bartholomew pursed his lips thoughtfully. 'A pictorial history,' he explained. 'With a particular leaning toward the countryside. Local folklore, that kind of thing.' Douglas nodded his understanding.

At the end of the bar Max spoke up. 'Tell him about Dixon's Point,' he said to Douglas.

Lord Bartholomew raised his eyebrows questioningly at Douglas, who sipped at his beer as he gathered his thoughts.

'Dixon's Point,' he said contemplatively. 'On the heath to the west of the village there is a large boulder, all on its own. Legend has it that a highwayman by the name of Tom Dixon died there.'

'Really?' came from the interested lord.

'So it is said.' Douglas shrugged. 'He was chased out of the village by the militia.' He paused to take a mouthful of beer and Mortimer interrupted with his claim to fame.

'Out of this very pub,' he declared before Douglas again took up the story.

'He got as far as that boulder before his horse was shot from under him. He took cover behind the boulder and there was a gun battle.' Douglas paused again as he ran his tongue along his cigarette paper. 'Tom Dixon was mortally wounded by a musket ball. The troopers told him that he would be put in the gibbet and he replied, "A curse on the gibbet, it will hold me not a day".' Douglas held a match to his cigarette before continuing. 'Anyway, they brought the body back and it was gibbeted. That night there was a terrible storm and the gibbet broke and was never repaired. Now, the gibbet stood on the other side of the river at the bottom of Poachers Hill. The lane became known as Broken Gibbet Lane, and then Bust Gibbet lane, and, when it was finally properly named, it was called Busjibber Lane.'

'Fascinating story,' Lord Bartholomew responded.

'That's not all.' Douglas smiled. 'Today, whenever there is a storm, the ghost of Tom Dixon gallops through the village but never gets any further than the spot where the gibbet stood.'

Lord Bartholomew was all smiles. 'Has anybody ever seen the ghost?'

'I've heard him,' Max said. 'You can hear the horse going over the bridge.'

'It may be true.' Douglas pulled on his cigarette. 'But who

really knows today?'

'These legends often have their basis in fact.' Lord Bartholomew nodded thoughtfully. 'It could well be true.'

'The militia were certainly around these parts,' Douglas replied. 'In the restaurant at the end of the road here, when they were renovating it, they found a false wall with one of those old three-pointed hats in it.'

'A tricorn?'

'That's it.'

'Obviously a village with a lot of history,' Lord Bartholomew observed.

'You've only got to look at Max,' Douglas quipped. 'He was around when it happened.'

Max grinned around the stem of his pipe. 'Less of your lip, young Cobden,' he growled playfully.

'How long will you be staying?' Douglas asked.

'Only a short while,' Lord Bartholomew answered. 'I have to be getting back to London.'

'We are having a knockabout cricket match this afternoon,' Douglas told him. 'You're welcome to play.' Lord Bartholomew thought it a splendid idea. 'We'll see you at three?' Douglas asked.

'Certainly! Look forward to it.' Lord Bartholomew said his goodbyes and made his way out of the pub.

Douglas could not help thinking that he waddled like a duck.

The early nip in the air was chased away by the afternoon sunshine and the game of cricket became a take-it-as-you-see-it affair. Twelve players in all. One batsman and eleven in the field. Highest scoring batsman the winner and, once out, the batsman became one of the fielders.

Maxwell had volunteered to do the duties of umpire, and Alwyn would keep the score from the bench beneath the sycamores at the same time as keeping the wasps away from the carafes of orange squash that Mortimer had provided.

'Ladies first,' Max suggested, and Susan skipped forward, insisting that cricket had probably not only been invented by a woman but was, and always had been, a woman's game.

Lord Bartholomew had used a pudgy hand to grab the ball before Douglas had driven the stumps into the ground, and now he stood some twenty yards behind Max and rubbed the ball on the crotch of his pinstriped trousers.

Rupert Bartholomew thundered towards the wicket, the spare tyre beneath his silk shirt wobbling like unset jelly, and the ball bounced halfway down the wicket and rocketed over Susan's head. Susan ducked instinctively, her eyes flaring with alarm.

'First ball,' said Bartholomew. 'Never mind, I'll get the next one right.' Susan smiled uncertainly, the unfamiliar bat held awkwardly in her hands.

The second ball was a yorker, delivered with devastating speed, and the middle stump was torn from the ground.

'Howzat!' Rupert Bartholomew bellowed, pointing his finger to the heavens as he implored Max to dismiss Susan from the crease. Max did not bother. Susan had already passed the bat to her uncle, and Douglas was as unimpressed as she was.

Rupert Bartholomew was all smiles. 'I used to play at Harrow, you know,' he boasted to Max.

'Really?' Max raised a weary eyebrow.

Douglas fared no better than Susan. The ball swung in with a vicious bounce and the leg stump only just remained in the ground. Rupert jumped as high as his belly would allow and his appeal echoed across the village.

Alan took the bat next. 'No problem,' he whispered to Douglas, and one minute later he hobbled back to his position in the field, his left shin bone aching painfully and Rupert's cry of 'LBW, umpire!' adding to his misery.

Mortimer managed two runs, his white beard bouncing on his chest as he ran the twenty two yards before the third ball shattered the stumps.

Mary stood, nervous and annoyed, and let out a frightened squeak as the ball destroyed her wicket without touching the ground.

Jennifer was next, and the bat was almost as big as she was. 'Take it easy, eh?' Max instructed the beaming lord.

'Of course,' Rupert replied. He dropped the fast pace,

choosing instead to prance gracefully around the wicket, and the ball spun in a high parabola, kicking sharply as it hit the green, and Jennifer never stood a chance.

Alwyn Jones removed his tweed jacket and rolled his shirt sleeves above his elbows as he strolled from the shadows. 'May I have a bat?' he enquired.

'By all means, Vicar,' Max sighed.

Alwyn picked up the bat from where Jennifer had dropped it and felt its weight in the palm of his hand. 'Hello, old friend,' he whispered, too low for anyone else to hear.

'Say your prayers, Vicar.' Rupert laughed, and then he charged towards the wicket. His arm came over his shoulder like a pendulum, the ball was released with perfect timing, and Alwyn launched it above the bowler's head and over the boundary.

'Six!' Max could not contain himself.

Mortimer was grinning through his whiskers. 'You mind my jugs of orange, Vicar,' he called. Alwyn smiled. 'They're in no danger.'

He drove the second ball through the covers for four and the third over the boundary for his second six. Rupert Bartholomew's face was lobster-red, a mixture of the effort of the extended run-up and his own rising annoyance, and as he let his fourth delivery go, his anger boiled over. The ball bounced halfway down the wicket, rising fast for Alwyn's head, and Alwyn pivoted his weight on his right leg and hooked the ball over his left shoulder.

'Six!' Max was now thoroughly enjoying himself.

Alwyn stared hard as Rupert Bartholomew made his fifth run. 'Forgive me, Father,' he muttered, and he drove the attempted yorker straight at Lord Bartholomew's head. Rupert flinched as the ball shot past his ear.

'Missed,' Alwyn muttered.

The ball bounced against the bark of one of the sycamores, and bounced again amongst Mortimer's jugs. 'You were saying?' Mortimer laughed.

Alwyn gave him a lopsided smile. 'Divine intervention,' he explained.

Rupert delivered his sixth ball with all the menace of the previous five, and Alwyn rested his weight on his back foot and brought the bat up underhand so that the ball lifted in a high, gentle lob. 'Catch,' he called to Jennifer.

Jennifer's face transformed itself into a study of childlike concentration and the ball plopped easily into her cupped hands.

It was all lost on Rupert Bartholomew. 'How is he?' he hollered, his arms raised in victory above his head.

Max grinned as Alwyn walked from the crease. 'Time for some orange juice, I think.'

October

Hedgehog snuffled his way between the trees at the edge of Wixley Wood. He avoided the fallen conkers in their half-open pods and left behind a vapour trail of frosted breath. The night was icy and he shivered involuntarily against the cold penetrating his bones.

He peered through the darkness, his eyes flicking left and right in the search for a home. Time was running short. His belly was full enough and the weather would only get worse from now on. He moved quickly through the wood, the dry fallen leaves rustling in his path, until he came upon a small glade.

The glade was well lit by the full moon, the air sharp and clear and, above all, silent. Hedgehog crept around the edge of the tree-line until he found what he was looking for.

The hollow base of the oak was almost totally obscured by fallen leaves so that he almost missed it; a fact that comforted him, for it meant that others might also overlook it. He worked his way through the leaves and between the roots of the tree.

He worked quickly. The bed was soon prepared, crudely fashioned but suitable, and the door would keep out the worst that Mother Nature could throw at him.

He looked out for one last time at the stars twinkling in the clear night-time sky and then firmly closed and bolted the door.

He set the alarm on his bedside clock for the month of March and then rolled himself into a ball beneath his thick blankets. Within moments his breathing was deep and regular as his heartbeat slowed, and his snores rolled contentedly around the bedroom.

Outside, Fox moved like a ghost, almost floating as he made his way across the glade and through the trees and their fallen acorns. The scent of Vixen's perfume lingered on his waistcoat and the silver tip of his cane shone beneath the stars.

Fox paused at the edge of Wixley Wood and looked out across the heath. The night was quiet and still, the cold causing almost everyone to stay indoors. He lit a cheroot and drew the smoke into his lungs, holding it there to savour its flavour and warm his body, and then he moved at a fast trot across the fields towards the small copse.

Alwyn sat in the study, looking out of the leaded windows at the seasonal change coming over the lawns.

The bright greens on the branches of the sycamores had turned to shades of coppery brown, reflecting the sharp autumnal sunshine with tints of gold and bronze, and the first fallen leaves lay crisp and forlorn on the grass. The flowers had lost their petals and long since withered and died, and now no insects, bees or butterflies buzzed about them.

The only consistency, Alwyn realised with a rueful smile, was the sudden appearance of the pair of grey squirrels as they bounded towards the bird table. Alwyn had fashioned a luridly coloured puppet which he had hopefully christened a 'scaresquirrel' and placed it at the foot of the upright support, but now he watched with an air of tired resignation as the two raiders ignored the puppet and sat insolently on the table, taking their time with the peanuts. Alwyn rested his chin on the palm of his hand and heaved a hopeless sigh. He could not even be bothered with opening the window and clapping his hands as that was proving ever more ineffectual.

The two grey squirrels vanished as quickly as they had appeared and Alwyn made his way through the old house before strolling leisurely along Church Walk. The day was brisk, the chill impervious to the sharp sunlight, and Alwyn walked with his hands thrust deeply into his overcoat pockets.

High in the branches of a tall elm the chattering rattle of a magpie carried along the lane. Alwyn followed the superstitious custom of the country and saluted the bird as he recognised the devil, and the magpie bobbed up and down as if in reply.

The bird kept pace with Alwyn until he reached the gates of the church and then it flew away in the opposite direction, as if contemptuous of his choice of venue. Alwyn laughed inwardly at the nonsense of it all as he watched the magpie disappear across the fields.

The sound of an approaching car caught Alwyn's attention and he forgot the magpie as a red BMW sped past. From the passenger seat Susan gave the Vicar a friendly wave before turning to Alan.

'He's got a good life,' she observed.

'Apart from the squirrels,' Alan added.

'All God's creatures,' Susan said with heavy irony.

Alan drove the car through Church Walk and past an old brick building that sat on a derelict site. A wooden sign had been erected in front of the building with the word 'Sold' displayed in bright red lettering.

'I cannot imagine who would want to buy that place,' Alan muttered, giving the building with its grimy broken windows a look of bemused horror. Alan dropped the driver's visor and donned a pair of sunglasses against the reflected glare of the piercing sunlight as the car left the village and turned onto an 'A' road.

'This is an old Roman road,' Susan commented.

The road was long and straight and was flanked on either side by rambling woodland and thick hedgerows.

'How long is it?' Alan enquired.

'Almost ten miles,' Susan answered. 'It leads directly past the Abbottsbury Paddocks.'

Alan drove the car at speed along the deserted road until a sign in the tree-line declared the following turn-off to be the route to the paddocks, and he slowed the vehicle and turned into a narrow twisting lane. He drove slowly along the pitted lane and into a courtyard formed by a surrounding collection of timber-framed buildings. Susan led the way across the yard, skirting a huge mound of manure and old straw that steamed in the cold day, before entering a long, high-ceilinged stable.

A tall woman in her early forties, dressed in riding breeches and boots, stepped out of a stall. Her long blonde hair was tied back into a ponytail that trailed over the collar of her Barbour jacket, and her manner was brusque and authoritative.

'Susan, I didn't know you were coming over today,' she opened.

'Spur of the moment, really,' Susan replied, before turning to Alan. 'Alan, this is Edwina. She owns the stables. This is Alan, a friend of mine.'

Alan held out his hand. 'Pleased to meet you, Edwina.'

Edwina's hand was firm and businesslike. 'Call me Eddie, everyone else does.'

'Eddie it is.' Alan smiled.

'Are you a rider?' Edwina immediately enquired.

'Chauffeur.' Alan grinned, and Susan gave him a slap on the arm.

'He's come to have a look,' she explained.

'Well, that's a start, I suppose,' Edwina decided. 'Bucephalus is in his stall. I'll see you later,' and she walked briskly out of the stable and across the yard.

Alan took a deep breath. 'What an intense woman!' he whispered.

'Oh, she's all right, typical horsey-type though.' Susan walked between the stalls with Alan a step behind until she reached a stall door which was painted sky-blue. The name 'Bucephalus' was imprinted in decorative scroll on the door and Susan leant over and called the name. The gelding was as black as tar and stood sixteen hands high. He responded to Susan's greeting with a shake of his mane before stepping forward and allowing her to caress his muzzle.

'He's magnificent,' Alan opined.

'Oh, he's more than that,' Susan replied softly.

'Why Bucephalus?' Alan asked, wrapping his tongue around

the word with difficulty. 'It sounds like a lung disease!' he added, an appalled look on his face.

Susan ignored Alan's remark and delivered another impromptu history lesson. 'Alexander the Great had a black stallion,' she explained patiently, 'and he was the only one who could ride it; the horse's name was Bucephalus.'

Alan was genuinely impressed. 'It suits him,' he said.

'Alexander named a city Bucephala after the horse when it died,' Susan continued.

She entered the stall and spoke softly to the gelding as she slipped the bridle on. Bucephalus stood still and patient as the saddle was buckled beneath his girth and then he allowed himself to be led out into the yard. The gelding snorted great clouds of steam into the autumn morning and Susan put one foot into the stirrup and vaulted nimbly into the saddle.

She smiled down at Alan from beneath her hard hat and he watched her walk the horse out of the yard and onto a bridle path that led into the surrounding countryside. Then he drove the BMW out of the paddocks and followed the directions for London.

The morning had brought the first hint of the forthcoming winter. A sharp frost had fallen during the night and Douglas paused to break a thin layer of ice on the cattle trough before tramping back along the lane.

High above, in the cloudless pale blue sky, a skein of white-fronted geese flew towards the west in arrowhead formation, their long migration almost over. Douglas picked up a fallen stick and threw it along the lane, and Piper sprinted after it. He played the game with the spaniel twice more before making his way across the cobbles and into the farmhouse.

Mary already had the stove glowing and Twinkle lay curled up beside it. Douglas gave the cat a dark frown. 'All that cat ever does is sleep,' he said.

Mary placed her husband's breakfast on the table. 'Don't you go picking on poor Twinkle,' she chided him.

'Poor Twinkle, my foot,' Douglas muttered. 'I wouldn't mind

so much if the lazy article actually caught some mice. The rodent population on this farm must be booming.' Twinkle opened his eyes a fraction and gave Douglas a black stare. Douglas stared straight back. 'And don't look at me like that,' he ordered, around a mouthful of bacon. 'Idle, good-for-nothing cat!'

Piper sat at his master's feet with a look on his face that Twinkle had come to loathe. Twinkle yawned and stretched in a show of uninterested nonchalance before sauntering across the kitchen. He drew level with the smirking spaniel and a deftly delivered right paw caught the dog on the tip of its nose. Piper let out a yelp and Douglas swivelled in his chair and let his left boot connect with Twinkle's backside. 'Ginger menace!' he snarled.

Mary was appalled. 'Stop that,' she shouted. 'We'll have no fighting.'

Douglas was unrepentant. 'It did that on purpose,' he insisted.

Mary opened the door and Twinkle stalked out in a haughty fashion. 'Lickspittle dog,' he muttered as he headed towards the warmth of the barn. 'I don't see him catching any mice either.'

Twinkle sprinted up the ladder and into the hayloft. He nestled himself into the folds of the old blanket that provided him with his favourite spot. 'And I don't sleep all the time either,' he complained, and he was instantly asleep.

It was the tiny scurrying of a late returning mouse that woke the sleeping cat. Twinkle's ears twitched and flicked once before his eyes opened into murderous slits. The mouse, busy amongst the loose wisps of straw, was oblivious to the danger that lurked only a few feet away.

Twinkle lay quite still, the muscles beginning to ripple along his flanks the only sign of the mounting tension. The mouse sat on its haunches and lifted its face to the air, and its nose caught the scent of danger. It crouched, its senses ringing with alarm as it turned to flee, and a million years of evolution descended upon it as the supreme hunter uncurled himself from his lair and moved with an almost indiscernible speed.

Twinkle carried his kill across the yard and scratched at the door. 'Let him stay out there,' he heard Douglas say. The door opened and Twinkle skirted Mary's ankles and dropped the dead mouse at Douglas Cobden's feet.

Mary arched an eyebrow and grinned at her husband. 'Well, well,' she said. 'Just look at that.'

Douglas did not know what to say, and Twinkle turned his back on him and strolled back out into the cold morning.

Mary was all smiles. 'That took you down a peg,' she said.

Douglas tried to appear unimpressed. 'One mouse,' he said dismissively.

'That's one more than you have ever caught,' Mary teased him.

Jennifer came through from the hallway and Douglas took the opportunity to change the subject. 'Morning, angel,' he smiled.

Jennifer immediately spotted the dead mouse. 'Has Twinkle caught another mouse?' she asked.

Mary looked quizzically at her daughter. 'Another?' she queried.

'He gets lots,' Jennifer replied. 'I usually bury them in the garden.'

Mary began to grin again. 'I didn't know that. How many have you buried?'

'Can't remember. About a hundred,' Jennifer exaggerated.

Douglas could not bear to listen to another word. 'I've got work to be getting on with,' he said, and he headed for the door.

'Watch out for the booming mice population,' Mary smirked. Douglas said nothing, deciding that he was in a situation that he could not win.

Twinkle was sitting on the cobbles watching as Douglas crossed the yard. Douglas cocked a rueful eyebrow at the ginger tom. 'All right, cat,' he said. 'You win.'

Douglas threw a coil of barbed wire and a bag of tacks into the back of his battered Land Rover, together with a claw hammer and a powerful winch, and the blue exhaust fumes lingered in the cold air as he drove out of the yard and along the track. The fencing that divided the field he kept for grazing from the fallow land was old and in places eaten away with rust. Douglas drew level with the fence before letting the engine die. The work was hard and painstaking, the heavy-duty gloves he wore protecting his hands from the sharp wire, and his shirt stretched across the bulging muscles in his shoulders as he worked the winch. He had discarded his jacket by the time Mary and Jennifer began to make their way along the track.

Douglas checked his watch. 'Eleven o'clock already,' he muttered.

Mary had with her a flask of hot tea and a round of sandwiches, and Jennifer had a basket with which she was already collecting the ripest blackberries. Douglas poured himself a full mug from the flask and let it stand to cool for a moment before using it to wash down a cheese sandwich.

'Halfway there,' he said, with a nod in the direction of the remaining hundred yards of rust-coloured fence.

Mary did not answer, her attention being focused across the fields in the direction of Wixley Wood. A rider atop an ebony-black horse was coming at the canter, and Mary shielded her eyes from the sharp autumnal sunshine as she watched the rider approach. 'We have a visitor. Susan, I should think.'

Douglas straightened up from the bonnet of the Land Rover and looked over his cup as the approaching rider put up a covey of partridges. The plump auburn birds throttled away into the distance and Susan brought Bucephalus up with ten yards to spare and allowed him to briefly clip at the grass as she slipped from the saddle.

'Lovely morning,' she greeted them, and grinned mischievously. 'Am I just in time for lunch?'

Douglas chuckled. 'Your sense of timing is superb,' he said.

Mary poured her niece a cup of tea. 'How's Alan?' she asked.

'Gone to London. Business or something,' Susan replied. 'I'm not quite sure. How's your fox?' she asked, turning to Jennifer.

Jennifer was always ecstatic when asked about Fox and she gave Susan a blow-by-blow account of his activities, imagined or otherwise, during the past month. 'And Twinkle caught another mouse,' she finished.

'Hooray for Twinkle,' Susan cheered.

'Hooray indeed,' Douglas said sourly.

The light from the street lamps reflected off the puddles forming on the dark London streets and rebounded from the shiny black umbrellas which hurried through the miserable night.

The fat man in the expensive suit turned away from the window in the twelve storey building and stubbed his cigar into a marble ashtray.

'If I can convince the powers that be that this motorway is necessary,' he began, 'then if I can secure the deal for the requirement of concrete...' He paused to settle his large body into a swivel chair which groaned beneath his weight. 'Then I can save the company from liquidation.'

The ill-lit room descended into silence as a tall middle-aged man with a closed file resting on his lap weighed up the odds. 'My company certainly needs an order of this magnitude,' he offered tentatively.

'Exactly!' The fat man leapt at the opening. 'We both need this motorway.' He dabbed at his brow with a silken handkerchief, a sharp contrast to the other man, who sat calmly, his face a mask which did not betray his thoughts.

'According to this file,' the tall man queried softly, 'this wood is centuries old?'

'You can't stand in the way of progress,' the fat man countered, waving a dismissive hand.

The tall man placed the file on the teak desk and looked up at the rain pattering on the window. 'Very well,' he concluded, and the walls closed in on the two men. 'If permission is granted for this motorway, you will get the order for the concrete.'

The storm. Always the storm. Black clouds heavy with the coming rain blocked out the weak light from the late October moon, and a wind with an edge like a knife lifted the mist from the river and blew it through the dark and silent streets of Little Wixley.

Chapter 4

November

Lord Dembury of Wixley, General Charles Randolph Tobias Dembury, MC, dressed in a knee-length black coat, a matching bowler hat set firmly on his head and a rolled umbrella held at the reverse slope beneath his left arm, stood stiffly to attention at the head of the regimental association of the Queen's Hussars and awaited the word of command from the uniformed guards officer at the head of the column.

General Dembury glanced down over his silver moustache at the row of medals gleaming brightly over his heart, and felt a warm prickle of pride course through his veins. He was not a man given to sentimentality. However, the annual Remembrance Day parade, when he marched at the head of what he firmly believed to be the finest regiment of cavalry in the world, never failed to bring a lump to his throat, so that he had to bring all his attention to bear on the proceedings to come lest his emotions overcome him.

From his position in the long parade, the General had already seen Her Majesty The Queen step forward on behalf of a proud and grateful nation and lay a wreath of blood-red poppies at the foot of the tall, silent Cenotaph. Whilst the nation's tribute was followed by the laying of wreaths from the armed services, the politicians and the representatives from the Empire and Commonwealth, General Dembury had waited with military patience and prayed silently that the slate-grey sky overhead would not turn to rain.

He braced himself, lifting his chin an extra notch as the stentorian word of command, which seemed to emanate from the very soles of the guards officer's highly polished boots, reverberated over the heads of the parade and along the crowded London streets. The parade moved off, a long precisioned line of stern-faced men, all with at least one medal pinned to their chests, all with their backs held straight, some with the paunch of middle age spreading over their belts, many with wisps of grey at their temples marking their generation, and a few, who revelled in the insult 'contemptible', flicking their head and eyes towards the proud monument from the comfort of the wheelchairs to which their great age had confined them, all with their own private memories, a domain which no other would ever enter.

The long column wound its way past the magnificent edifice emblazoned with the flags of the armed forces and down the narrow London streets until it passed out of sight of the respectful, adoring crowds and dispersed, the officers retiring to their respective clubs, the other ranks heading for the nearest public houses, there to swap stories and reminisce with old and trusted friends.

General Dembury made his way through the ranks of his own regiment, pausing to shake hands or pass a word with an old comrade, before climbing into the back of his limousine and allowing his driver to set off at a sedate pace for the hallowed surrounds of the Wellington Club.

Douglas walked Piper down Poachers Hill with his hands pushed deeply into the pockets of his sheepskin coat, his breath fogging the moist morning air. Below him Little Wixley sat silent and still, the grey tower of St Mary's Church rising through the thin mist that had risen from the river and now enveloped the village. Douglas walked through Busjibber Lane, the smoke rising from the chimney pot of the end cottage causing him to think of the open fire in the Three Pheasants, so that he quickened his pace, lengthening his stride as he crossed the mist-shrouded stone bridge and the swollen waters of the Wix that poured fast and cold beneath. He walked quickly through the village, nodding a greeting to a passer-by who was out walking a wet and miserable-looking Border collie, before entering the pub.

The lounge was warm and snug and the aroma of the woodsmoke rising from the logs already burning brightly in the fireplace added a comforting welcome. Apart from Max, who sat in his customary position at the end of the bar, the maroon tie of the parachute regiment knotted at his throat and a row of gleaming medals pinned to his chest, Mortimer had no other customers.

'Morning, Doug,' he said. 'Cold out today.'

'Winter is upon us, Mortimer,' Douglas replied, hanging his coat and scarf on a hook beside the door before settling himself onto a barstool. 'Guinness, please, Mortimer. Morning, Max, very smart.'

'Morning, Doug,' Max answered through his teeth, which were clamped tightly around the stem of his pipe.

'Something wrong?' Douglas enquired, detecting a certain tension in the two men.

Mortimer reached below the bar and produced a copy of the previous evening's newspaper. 'That's what's wrong, my friend,' he said, a dark frown creasing his brow.

Douglas unfolded the newspaper and the headline on the front page leapt out at him.

'Motorway?' Douglas's frown matched the landlord's. 'What motorway?'

'Exactly!' Max glowered, blowing out a cloud of angry blue smoke.

'I've heard nothing about a motorway,' Douglas remarked, his eyes traversing the article's opening lines.

'That goes for the lot of us,' Mortimer said, his tone indignant.

'Wixley Wood!' Douglas suddenly shouted, his eyes widening with shock. 'They can't lay a motorway through Wixley Wood.'

'Bloody criminal, I call it,' Max fumed, his eyes boring into the paper lying on the bar.

Silence descended in the room as Douglas continued reading the shocking news until he reached its startling conclusion. 'Compulsory purchase order of property in Busjibber Lane!' he shouted, aghast. 'They can't do that.' He looked up from the paper, his face registering his astonishment.

'They can and they will, given half the chance,' Max growled.

Mortimer picked the paper up from the bar and passed his

eyes over its stupefying contents for the fourth time since it had landed with such innocent piety on his doormat. 'Who needs it anyway,' he said, with a rhetorical grimace. 'We don't need a motorway, least of all between the village and Poachers Hill. It will ruin everything, the noise...' He tailed off, appalled at the form the nightmare he was conjuring up was taking.

'There won't be a minute's peace!' Max agreed, tapping furiously with the stem of his pipe at the pint of untouched brown ale which sat forlornly on the bar beside him.

'You realise, Douglas,' Mortimer said weightily, 'you will be affected.'

Douglas nodded slowly. He was only too aware of whose farmland the proposed motorway's path would affect the most. 'If it happens,' he commented ominously.

'That's right!' Max rejoined, his old, lined face dark and foreboding. 'We can't just sit back and let it happen.'

'We shall have to organise some sort of petition,' Mortimer suggested.

'That will do for a start,' Douglas agreed.

'This sort of thing takes money,' Max observed dryly.

'Start a fund,' Mortimer replied. 'I could put a bottle on the bar here.'

'It will take more than that,' Douglas remarked, pausing to take a swallow of his beer. 'These motorway types have got more clout than a jarful of loose change.'

Douglas's observations brought silence down upon the room again as the three of them contemplated the size of the task that they were faced with.

The sitting room of the Wellington Club, bedecked with huge portraits of British military figures throughout the ages and warmed by the wood crackling brightly in the fireplace, rustled gently to the sound of folding newspapers, the quiet clink of cut-glass decanters, and the shrill voice from the top of the room of Lord Bartholomew holding forth on his favourite topic.

Apart from a small group of younger men gathered around the corpulent lord, who stood in his customary position beneath a portrait of Winston Churchill, the members of the club seemed largely to be ignoring him. One man in particular was oblivious to what he always described as 'Bart's meandering waffle'. From his position beside the fireplace, the octogenarian Sir Montague De'Ath had already given up, having heard it all before, and was snoring loudly, his pince-nez slipping slowly down his aquiline nose, his long angular frame disappearing into the folds of a deep armchair.

'So pater said: come up on the left flank, the left, by God, but would Monty listen? Oh no!' the fat Bartholomew paused for effect before continuing his account of how his father could have won the war single-handedly had people only bothered to listen.

Sitting across the room in a deep leather-buttoned armchair away from the direct heat of the fire and wreathed in a cloud of blue cigar smoke, General Dembury stifled a yawn. He too had heard it all before, many times at that, he thought sourly, knowing that very little, if indeed any of it, was true. Judging by Bartholomew's long-winded stories, his father must have been in half a dozen places at once. The General allowed a flicker of a smile to touch his lips as he mentally predicted that at any moment the smug Bartholomew would make a grand sweep from Alamein to the Normandy beachhead without pausing for breath.

The General lifted a balloon glass to his lips and allowed a strong brandy to trickle across his palate. He took another pull on the huge Havana he held between the two only remaining fingers of his left hand and returned his attention to the open copy of the *Sunday Times* resting on his lap. The front page had held little to interest him and he had already turned to that part of the paper which catered solely for those of its readers who felt they had an opinion worth giving. The first two letters concerned Britain's ties with its Commonwealth and expressed views which he felt himself generally in agreement with and he read through them quickly.

The third correspondence caused him to sit bolt upright in his chair, the brandy rolling in his glass, his eyes widening as he read each line. 'What's this? Wixley Wood? What "mooted plans" for Wixley Wood?'

From the top of the room Lord Bartholomew's account of how his father had personally led the breakout from Sword Beach was cut brutally short by a thunderous bellow from the array of chairs on the far side of the room.

General Dembury, his face flushed crimson behind his silver whiskers, had risen from his chair with the copy of the *Sunday Times* held in the white-knuckled grip of his right fist.

'Motorway!' he roared again, the words ricocheting around the room. 'Over my dead body!' The paper, resembling a rising cock pheasant shot at its zenith, flew across the carpet in disarray as the furious General stamped out of the room.

Slumbering peacefully in his chair beside the fireplace, Sir Montague awoke with a start to find the dishevelled newspaper scattered about his person. He adjusted his pince-nez and craned his long neck over the back of the chair and peered myopically around the assembled company. 'What's all the fuss?' he enquired testily, lifting the centre pages of the newspaper from atop his head, where, following its short furious flight across the room, it had come to rest.

'I do believe,' Lord Bartholomew murmured, 'Charles found some concrete in his brandy.'

'Concrete, by Jove!' Sir Montague was already drifting off again. 'No need to take it out on me, what? Why not simply thrash the waiter,' he mumbled, before succumbing once again to the comforts of his armchair.

A gentle rustling of paper ensued as the gentlemen of the club returned to their reading matters, settling themselves like a clutch of broody hens who had been disturbed at their labours.

Lord Bartholomew placed his glass upon a low mahogany table and made his excuses. 'You'll have to forgive me, gentlemen, I've business to attend to,' he said, adjusting his monogrammed cufflinks and turning for the door.

'Oh, do tell of Arnhem before you go,' squeaked a young subaltern on leave from his regiment, his eyes still shining at the tales of Bartholomew Senior's derring-do at Normandy.

'Some other day, my boy.' Rupert Bartholomew consoled him with a fatherly pat on the elbow. 'I've a call to make. Arnhem will have to wait.'

Outside on the pavement the General buttoned his overcoat against the chill and pulled on his black leather gloves. The London street looked grey and dismal, the ground still wet from the rainfall. Setting his bowler firmly on his head and gripping the umbrella by its neck, he set off along the road, his step short and rapid, the look on his face matching the dark foreboding clouds rolling across the oppressive afternoon sky.

General Dembury turned a corner into an adjoining cul-de-sac and his driver sprang from the driver's seat and opened the rear door of the limousine. 'Pleasant lunch, M'Lord?' The chauffeur touched the peak of his cap respectfully as the General climbed into the back seat.

'Home, Hodges!' snapped the General. 'Best speed. I want to be there before nightfall.'

'Very well, M'Lord.' Hodges jumped behind the wheel of the car. He had seen the old man in this sort of mood before. Somebody was for the high jump and no mistake.

Hodges gunned the engine into life, put the car into gear and the Rolls-Royce shot out of the cul-de-sac and up the street, past the twin portals marking the entrance to the Wellington Club, just in time for the General to catch a glimpse of Lord Bartholomew speaking into the portable telephone he always carried and climbing into the back of one of London's numerous black taxis.

Mary tied Jennifer's woollen bonnet beneath her chin and then pulled her own gloves on before opening the kitchen door and allowing the cold day to rush in.

'Quickly, let's not let all the heat out,' she ordered.

Jennifer obediently hurried through the door and immediately clutched her mittened hands to her face. 'It's freezing,' she shouted.

'I know it is,' her mother answered. 'You should have thought of that earlier.' Mary pulled the door shut and wondered why on earth she had allowed herself to be persuaded into even stepping out of the house on such a day. 'Come along then,' she said resignedly, 'let's go.'

Jennifer walked at her mother's side as they crossed the fields towards the bare branches of Wixley Wood with her hands pushed deeply into her pockets and her coat buttoned to her throat. The wood offered a shelter from the wind and Mary was so grateful that the thought of having to walk back seemed all the more daunting.

Jennifer immediately ran ahead, following the course of the damp muddy tracks until Mary heard her urgent summons from the trees. Mary caught up with her at a bend in the track to find Jennifer pointing to a wet clearing where the grass was embellished with ring upon ring of wild mushrooms.

'Yes,' said Mary. 'That's what we're looking for.'

'I'll see if I can find some more,' Jennifer declared, and then she galloped off along the track. She made her way quickly to the clearing where she usually met with Fox and then called his name. Fox appeared from the edge of the trees and the two friends met with a mutual squeal of delight.

'It's very cold, Mr Fox,' Jennifer said, and she produced a ham sandwich for him. 'My mummy said it was so cold that we couldn't come today, but I told her you would be hungry so we came anyway.'

Fox accepted the sandwich and then his ears pricked to what the child was saying.

'If they do put a motorway through then my daddy says I won't be able to come any more but I'll try to anyway.'

'Motorway?' Fox puzzled.

'Daddy says that it will be too dangerous,' Jennifer continued, 'because a motorway is a big road, and I saw a picture of it in the newspaper.'

Fox's eyes grew wider as Jennifer rambled on in her sing-song voice, telling him everything she knew about the motorway until, by the time she had finished, he was in an almost complete state of shock.

'This is horrendous...' he spluttered.

'Daddy says it shouldn't be allowed,' Jennifer agreed.

'You say it was in a copy of a newspaper, Jenny?' Fox queried earnestly.

'I've brought it for you to see,' Jennifer replied, and she pulled the pages from her pocket before blowing on her fingers. 'You're lucky,' she observed as Fox studied the newsprint. 'You don't get cold fingers.'

'I do get a cold nose,' Fox replied.

'So do I.' Jennifer nodded in sympathy.

Mary's call echoed through the cold afternoon and Fox turned to leave. 'Thank you for bringing me this,' he said. 'I'll see you next week?'

'I expect so,' Jennifer told him.

'Let me know if you hear anything else about this motorway, won't you?'

'I will,' Jennifer replied, and Fox vanished into the trees.

Fox leaned back in the high-backed chair and blew a thin stream of blue smoke from between his lips before inspecting the ash at the end of his cheroot. Satisfied with the level draw of the cigar, he turned his attention to the open newspaper lying on the table before him. He lifted the newspaper and began reading, ignoring the smaller details and concentrating on the major revelations of the article with which he was concerned.

Fifteen minutes later Fox extinguished his cigar and threw the paper back onto the table in disgust. Across the room Weasel looked up from beneath his cap and squinted through the smoke rising from his thinly-rolled cigarette.

'Well?' he asked.

'See for yourself,' fox replied absently.

'You know I can't read!' Weasel snapped.

'Oh yes, I am sorry, old man,' Fox apologised. 'I do believe we have a problem,' he continued, his eyes still fixed on the newspaper. The dark frown which had spread across his face turned into a sharp scowl. 'We shall have to arrange a meeting with the others as soon as possible.'

'We could go now,' Weasel suggested, looking at his wristwatch. 'There's hours of darkness yet. Cut across Dembury's estate and we'll be there in no time.'

'Yes, you're right.' Fox stood up, picked up the newspaper

and his cane, and made for the door.

'Let's not waste any time then' said Weasel, opening the door. 'Badger's first, I suppose?'

'Badger's only tonight, I think. This may take some time.'

The Rolls-Royce swung majestically through the open gates of Blackthorn Estate and on up the long driveway, its path flanked either side by a series of stately, evenly spaced oaks. The car's headlights pierced the dark, revealing a fox and a weasel scampering across its path, until it came to a graceful stop on the white stone chip forecourt to the front of the large, ivy-clad house.

General Dembury scorned the services of his chauffeur and jumped out of the limousine impatiently before striding purposefully across the forecourt and up the steps towards the ornate oakwood doors. The doors opened as Lord Wixley mounted the steps and he marched through, ignoring the platitudes of the butler.

'Catherine!' the General bellowed, his voice ringing the length of the long hallway. 'Catherine, where are you?' His shouted demand carried throughout the house.

In her bedroom on the first floor, lady Dembury, a tall willowy blonde some twenty years younger than her husband and still possessed of a figure for which she was justly proud, reacted to the sound of her husband's voice in much the same manner as she would have reacted had she just poked one of her long manicured fingers into an electrical socket.

'Charles!' she gasped, pushing at the handsome footman. 'Off!' she ordered in hushed tones, regretting the interruption as she was just beginning to enjoy herself. Still, she consoled herself, there would be other times. She rolled the breathless Guido aside, jumped off the bed and began smoothing her skirt.

'What is it?' asked the bewildered footman.

'His Lordship's back,' Lady Dembury hissed as she began tidying her hair in front of the gilt-edged mirror on the dressing table.

Guido leapt off the bed as if he had been stung by an angry

hornet. '*Mein Gott!*' he whispered, 'I thought he was not due back until tomorrow.'

Lady Dembury turned from the mirror and gave the footman a quizzical look. 'What do you mean, '*Mein Gott?*' That's German.' She frowned as she slipped her stockinged feet into a pair of black stilettos. 'You told me you were Italian.'

'My mother was German,' Guido lied, as he buttoned his shirt over the dense black curls which covered his muscular chest. 'My father was Italian,' he lied again. 'I learnt the language on my mother's knee.'

Another resounding bellow from downstairs cut short Lady Dembury's interrogation and much to Guido's relief, she shot out of the bedroom door and down the winding staircase.

Guido, or Mustapha, as he was known to his Turkish parents, crept out of the perfumed bedroom and disappeared along the corridor, reflecting that being an illegal immigrant in Germany had never been as taxing as being a footman in England.

'Catherine!' the General was rapidly running out of patience.

'What on earth is the matter, darling?' Lady Dembury appeared, flushed and breathless, at the foot of the stairs.

'A bloody motorway, that's what the matter is,' His Lordship roared, working himself up into a fine fury.

'Calm down, dear.' Lady Dembury laid a restraining hand on her husband's elbow and guided him towards the sitting room door. 'Come and sit down and tell me all about it,' she soothed as she led her husband into the room.

In the sitting room, Benton, His Lordship's butler for twelve years and well-attuned to the moods of his master, had already placed a large Irish whiskey on the round table beside the General's armchair, along with a neatly clipped Havana, before quickly making himself scarce.

The General paced furiously across the room, snatched up the drink and took a long swallow before launching himself into another tirade.

'A motorway, no less. What do they think they're playing at? I've heard nothing of it. Well, they will have to cross swords with me first, I can tell you. If they think they can just -'

'Charles!' Lady Dembury shouted, interrupting her husband's

angry mood. 'Will you please calm down,' she said, before taking a deep breath. 'Now stop shouting and explain to me what on earth you are talking about.'

Lord Dembury lowered himself into his chair and looked up at his wife. 'I am sorry, my dear. I didn't mean to shout at you,' he apologised, putting down the glass and placing the large cigar between his lips.

Lady Dembury waited patiently while the General located a box of matches from the pocket of his tweed jacket and lit the cigar.

'It would appear, my dear,' he began, leaning back in the chair and exhaling a thin stream of blue smoke, 'that there are plans afoot to lay a motorway through Wixley Wood.'

Lady Dembury, her eyes resembling the glassy stare of the stag's head which hung above the fireplace, picked up her husband's empty glass. 'Another?' she asked, thinking that she could probably do with one herself. Two shocks in the space of five minutes was more than she could bear.

'Yes please, my dear.' The General waited for his wife to return from the drinks cabinet before continuing. 'I've no confirmation yet, of course, but I shall find out more in the morning.'

Lady Dembury sipped delicately at a large gin then sat down opposite her husband. 'But that's awful,' she began, before being interrupted by a knock at the door.

'Come,' the General ordered, his voice calm. Guido, the footman, appeared in the doorway, having been pressed into service by Benton, with a copy of an evening newspaper held before him.

'Yesterday's evening paper, M'Lord,' Guido explained, offering the paper to the General. 'Mr Benton thought there was something you should see, M'Lord,' he said, dropping the butler's name into the sentence, having had no intention of entering the lion's den alone.

The General shook the paper open at its front page and found the very confirmation he had been seeking.

'I thought badgers were supposed to be nocturnal!' said Fox

irritably, knocking on the door to Badger's sett for what seemed like the hundredth time.

'Not at his age,' observed Weasel, who was hunched down in the folds of his coat against the cold.

'Oh, do come along,' Fox said irritably, again threatening the door with the cane.

From behind the heavy door badger's angry shout stilled Fox's paw. 'All right, all right, I'm coming.' The words rumbled like distant thunder.

'At last,' Fox breathed.

The door swung open and Badger blinked up at the two figures on his doorstep. 'What bloody time do you call this?' he roared.

'No time for that, old man. May we come in?' and Fox walked into the hallway without waiting for an answer.

'Looks as if you already are!' Badger roared again.

'Oh, do stop shouting, old man, this is urgent. We must talk,' said Fox earnestly.

'And what is so urgent that it can't wait until morning?' Badger grumbled, slamming the door shut and pushing past his two visitors.

'I do apologise for the unseemly hour,' Fox began as Badger led them into the sitting room, 'but we have a problem of the first magnitude.'

'We!' said Badger gruffly, as he lowered himself into a floral-patterned armchair beside the glowing embers in the fireplace.

'Yes, we.' Fox went on: 'All of us on the heath. I would like you to look at this.' Fox handed the folded newspaper to Badger and sat down beside Weasel on the matching patterned settee opposite the fire.

Badger opened the paper and settled his half-moon spectacles onto his nose. 'What is all this about?' he demanded, looking suspiciously over the top of his glasses at Fox.

Fox paused and took a deep breath before looking at Badger sitting in the half-light across the room. Badger might be old and slower than in his youth but he was still a powerful animal and Fox was well aware of his temper. 'It appears to be, I am afraid, Badger, a plan for laying a motorway through Wixley.'

The silence in the room became instantly oppressive, the ticking of the carriage clock on the mantelpiece suddenly deafeningly loud. Badger sat like a stone, his features expressionless, his eyes fixed somewhere in the distance. The silence continued for what seemed like an eternity, causing Weasel to shift uncomfortably and reach into his pocket for a cigarette.

'I hope you're not going to light that filthy thing in here!' Badger glowered.

Weasel hesitated, glancing nervously about the room. 'No, no, not at all, mate.'

'I thought not.' Badger looked down at the paper and began reading the front page.

Weasel rose silently from the settee and stole out of the house before reaching into his pocket for the cigarette. He drew the smoke into his lungs and blew out appreciatively. 'I needed that,' he muttered. He shivered against the cold night air and looked up at the bright moon riding high in the dark, cloudless sky. 'A deep frost tonight,' he said to himself, before flicking the finished cigarette across the ground and turning back into the sett.

He walked back into the sitting room to find Badger sitting deep in thought, his chin resting on his fist as he stared into the fire, and Fox leaning back in his seat, his legs crossed at the ankles and a cheroot held between his white teeth.

Bloody rich! thought Weasel, frowning. Why should I have to go and stand out in the cold? He lowered himself onto the settee and held his paws out towards the flames in the fireplace which were licking their way around a fresh log.

Badger stirred in his chair and looked around the room. The ceiling was low and crossed with broad oak beams, the walls decorated with old black-and-white photographs of the heath in bygone years. Badger's gaze settled on a small framed picture above the writing bureau in the corner of the room; the shadows cast by the fire were flickering across it.

'That photo was taken by my grandfather some eighty years ago,' he said. 'Do you both recognise it?'

Fox and Weasel followed Badger's gaze and contemplated the

small photograph.

'Can't say as I do, old man,' Fox demurred.

'Me neither,' Weasel agreed, and they both turned back to the old brock sitting opposite them.

'Hardly surprising, really,' said Badger, his tone somewhere between scathing and weary. 'It's not there any more.' He paused and stared again into the fire. 'It's a photograph of old Abbott's Wood.'

'Abbott's Wood?' Fox puzzled.

'Yes, Abbott's Wood, where now you'll only find the Abbott's Way Trading Estate!'

The silence enveloped them again as Fox and Weasel looked again at the small photograph and tried to picture it before the industrial lorries which now called there every day had arrived.

Badger broke the long silence. 'That's where my grandfather used to live, before he brought my father out here, on the other side of the heath, and now it looks as if they are going to do it again.'

'Well, that's just it,' said Fox. 'What can we do? You're the oldest resident badger. Any suggestions?'

'I shall have to think on this one,' Badger replied. 'I shall have to think on this one very hard!'

Alan turned up the collar of his sheepskin coat against the winter's chill and took hold of Susan's gloved hand. Their fingers interlocked in a soft and tender embrace. Alan kicked absently at a fallen fir cone, his mind locked into the prospect of losing everything he had worked for, a prospect which seemed as bleak as the steel-grey clouds scudding low above the melancholy wood.

Alan and Susan turned a corner of the winding track and a pair of roe-deer vanished into the trees, their winter coats blending perfectly with their quiet surroundings. They walked on in silence, their mood reflecting the brooding clouds until the rain broke and began pattering on the bare branches and the damp fallen leaves.

The two lovers sheltered against the broad trunk of a mighty oak, Susan resting her back against Alan's chest with his arms wrapped around her waist.

'I like the rain. It makes everything clean and fresh,' Susan said softly.

Alan nuzzled the chestnut curls at the nape of Susan's neck, breathing in her warm female scent, and held her closely.

The rain trailed off into a fine drizzle and they walked back to the car. Alan drove through the wet country lanes at a sedate pace before parking the BMW outside the Three Pheasants.

Mortimer already had the fire burning brightly and Max sat at the end of the bar, wreathed in a cloud of aromatic smoke from his briar.

'What's this?' Alan tapped at a large bottle on the bar with a note glued to it which read 'Campaign Fund' in large red ink.

'All monies gratefully received towards the saving of Wixley Wood,' Mortimer replied as he placed a foaming pint of bitter in front of Alan. The bottle already held an inch of change and an assortment of notes, one of them a German note for twenty marks. Alan added the change from his ten pounds, the coins clinking loudly against the glass.

'How will the money be used?' Susan enquired, looking from Mortimer to Max as she sipped at a gin and tonic.

Max lifted his pipe from between his teeth before replying. 'I am going to raise a petition, as many signatures as I can get, against this motorway and a delegation of us will take it personally to Downing Street.'

The door opened and Douglas shook the rain from his shoulders and sent Piper to sit beside the fireplace. 'Miserable day,' he opened as Mortimer began pulling a pint of jet-black Guinness. A collection of wan smiles answered Douglas's greeting. 'Not much better in here,' Douglas sighed as he positioned himself on a stool.

'Motorway blues,' Mortimer explained.

'I see they've acquired that waste ground at the top of Church Walk,' Douglas remarked between mouthfuls of beer.

'That didn't take them long,' Max agreed sourly.

The room fell into silence as the company contemplated the march of progress before Susan dragged her eyes from the flames dancing on the logs in the fireplace and aired her opinion.

'We need some posters, posters we can put up all over the village,' she said, looking around the room for approval.

'Good idea.' Mortimer nodded, a little hesitantly, his eyes wandering to the glass bottle.

Alan followed Mortimer's gaze and train of thought. 'I can organise that,' he decided. 'I know somebody in London. It shouldn't take too long.'

'Good man,' Max rejoined, returning his attention to relighting his pipe.

'Let's say a thousand to begin with,' Alan said, 'one in every window.'

'One for me,' Mortimer demanded stoutly. 'In fact, make that two.'

'The best idea would be to put a pile of them on the bar and people could help themselves,' Alan suggested to a chorus of nodding heads.

'Good idea, will do,' Mortimer agreed.

The door opened and Timothy Dembury rushed in, his lank hair hanging in wet rat's tails and his blue windcheater dripping with rain. Alan took a deep weary breath and Susan rolled her eyes heavenwards. Timothy sidled up to the bar, his Reebok trainers squelching on the carpet, and Mortimer gave him a baleful stare.

'I feel like a drowned rat,' Timothy squeaked, beaming his toothy grin around the room, and Alan thought he could not have come up with a better description himself.

'Half a lager?' Mortimer enquired wearily.

'*Exactimundo, amigo,*' Timothy beamed. 'Can I buy anyone a drink?' he asked, looking around the bar.

Douglas's eyes remained rooted to the bar whilst Max made a great fuss of relighting his pipe. Susan had suddenly found something out of the window which required her undivided attention, and Alan seemed intent on contemplating the texture of the ceiling.

'Anybody?' Timothy smiled again, and whatever Susan had seen out of the window seemed suddenly to materialise on the carpet at her feet. 'Oh well, never mind.' Timothy grinned broadly, but his eyes registered the hurt of rejection and Mortimer felt a pang of sympathy for the younger man.

'I'll have one with you, son,' he said, a little grudgingly, and Timothy's face lit up.

'What will you have, *amigo*?'

'Ill have half a bitter, and no more *amigo*. Okay?' Mortimer said gravely, and Timothy nodded weakly. He dropped his change into the bottle and sipped at his lager before feeling bold enough to give his opinion.

'Disgraceful, isn't it, this motorway plan?' he said.

'Bloody criminal,' Max growled, using his favourite phrase to describe his viewpoint with regard to the motorway.

'I agree,' Timothy concurred. 'It isn't as if a motorway is even required, and Wixley Wood is far too magnificent a wood to desecrate in this fashion. Besides, you can't keep laying everything under concrete just to accommodate the motor car. The traffic just expands to fill the available space. What you have to do is reduce the volume of traffic. The three-car family is becoming the accepted standard and that has to stop.'

Alan nodded slowly, finding himself in agreement with the words.

'What is required,' Timothy continued, 'is a preservation order. That would put a stop to it. It is simply wrong to destroy the environment like this.'

Douglas rolled a cigarette and listened to the opinion with a grudging respect.

'The more and louder we complain,' Timothy said with a passion, 'the greater the chance of it being picked up on by the national media. What we need is a major event to bring it to the media's attention.'

The room fell silent as the others paused to consider Timothy's words, before Alan voiced his agreement. 'Good thinking.' He looked at Timothy. 'Any ideas?'

'Not yet, I must admit.' Timothy shook his long hair. 'But then it is too early anyway. We don't know their plan of action yet and until we do we can't counter it.'

Alan drained his glass and, with Susan, turned for the door. 'I look forward to hearing your ideas,' he said.

'I'll keep you posted.' Timothy smiled.

Alan held the car door open for Susan before running quickly through the rain and into the driver's seat.

'Maybe he's not so daft,' he remarked as he pulled away from the kerbside.

'It did make a change, I must say,' Susan admitted as if she were still finding it hard to believe.

'Media attention,' Alan said thoughtfully. 'Media attention.'

Blackthorn Estate echoed to the clash of bone as the rutting stags locked antlers, forcing each other back and forth as they vied furiously for the right to mate.

General Dembury guided the chestnut mare through the trees, beneath the copper leaves and the slanting rays of late autumn, and pointed the animal's head for home. He allowed the mare to move at its own pace as he enjoyed the golden afternoon peace, and so it was an hour before one of the stable lads put two fingers to the peak of his cap.

Lady Dembury sat beside a crackling fire and sipped at a gin and tonic as her husband clipped the end from one of his favourite cigars.

'Bit early in the year for a fire, isn't it?' he enquired as he lifted a brand from the flames.

'There was a chill in the air. I thought it would be nice.' Lady Dembury smiled sweetly.

The General threw the brand back into the flames and nodded absently. 'Quite right, quite right,' he murmured.

'How was your ride?' Lady Dembury asked.

'Splendid. It gave me time to think,' he replied as he poured whiskey into a glass.

'Go on.'

Cubes of ice chinked against the crystal and the General crossed to his chair as he gathered his thoughts. 'I would like to know who is behind this motorway business.'

'Wouldn't we all!'

'How to find out, that is the question.' He sipped at the

whiskey and stared thoughtfully into the fire. The flames danced around the logs, the yellow and blue flickering on the General's glass. 'And what to do about it,' he finished the sentence.

Chapter 5

December

'Our home is threatened, my dear,' said Badger.

He sat in the kitchen with his feet immersed in a bowl of hot water and the newspaper open on his lap as he read again the article concerning the proposed motorway. He looked up at his wife from over his half-moon spectacles and laid the paper to one side.

Mrs Badger finished with the knife she had been using to slice the root vegetables and wiped her paws on her apron before turning to her husband. The two of them had been together many years and both were well tuned to each other's moods. As she patted her steel-grey hair, she could see in her husband's eyes the same sense of unease as she herself felt.

'What are you going to do?' she asked.

'I shall have to organise a meeting with some of the others, I suppose,' Badger replied. 'Thrash out some plan of action.'

Mrs Badger hesitated, unsure of her own opinions. 'Is there anything we can do?' she queried, her long black eyebrows knitting into a doubtful frown.

'We must try, my dear,' Badger observed softly. 'I will have a word with one of the hares. They can pass on the message quickly.'

The two of them raised their eyes to the ceiling as the sound of a horse galloping through the rain overhead passed nearby.

'Not a nice day to be out riding,' Mrs Badger remarked.

'There will be none of that at all if this road goes through,' Badger said.

'When will you speak with Hare?'

'At dusk.'

The hares had fanned out into the early night and the news had spread like a forest fire.

Otter was incensed. He was heartily sick and tired of being hounded out of one home after another. 'Never a moment's peace,' he fumed.

Stag had listened to the message with a lofty, almost regal, silence, and then he had given a curt nod before turning back to his does, and Polecat, who had only recently come to live in the wood, gave his assurance that he too would attend. He had had enough of running. The squirrel twins had agreed to represent the village.

Now hare was knocking on Badger's door as the first grey streaks of dawn ushered in another cold day. 'They're all coming,' Hare reported, ' except Stag, of course, but he wanted to be kept informed.'

'Of course,' Badger replied, realising that it was a ludicrous notion to try to squeeze Stag into his sett. 'Well done, Hare.' Badger nodded. 'I'll see you at the meeting.'

A deep frost, impervious to the weak winter sunlight, covered the ground, adding an icy sharpness to the chill early hours of the day.

Fox sat on a fallen fungus-covered log near the edge of the small copse, his breath steaming in the cold morning air, and looked out across the silver frosted fields. He was not accustomed to being out at this time of the day, preferring the cover of darkness, but as he gazed out across the wintry landscape he comfortably decided that, apart from the raucous cries of the rooks wheeling overhead above the treetops, all was quiet.

He noted the thin wisp of smoke rising from the chimney of Douglas Cobden's farmhouse far in the distance before lifting the gold hunter from the fob pocket of his waistcoat. Eight-thirty! Fox snapped the watch closed, his irritation at the hour returning.

He would have preferred it if Badger had called his meeting at a more convenient hour. He had no desire to cross the open country towards Wixley Wood in the daylight, but Badger had left him with little choice.

Fox jumped down from the log and eased his way through the dense bracken which flanked that side of the copse before emerging into the open field. He paused and checked the terrain and, satisfied that all was quiet, set off at a slow trot.

Four hundred yards out Fox stopped in mid-stride and stood tense and still, his head cocked to one side and his ears pricked; the sound caused his blood to ice over and a bead of sweat as cold as the surrounding frost to fall from his brow. He knew that sound. He had heard it before, and the memories of sitting at his grandfather's knee came flooding back. He could see him clearly, the old greybeard, telling him, the young cub, how there was no outwitting it, no fighting it, nothing but full flight as the only response to what he could now clearly hear as the clarion call of the Wixley and Abbott's Hunt.

Fox looked to his left and strained his eyes against the cold air. Five thunderous beats of his heart later he could see them, the dappled hounds, their stiff upright tails slicing through the air, and the huntsmen riding tall in their saddles a hundred yards behind. Fox's brush twitched as then he heard the baying of the pack as the hunt wheeled sharply and headed directly towards him.

Fox sprang to his right and began racing in the direction of Douglas Cobden's land. He could see, low in the distance, the drystone wall which marked the boundary of Cobden's smallholding and he knew that there he would be safe. Cobden never allowed the hunt onto his land, it was well known. If he could escape the hunt he could worry about Cobden's shotgun later.

Fox sped across the hard frozen ground, his stride long and agile, his eyes fixed on the wall in the distance. He crested the small rise at Dixon's Point and ducked behind the large boulder and the ragged collection of bramble bushes before looking over this shoulder.

The pack were gaining on him, the horses now at the gallop, and the bright red tunics of the huntsmen blazed in the winter sunshine like fresh blood spilt on a butcher's apron.

Fox faced his front again and judged the distance to the

drystone wall. He was over halfway there now, he decided. 'Time yet, old man,' he muttered. Fox sped on, his breath coming in short sharp gasps, ignorant of the low bracken which snatched at his waistcoat, oblivious to their sharp pricks of pain, his mind set on one thing: making for the drystone wall, which grew larger with each pace.

He bounded down the short slope and across the level field, covering the last mile to the wall without slowing his pace, and then he turned to look back at his pursuers. 'Two hundred yards,' he muttered, gulping down great lungfuls of air. 'My race, I think!' and he vaulted up onto the wall and down the other side; his legs, weak from the chase, buckled a little as he landed.

Fox gathered himself and ran on, away from the insane howling of the hounds and the shrill cries of the hunting horn, and the drystone wall fell away behind him. They would come no further, he was sure.

'Well done, old man,' he said, allowing himself a thin smile as the elation of his escape coursed through his veins. 'Grandpa would have been proud.'

Fifty yards on the smile had slipped from Fox's face. The baying of the hounds had not receded and he realised with a sickening dread that the heavy thump which shook the ground behind him was the first rider clearing the drystone wall.

Without breaking his stride, Fox glanced over his shoulder. The hounds, their howling rising in a crescendo, were only twenty yards behind and he knew that his strength was failing. 'Sorry Grandpa,' he muttered, the words catching in his throat as he changed his grip on the silver-topped cane. 'This far and no further.'

Fox turned to face his tormentors with an élan he did not feel and, with the blood roaring in his ears and the cane held before him in trembling paws, found they were upon him.

'Flea-bitten cat!' Piper barked.

'Yes-man of the animal kingdom!' Twinkle hissed, knowing that this was the insult which would infuriate Piper the most.

'Mange-ridden feline sponger!' Piper snapped menacingly.

'Mange is for dogs, you performing canine clown. Sit, Piper,' Twinkle mimicked. 'Beg, Piper. Shake hands, Piper. Roll over, play dead, stupid dog!'

Piper bared his teeth, his snout rolling back over the gleaming white fangs. 'Oh, Mr bloody cool.' The low growl came from the back of his throat. 'A simple trick like that earns me extra titbits. You ought to try it some time, if only you had the brains.'

Douglas put a stop to it. 'Always bloody arguing,' he bellowed. 'Cut it out, the pair of you.'

Piper flopped onto his stomach and looked at Douglas with innocent and devoted eyes.

Twinkle was not impressed. 'Yes, go on, play the part. If you're really good you can chase a stick later!'

Douglas stamped his boot on the floor. 'Enough!' he roared. 'Or I'll send you both to the knacker's yard.'

Twinkle sprang up beside the open window and dropped into the cobbled yard. 'Out of the way, chicken!' he hissed at one of the scruffy red hens. The startled hen sprinted across the yard and into the chicken run. Twinkle settled himself in the hayloft, content to spend the rest of the day snoozing on the old blanket.

Douglas watched Twinkle disappear into the barn before turning to Piper. 'A little shooting this morning?' he asked, and Piper wagged his tail. 'Like that idea, do you?' Douglas grinned and Piper barked his approval.

Douglas carried a canvas bag of fat red cartridges over his Barbour jacket and the Purdey clutched in his right fist, and Piper scampered in front of him. Douglas's boots crunched on the hoar frost, leaving tracks across the fields.

The first wood pigeon had soared high from the small spinney before jinking left and right across the wintry sky, and Douglas had brought it to earth with his first shot. A second had shortly followed, Piper dutifully collecting the fallen birds, before Douglas first heard the sound of the hunting horn.

'Best take a look,' he muttered. He cradled the Purdey in the crook of his right arm and the two dead pigeons dangled by their necks from his left hand.

Before he had reached the drystone wall he could see the drama being played out on the far side. The sleek red fox was darting across the open, frosted fields, the dogs, forty or more, only two hundred yards behind and in full chase. Douglas dropped the pigeons to the ground and strode forward at the same time as the fox, its strength clearly flagging, cleared the wall and ran on.

'Not on my land,' Douglas muttered darkly, and he loaded two fresh cartridges into the Purdey. Then, realising that there would be no checking the dogs, he snapped the gun closed and broke into a run, his long legs quickly covering the ground.

The hounds were upon the fox before he had covered half the distance and, even as he ran, the first horses were clearing the drystone wall, the riders standing tall in the stirrups, their red tunics blazing against the white background.

'Not on my land!' Douglas roared, ten yards from the spot where the encircled fox was snapping and spitting at its tormentors, and, scorning to bring the gun to the shoulder, he fired both barrels over the heads of the frenzied dogs.

Fox had brought the silver-topped cane down on the skull of the leading beagle with a power found only by those in mortal danger, and it had felled the dog instantly. His second blow had sent another hound tripping sideways into the darkness of unconsciousness, but they were many and Fox was blown from the chase. Now Fox was snapping at his enemies and swinging the cane in a wide arc in a desperate bid to keep the hounds at bay, and the pit of fear in his stomach threatened to smother him with panic.

The deafening thunderclap which suddenly erupted over his head shook his senses so, he almost dropped his weapon, and he braced himself for the final onslaught.

It never came.

The dogs, stunned – Fox saw the slavering grins fall from their manic faces- had frozen into an eerie tableau, their obscene tongues lolling from their open mouths. Fox, realising that this, his last chance, would last but the length of a heartbeat, leapt over the heads of the pack, which stood three deep, and was gone.

As big a man as he was, the recoil of the gun in such an unwieldy grip had knocked Douglas back a pace but he thought that the effect of the shot on the pack had been worth the jolt to his arms.

The attention of the hounds had been momentarily diverted from the fox and, as Douglas opened the breach and the two smoking cartridges spun over his broad shoulders, the fox leapt the pack and was even now streaking across the fields.

The silence lasted but a second as the dogs, their baying rising again, turned towards their quarry. Douglas heaved the reloaded shotgun to his shoulder and let loose both barrels over the heads of the pack a second time and watched as the hounds broke in panic.

'Enough with that gun, damn you!'

Douglas turned towards the sound of the angry voice as he ejected the two spent cartridges. Trotting forward astride a magnificent chestnut mare, the General, Lord Dembury of Wixley, MC, glared at him from over the silver whiskers which climbed his cheekbones.

'Not on my land. You're trespassing,' said Douglas calmly, and the sound of the shotgun's breach closing on two fresh cartridges reinforced his words.

General Dembury glared at the big farmer with impotent fury at the hopeless situation he found himself in. The hounds would go no further now, their weak whining was testimony enough to that, he thought, and the look in this farmer's eyes, not to mention that bloody shotgun held at the port across his chest, was proof enough that he would not be browbeaten.

Damn the man, thought the General, time to play the gentleman. 'It would appear we grew a little overzealous,' he said, and he pulled at the reins so that the mare danced in a tight circle away from the unflinching farmer.

'That you did, M'Lord,' Douglas replied. 'I'd be obliged, sir, if you'd lead your hunt from my property.'

Manners as well, thought the General looking down at the farmer. Not that far down either, he thought. Damn me, but the fellow stands as tall as my mounted waist.

'I'll bid you good day, sir,' said the General, and he looked at Douglas for a long moment before turning the mare at the gallop and clearing the stone wall with ease, and the hunt followed in his wake.

'He's late,' Badger cursed. 'Bloody rude, I call it.'

'He'll have his reasons.' Weasel glanced across the table.

'He always has bloody reasons,' Badger shot back. He had no time for the shifty Weasel. Bloody thief, as far as he was concerned, and that pretentious dandy Fox was no better.

'Let's get on,' Badger suggested, looking around the table at the others present.

'Another five minutes perhaps,' Hare ventured. 'After all ...'

'Another five minutes my arse!' snapped Badger, cutting Hare short. 'He's had enough time.'

The door to the room opened and Fox stepped through.

'My apologies for my tardy arrival,' said Fox. 'I'm afraid I was unavoidably detained.'

Badger looked hard at the canine.

Fox removed his bright scarlet waistcoat and handed it to Badger's plump wife. 'My dear Mrs Badger, I wonder if you would be so kind as to put a stitch in that for me, please?' He smiled. 'I rather clumsily caught it on a bramble.'

Badger took in the torn waistcoat, the strained smile and the sheen in Fox's eyes, and knew. He was covered in too many old scars from the baiters and their dogs not to be able to recognise the look of the hunted.

'My pleasure, Mr Fox,' replied Mrs Badger, succumbing to Fox's easy charm.

'Many thanks. You're very kind.' Fox smiled again.

'Take a seat, Fox,' said Badger. You had to hand it to him, he certainly has some pluck, he thought, as he watched Fox ease himself gently into a chair. 'Glad you made it, Fox,' said Badger, looking into Fox's eyes.

Fox returned the searching gaze. 'Thanks, old man. Glad to be here.'

'Let's get on,' said Badger.

Alwyn glanced out of the vicarage window for the umpteenth time that morning and still there was no sign of the squirrels. He was unsure as to whether or not he was happy with their sudden disappearance. He had become so accustomed to their antics that he found he was missing them already.

Alwyn forgot the squirrels as he made his way along Church Walk. The morning was still young, the streets not yet aired, and he shivered against the cold. He unlocked the church doors and blew on his fingers before emptying the collection box. 'Every little helps,' he told himself as he studied the meagre amount. 'A lot would, of course, be of more help.' He raised his eyes heavenwards. 'A gentle hint, Father,' he mused.

Alwyn returned to the vicarage to find the day's post waiting on the carpet. The first three were Christmas cards and he placed them on the mantelpiece with those that had arrived earlier in the week.

The fourth was a letter and Alwyn's hand trembled slightly as he read it. Lord Dembury had enclosed the season's greetings and a cheque which would more than cover the cost of the repairs the church roof required.

Alwyn dragged his eyes away from the bold signature and glanced heavenwards. He did not even know what to think, let alone say.

Fox leaned nonchalantly back in the hard chair, his ankles crossed on the long wooden table and a Monte Cristo held between his sharp white teeth.

At the head of the table Badger was waving the month-old newspaper in the air. 'This can't be allowed to happen,' he barked, looking around the table at the others from beneath his heavy black eyebrows.

'Badger, old boy,' Fox interjected, 'none of us are deaf. Do please stop shouting. What we need is a plan of action.'

'Well, you're the one who is friends with this farmer's daughter,' Badger replied. 'Can't you make some sort of contact with her?'

'What on earth can she do?' Fox asked, raising his eyebrows incredulously.

'Well, I don't know!'

'Neither do I, old boy.' Fox drew on the mild cigar. 'She is only a child.'

'But she is a contact with the villagers,' Otter interrupted, 'no matter how small, and we do need their help.'

'I agree.' Badger nodded. 'We can't do this on our own.'

'I still do not see how a seven-year-old child can be of help,' Fox queried.

Weasel looked up at Fox and ran a thoughtful finger along his chin. 'I do,' he said softly. All heads turned towards the slender figure beneath the flat cap.

'Well,' Badger growled, 'let's hear it.'

Weasel leaned forward and rested his elbows on the bare table. 'The motorway construction company has built a site in Church Walk in the village,' Weasel began. 'The plans for this road must be held in there.'

'And?' Badger frowned.

'We borrow a camera from Foxy's girlfriend, photograph the plans, pass them back to her.' Weasel spread his paws eloquently. 'And she can pass them on.'

'You mean break in?' Fox murmured, looking at Weasel questioningly.

'Well, obviously,' Weasel stated with a matter-of-fact voice.

'I like it.' Fox smiled, excited by the daring adventure of the idea.

'Surely the site will be guarded?' Mole ventured from behind his thick spectacles. 'They must have security patrols there.'

'A minor problem, old boy,' Fox said smoothly.

'A minor problem, my arse!' Badger shouted. 'That site is probably crawling with dogs.'

'Oh, Badger, do calm down. It will be fun.' Fox blew a perfect smoke ring which rose and dissipated against the low ceiling.

'Fun!' Badger said, aghast. 'This isn't supposed to be a holiday trip!'

'Has anybody ever used a camera?' Otter looked around the table.

A chorus of shaking heads met his enquiry.

'You have Badger.' Fox looked at Badger with twinkling, mischievous eyes.

'You must be joking!' Badger bellowed.

'Oh, don't be so wet, old boy.' Fox smiled. 'You can do it.'

'Can you really use a camera, Badger?' one of the squirrel twins asked curiously.

'It doesn't matter if I can or I can't.' Badger rounded on him. 'The whole idea is ridiculous!'

'Oh, come on, Badger,' Hare pleaded. 'You can give it a go, surely?'

Badger glowered at Fox from over his half-moon spectacles, furious that the canine had outmanoeuvred him. 'This had better work!' he growled, menacingly.

'It will, old boy, it will.'

Jennifer reached into the drawer and rummaged through its contents before finding what she was looking for.

The camera was a small pocket Instamatic and the film it held was unused. Jennifer pocketed the camera and pushed the drawer closed, making sure she left no trace that the camera had gone missing, and made her way through to the kitchen and out into the yard. The day was cold, the cobbles still wet from the morning rain, and Jennifer hurried across the yard and into the barn.

She had chosen her moment with care. Douglas had left the house for his customary lunchtime pint an hour earlier, and Mary was engrossed in the Sunday newspapers.

Jennifer picked up the ball she had left in the barn the previous afternoon and began to kick it through the gate towards Wixley Wood. She continued to kick the ball across the fields until she had reached the drystone wall that marked the boundary of her father's property, and then she forgot the ball as she began to search the small gaps in the wall until she found what she was looking for.

'Mr Weasel?' she called, and Weasel's beady eyes blinked back at her from his home within the wall. 'I've brought you the camera that Mr Fox wants,' she said, and she slipped the camera into the space between the stones.

'Make sure he gets it,' she commanded, and then she collected the ball and ran back towards the farmhouse as the rain began to fall for the second time that day.

Night had fallen by the time Weasel jumped down from the wall, and now he stood at the edge of Wixley Wood waiting for Fox to arrive.

Fox came through the trees at a leisurely pace. 'Weasel, old boy, well met by moonlight,' he quipped.

Weasel gave Fox a confused stare. 'What by moonlight?' he queried.

'Never mind,' Fox sighed. 'At least the rain has stopped, eh?'

'If it had not, I wouldn't be here.' Weasel sniffed disdainfully. 'Is this what you want?' he asked, and he produced the camera from inside his camel-hair coat.

Fox's eyes lit up. 'Splendid,' he said, as he inspected the small Instamatic. 'That is ideal.'

'How does it work?'

'Damned if I know, old boy.' Fox shook his head. 'It's up to Badger, I'm afraid.'

It took less than thirty minutes for them to make the journey through the wood to Badger's sett.

'Fit and raring to go, Badger?' Fox enquired.

'This is madness,' Badger growled as he readied himself.

'Nonsense, old boy,' Fox insisted. 'It'll be a piece of cake.'

Badger was far from convinced and he grumbled about the entire scheme all the way to the village.

Alan lay on his belly on the floor, a look of bewildered

frustration on his face as he read again the long and convoluted instructions.

'All video recorders should come pre-packed with a ten-year-old child!' He scowled at the machine. 'It would make this programming malarkey all the easier.'

'Patience,' Susan said from her perch on the edge of the settee.

'Patience, my foot!' Alan growled. 'I'm sure they write all this in double Dutch deliberately just to confuse you!'

Susan pulled a face and decided it was probably better to remain silent. Men, she thought, hopeless!

The kettle began to whistle from the kitchen and Susan walked through the hallway and lifted it from the gas. 'Why don't you get an electric kettle?' she called as she poured hot water over the coffee grounds. 'This thing looks older than the cottage.'

Alan did not bother replying, his attention still focused on the legion of buttons on the face of the recorder. Susan glanced out of the kitchen window at the cold darkness merging with the night-time profiles.

'Alan, come here quickly,' she called, her voice urgent and hushed.

He threw the pamphlet onto the settee in exasperation and padded quickly into the kitchen. 'What is it?' he asked, whispering automatically.

'Over there.' Susan pointed at the long dark garden. Alan peered through the window, craning his neck and pivoting his head. Towards the end of the garden, before the reflective waters of the pond, Alan could see a fox and a badger hurrying across the lawn.

'Well, look at that,' he marvelled, placing an arm around Susan's waist.

She snuggled against him. 'Isn't that lovely,' she whispered.

The pair of nocturnal visitors were suddenly joined by a third, a small brown weasel, its agile contours moving nimbly beneath the moonlight.

'That's amazing,' Susan gasped, her eyes wide and shining.

The trio of stealthy night-time callers passed wraithlike

through the low wooden picket fence at the bottom of the garden and dropped out of sight into the wide, murky field.

'I have never seen the like of that before,' Susan said wonderingly as she walked back through to the sitting room with a mug of steaming coffee in each hand. Alan sat down beside her on the long settee, the flames from the log fire matching the warm glow in his heart, and accepted the proffered mug.

'Did you programme the video?' Susan asked, sipping at her coffee.

'To hell with the video.' Alan prised Susan's mug gently from her fingers and placed it on the table beside his own. 'And to hell with the coffee.' He laid Susan beneath himself in the folds of the sofa, and her lips were soft and warm.

A solitary barn owl, silhouetted against the watchful eye of the moon, made a low, ghostly pass over the cold headstones standing stark in the darkness, as Fox led Weasel and Badger through the small silent churchyard.

'Is this entirely necessary?' Badger grumbled quietly, his heavy grey bulk bringing up the rear.

'Do stop complaining, old man,' Fox whispered. 'This way is safer, away from the road.'

Badger scowled. 'Safer it may be but I am not particularly fond of creeping about in graveyards in the dead of night.'

Fox chose to ignore Badger's complaining and carried on, quickly passing through the churchyard and over the flint wall which surrounded it.

'How do you expect me to get over that?' Badger hissed. The wall was at least five feet high.

Fox jumped back into the churchyard and, with Weasel helping, boosted Badger up and onto the top of the wall. Badger was puffing and panting all the while. 'You should lose some weight, old boy,' Fox commented, sitting atop the wall next to the old brock.

Badger frowned at the long drop. 'Now I'm up here, how do you suggest I get down again?'

'You jump, old boy, you jump,' and Fox leapt down from the wall and landed lightly on his nimble feet.

'Why the hell couldn't we just go around the bloody thing?' Badger moaned, lowering himself gingerly down the side of the ivy-clad wall.

The trio moved on quickly and quietly, the inky black night affording them ample cover until they came up against the wire fence that surrounded the collection of prefabricated huts and the single red brick building. The three of them stood silently peering through the mesh.

'What do you think?' Weasel asked quietly.

'Seems quiet enough,' Fox replied, his eyes searching the moonlit compound.

'That doesn't mean to say it's deserted,' Badger said testily, his heavy black eyebrows meeting in a dark frown.

Fox's whiskers bristled. 'Badger, I do wish you would show a little more enthusiasm,' he seethed.

'Enthusiasm!' Badger shot back. 'For this hare-brained scheme? I don't know how I ever let you talk me into it.'

'Keep your voice down!' Fox scolded him. 'You'll wake the entire neighbourhood.'

'It's not the neighbourhood you should worry about,' Badger hissed, pointing to the compound. 'It's what's inside there!'

Weasel stepped between the quarrelling pair. 'Cut it out, both of you, it's a bit late for all this –,'

'No, it's not,' Badger interrupted him.

'Yes, it is...'

'No, it's not.'

'For God's sake,' Fox shouted. 'Will you two pull yourselves together!'

'You're a fine one to talk.' Badger turned on him. 'This was all your crackpot idea in the first place.'

'It is not a crackpot idea!' Fox shot back.

'Of course it is, we could all get ourselves killed.'

'Nobody is going to get killed!'

'Not me, that's for sure!'

'Will you stop it!' Weasel yelled, his voice carrying clearly through the cold night air. 'Are we doing this or aren't we?'

'Yes!'

'No!'

'Yes, we are,' Fox snapped, 'and that's final. Now come on.'

The three confederates crept furtively along the edge of the fence, Badger continuing to voice his doubts as to the sanity of his two companions, until they reached the wide double gates. Weasel scurried forward and passed an expert eye over the large padlock as Fox and Badger kept watch on the silent compound. The lock was no match for Weasel's shady talents, giving up the fight almost immediately, and Weasel led the way through the open gates.

They scampered quickly across the compound, Badger cursing the bright moon, and into the dark shadow of the brick building. Weasel set to work on the lock and within seconds the door eased open and Fox and Badger hurried in behind.

The office was dark and spartan, decorated with only the essentials: a table, two chairs and a single tall filing cabinet, beside which stood a short square iron safe, its dark green hue disguising it in the dark of the night.

'This is what we are after.' Fox gave the safe a perfunctory tap with the silver tip of his cane. 'Think you can do it, old boy?' He looked at Weasel.

Weasel pushed his cap onto the back of his head and squinted through the dark at the large dial on the face of the door, his whiskers twitching. 'Might take some time,' he murmured.

Badger scowled. 'Time is not something we have a lot of,' he muttered, his eyes searching the compound beyond the single window.

'Well, it can't be rushed,' Weasel stated, and placing his ear to the safe he began to feel for the mechanism. The silence in the room was broken only by the faint clicking of the dial beneath the light, caressing paws of the master cracksman and the shallow breathing of his two collaborators.

The minutes ticked by. Fox pulled up a chair and sat with his ankles crossed on the top of the safe and watched as Weasel, a tightly-rolled cigarette glued eternally to his bottom lip, felt delicately for the tumblers.

Badger looked at Fox with ill-disguised disdain. 'I don't know what you are looking so casual about,' he whispered scornfully.

'Everything will be all right, Badger,' Fox replied confidently, and he held a match to the tip of a cheroot.

'I hope you're right!'

'Do have a little faith, old boy,' Fox sighed as he inspected the ash on his cigar.

Weasel leaned away from the safe, a triumphant gleam in his eye, and the heavy green door fell open.

'Well done, old man,' Fox congratulated him. Fox reached into the safe and produced a sheaf of neatly typed white papers. 'Now let's see what we have here.' He laid the large pristine pages on the table and began to sort through them. 'What do you say?' he asked Badger, who was peering over his shoulder.

Badger picked up one of the loose-leaf copies and read through it quickly. 'This one, definitely,' he decided, before placing it to one side and continuing with another.

Moments later Badger and Fox had created a neat pile of papers they considered worth recording and then Badger produced the small pocket-sized camera and began photographing them in rapid succession.

'That's the lot,' he whispered, pocketing the Instamatic, and Fox gathered the sheets and placed them back in the safe. Weasel pushed the door gently closed and spun the dial, and the three of them tiptoed towards the exit. Weasel pulled the door open a fraction and peered through the gap, his sharp eyes darting around the compound.

'All quiet,' he whispered, before stepping out into the cold night. Fox and Badger followed silently and then waited in the shadows as Weasel closed and locked the door.

'All done.' Weasel nodded at the pair, and he set out quickly across the open compound.

'Steady, old boy,' Fox cautioned from the shadows. 'Let's take our time.'

Weasel hesitated, his agile form outlined on the grey concrete by the bright moon, and the first Alsatian stepped alert and menacing from behind one of the prefabricated huts.

'Bugger!' Badger cursed. 'I just bloody well knew it!'

Weasel emitted a short frightened squeak and bounded

towards the gates, his tail stiff and upright and his beady eyes suddenly wide beneath the peak of his cap.

'Time to leave, old boy.' Fox smiled before racing out across the bare moonlit compound. Badger needed no prompting and he followed close on Fox's heels. Weasel ducked between the gates and then vanished into the night just as the Alsatian stepped suddenly and powerfully into Fox and Badger's path, blocking the route to the open gates.

Fox and Badger came to a dead stop. The Alsatian stood rigid and unflinching, like a sentry at the gates of Rome, its feet planted four square on the ground, its back ramrod-straight and its chin held high in open and daunting challenge.

Fox passed a critical eye over the resolute and unwavering Alsatian. 'Not quite as I had planned,' he murmured, smoothing a long white whisker.

'You don't bloody say!' Badger fumed, and he glared at Fox from beneath his beetling eyebrows. 'I told you something like this would happen...' Badger trailed off, his voice lost in the night as the stern, steadfast Alsatian was joined by a further two equally taut and compact dogs.

'And then there were three,' Fox observed wryly, his eyes meeting those of the two new arrivals.

'Four, actually!' Badger rejoined archly. 'Take a look over your shoulder.'

'Well, well.' Fox glanced behind his back. 'We warrant the full works, obviously.'

Badger gave Fox a poisonous look. 'We are in it up to our necks, you little git!'

Fox's smile did not falter as the four Alsatians, all of them bearing the hallmarks of a former career in the police force, launched themselves, fast and agile, across the moon-washed compound.

'No need for panic, Badger old boy.' Fox adopted a rakish smile as he gave his silver-tipped cane a confident twirl. 'I think you will find we have them surrounded.'

Mortimer always claimed that Carol Night was the best night of the year. Max agreed. So did Alwyn, who, being Welsh as well as a vicar, was always in fine voice.

Mortimer passed the song sheets along the bar before the organist struck up, and the Three Pheasants rollicked into the first verse of 'Once in Royal David's City'. Douglas bellowed between mouthfuls of Guinness and Alan, who had never come across anything like it, thoroughly enjoyed himself.

By the time Mortimer called time, the assembled company had exhausted well over a dozen carols, as well as themselves into the bargain.

Max had stood on the pavement sucking merrily on his inevitable pipe, having secured a goodnight kiss from Susan, and Douglas had struggled over the style at the top of Poachers Hill.

It was a long, shuffling walk home.

Now Douglas lay snoozing on the settee as Mary busied herself with the wrapping of her daughter's Christmas presents. Mary paused as the thought struck her that she was unsure as to whether or not the camera had any film in it. She finished tying blue ribbon around a large parcel and laid it away from the fire before crossing the room and pulling open the top drawer of the sideboard.

'That's odd,' she said, and Douglas opened one eye.

'What is?' he enquired in a sleepy voice.

Mary searched again through the drawer before answering. 'I could have sworn that the camera was in here,' she said, almost to herself.

'No idea,' was Douglas's response, and his eyelid dropped closed.

'We must have a film for Christmas,' Mary said thoughtfully.

'Plenty of time yet,' Douglas remarked. 'We'll find it sometime.'

Fox and Badger stood back-to-back beneath the pale moon, braced against each other, as the four dogs hurtled, strict and supple, towards them. Badger launched a wide-ranging and powerful punch and his huge right fist caught the first charging

Alsatian cleanly on the line of its jaw. The dog tripped and stumbled, its knees buckling slightly, and Badger landed a slicing left uppercut on the dog's chin. The dog's head snapped backwards. Badger stood like a prizefighter, high on the balls of his feet with his bunched fists held defensively in front of his chest, as the Alsatian reeled and fell at his feet.

A second dog closed in at a tight angle and loomed into the periphery of Badger's vision. Badger danced nimbly to his right to face the attack.

The silver tip of Fox's cane flashed through the darkness and caught the dog a glancing blow on its kneecap, causing it to lose its footing so that its rapid charge hesitated and faltered.

'Now's your time, old boy,' Fox said over his shoulder, and Badger scored a short, sharp blow to the side of the stumbling Alsatian's head. The dog toppled to the ground, its eyelids fluttering closed over its sightless eyes. Fox swung the cane back across his front in a wide backhanded arc and the heavy silver tip cracked on the hard bony skull of the third dog, and it crashed to the ground like a felled oak.

Fox stepped back a pace to allow himself space as the fourth and largest of the guard dogs sprang forward, its paws slapping on the grey concrete. Fox swung the cane upwards in an underhand grip and the silver tip ricocheted against the Alsatian's sharply bared fangs. The dog howled with the sudden icy pain, its furious onslaught checked, and Fox brought the cane down on to its drooping head with a confident finality.

He glanced over this shoulder at Badger, who stood over the two motionless figures lying at his feet. 'The field is ours, I think, old man,' Fox remarked, and he placed a triumphant cheroot between his smiling white teeth.

'Let's get out of here before they come round.' Badger massaged his right fist and stepped warily over the prostrate Alsatians.

'Nice meeting you chaps.' Fox flicked the dead match at the unconscious dogs. 'Must do it again sometime,' and he followed Badger out through the swinging gates and into the night.

General Dembury gathered the reins and clutched at the pommel. He slipped one booted foot into the steel, hoisted himself into the saddle, and the leather creaked beneath his weight. He put his heels to the flanks of the chestnut mare and turned its head towards the gate.

The water from the fountain tinkled into the pond as the General walked the horse out of the paddock and onto the path that circled Blackthorn Estate. The previous night's rain had left the estate clean and fresh, and he savoured the damp musky smell of the woods as he rode between the dripping trees. He rode at a sedate pace, pausing once to watch a woodpecker hunting for beetles, and so it was an hour before his nostrils flared to the rank odour of woodsmoke.

A hundred yards along the woodland track and off to one side, smoke was drifting from behind one of the old woodcutters' shacks that dotted the estate. The General walked the horse forward, a frown of suspicion beetling his eyebrows. The door to the ivy-clad shack was open and he could see it was deserted. Five yards from the shack the smoke was rising from a weak fire of damp branches and broken twigs. He looked slowly around the surrounding trees. The wood was quiet and still. 'Odd,' the General murmured.

The fire was not that old, with only a small puddle of ash at its base. 'Somebody must have started it,' the General mused aloud and then checked himself as an untidy figure stepped from between the trees. The man stopped in his tracks, his eyes widening with surprise, and he guiltily pushed the dead rabbit behind his back out of sight of the General's accusing glare.

'This is private property!' the General barked, and the mare jinked beneath him as it scissored its ears toward his voice. He patted the mare's withers and whispered soothingly, but without once taking his eyes from the trespasser.

The man was dressed in clothes that he had obviously been wearing for some time. The coat was threadbare and shiny with age and the collar of the shirt was grimy and frayed. The sole of one shoe was bound with string and the knees of the trousers were ragged and torn. The man's hair hung long and matted around the beard that had never seen a razor. The General was sure that the hands that held the rabbit behind his back would be crusted with dirt, the nails broken and the fingers cut and bleeding.

'Well, man,' the General demanded, 'explain yourself! What are you doing here?' The man looked down at his scuffed shoes and shuffled his feet. 'Apart from poaching, that is!' and the man looked away, unable to meet the General's stare.

'Sorry,' the man whispered.

'Sorry!' the General growled. 'That won't do,' he said, and then he took a deep calming breath. It was obvious that the man posed no threat. It was also obvious that he knew he was in the wrong and that he was in desperate straits. At least he was not one of those traveller types, the General thought wryly. The last time the travellers had pitched camp on the estate he had had to be forcibly restrained by his wife from evicting them at the point of a shotgun. Lady Dembury had no doubts as to who would have been on the receiving end of the first salvo.

The self-styled leader and spokesman for the travellers went by the name of Styx and had addressed His Lordship as 'man'. The General had engaged in a most undignified slanging match until his patience had run out and he had marched into his study and snatched up one of the Holland and Holland's. Lady Dembury and Benton had caught the General as he moved at a furious pace across the lawns.

The General had a merry twinkle in his eye as he recalled the occasion. 'Haven't shot anybody in over forty years,' he mused aloud, and the man with the rabbit visibly quailed. 'Don't fret yourself.' The General looked at him. 'What's your name?' he demanded.

'Smith,' the man answered in broad Irish.

'Smith, my foot!' the General snapped. 'What's your name? And don't lie to me again!'

'Murphy, sir. Liam Murphy,' the man whispered.

'And where are you from, Liam Murphy?'

'Cork, sir.'

The General ran a keen eye across the Irish lad. 'How old are you, Liam Murphy?' he demanded.

'Eighteen, sir.' Liam was still looking at his feet.

'Look up when I am speaking to you,' the General ordered, and Liam's chin sprang up like a guardsman. 'How is it that you are reduced to these circumstances?' the General continued.

'I came over looking for work, sir,' Liam answered, and then his chin dropped again, 'but there is none.'

'There is always work,' the General told him. 'And look up, lad! If you are to work for me, you had firstly better learn that I do not give an order twice.'

Liam walked at His Lordship's stirrup as they made their way through the wood. 'Who taught you to catch rabbits?' the General wanted to know.

'My grandfather, sir.'

'A master poacher, no doubt.' The General smiled down at Liam for the first time but Liam's answering smile was hesitant and uncertain. He's like a frightened puppy, the General thought, but his eyes are clear and he looks strong enough.

Lady Dembury was appalled. 'What do you intend doing with him?' she asked, her voice full of amazement.

'Well,' the General gruffed, 'I thought perhaps he could replace that footman who resigned in such a hurry. What was his name? Gideon or something?'

'Guido!' Lady Dembury could hardly believe it.

'That's the chap.' The General nodded. He had still not fathomed why Guido had left in such a hurry. He had seemed happy enough to begin with, and his reasons for leaving seemed most curious. Something or other about a sick aunt.

'Charles, you cannot be serious!' Lady Dembury was saying. 'He's a tramp!'

The General chuckled indulgently. 'He will turn out all right, you'll see.'

'He's filthy!'

'Benton will sort him out.'

'Madness.' Lady Dembury sighed at the intransigence of men. 'Sheer madness.'

The General however, was right. Benton had put Liam in a bath of near-scalding water, feeling that it would probably take a blowtorch to get the grime that he would leave behind off the enamel, and had thrown the foul-smelling clothes onto one of the head groundsman's ever-present bonfires. With ten pounds in his pocket, Liam had been virtually frogmarched into Little Wixley to be cut and shaved, and the following morning he stood at the position of attention as Benton ran his experienced and all-seeing eyes over the uniform that had been found for him.

Benton brushed a speck from Liam's shoulder. 'You'll do,' he decided.

Within a week Liam had learnt the rudiments of his position and Benton, who was well pleased with his ability to learn quickly, gave this answer to His Lordship's question.

'Murphy is doing well, M'Lord. He is able and keen to learn.'

'Splendid.' The General smiled in triumph at his wife. 'What did I tell you?'

Liam had the use of a bicycle kept in one of the outbuildings and, with his first wage packet, he pedalled into Little Wixley.

'New face?' Mortimer enquired as he poured Liam a pint of lager.

'I've landed a job at Blackthorn House.' Liam beamed, his good fortune still something that surprised him.

'Lord Dembury's place.' Mortimer nodded as he placed the pint of golden coloured lager on the bar. 'I know it.'

Liam paid for his drink and took what he presumed to be a manly swallow, before blushing scarlet.

Susan Hamilton was giving him her unashamed appraisal from across the bar and Liam could feel his cheeks burning.

'Hello,' Susan said softly, well aware of the effect she was having, and Liam felt like a rabbit when it comes face to face with a ferret: hypnotised and unable to move.

'Hello,' and his tongue felt too big for his mouth.

'My name's Susan,' and Susan raised a questioning eyebrow.

'Liam.'

'Wonderful accent,' Susan purred, and Liam felt as if his head was going to explode.

The landlord was wearing an indulgent smile and the old man in the corner was looking over his pipe with ill-concealed amusement.

'I'm Irish,' Liam explained, hating himself for making it sound like an excuse.

'A wild colonial boy,' Susan purred again, and a forceful but playful voice cut her short.

'Stop teasing the lad,' Alan told her as he returned from what he always referred to as the little boys' room. 'Don't you worry mate.' He grinned at Liam. 'Her bark is worse than her bite.'

Liam suddenly felt a pang of jealousy and cold anger.

'I'm not a colonial.' He looked at Susan.

'Oh my.' Susan tittered. 'I was only joking, really.'

Liam took another mouthful of the cold lager. 'And I'm not a boy either.'

'All right, lad,' Mortimer cut in. 'That will do.'

'Why don't you tell her that?' Liam snapped, and the atmosphere became instantly tense.

Mortimer placed his bunched fists on his hips and gave Liam a cold stare.

'Aye, I know.' Liam emptied his glass. 'Pick on the newcomer, why don't ye.' He turned and slammed the door on his way out.

Liam stamped through the village seething with rage and humiliation. She was beautiful but she was not interested in him other than as a butt of her jokes. The boyfriend was a big-headed bastard. Last time I'm going in that dump, he vowed. All of Liam's youthful and untried masculine pride was a turmoil of frustration and hurt.

He had to walk back to the Three Pheasants to collect the bicycle.

Jennifer bounded barefooted down the stairs in her pink dressing gown with her blonde curls bouncing uncontrollably.

The sitting room was already warm, the fire in the grate having been prepared by Mary an hour earlier, and Jennifer burst into the room in a frenzy of excitement. The baubles hanging from the tree reflected the flames from the fire and the fairy lights lit up the array of prettily wrapped parcels which lay beneath the tinselled branches.

'Merry Christmas,' Jennifer said, as Mary took the first photograph of the day with the camera she had found twenty four hours earlier. Douglas and Mary smiled indulgently at their daughter as she proceeded to tear the wrapping paper from the largest gift.

Douglas winked at Mary. 'Patience not being much of a virtue in this household,' he grinned.

Jennifer squealed with delight and clutched the doll to her chest before rewarding both her parents with a smothering kiss.

The day descended into organised chaos. Douglas had first his toe and then his head bandaged before Jennifer tired of wearing her nurse's costume and left him to snooze in front of the fire with his feet encased in his new slippers, and Piper ran around the house like a dog possessed as he played havoc with the rubber bone that squeaked every time he picked it up.

Only Twinkle seemed to keep a cool head, eyeing the whole business with a lofty air and preferring to spend his time sleeping beside the kitchen stove.

'I know what will get you up,' Mary said, giving Twinkle a fond look, and she placed a bowl with the giblets from the turkey beneath Twinkle's sleeping nose. Twinkle's whiskers twitched once, and then once again, before his eyes flew open and he sprang like a jack-in-the-box from the wicker basket.

'Thought so.' Mary smiled as Twinkle began chewing on the warm titbits.

Mary turned and looked out of the window at the sound of a car drawing into the yard. Alan brought the BMW to a stop and Susan leapt out of the car and ran across the frozen cobbles before he had switched the engine off.

'Don't know what all the rush is,' Alan muttered.

Mary held the door open and Susan ran in and stood in front of the stove. 'Merry Christmas, everyone,' she called, and Jennifer immediately came running through from the sitting room.

Alan entered with a large bottle of wine and made his way through to the sitting room. 'Wakey, wakey,' he said with a wry smile. 'You can't have had enough already.'

Douglas eased himself out of the armchair with a great show of weariness. 'You haven't been used as a guinea pig by Florence nightingale out there,' he groaned. He poured sherry into two glasses and the two men toasted each other.

'You got slippers,' Alan observed.

'Again,' Douglas replied. 'What about you?'

Alan gave the scarf around his neck a vigorous shake.

'Very nice,' Douglas commented.

'And a box of monogrammed hankies,' Alan added, with a deadpan expression.

'Snap!' Douglas nodded, and the two men burst into laughter.

Jennifer appeared in the doorway with a look of anticipation in her eyes. 'Susan said that I should ask you to come outside, please,' she said.

'Ah,' Douglas said with a pantomime voice, 'what's outside?'

Susan took Jennifer's hand and, with Alan, Douglas and Mary following behind, led the child to the barn. 'Can you guess what's in here? she asked, and Jennifer shook her head wonderingly. Susan opened the door and the small group entered the barn. The air was warm and musty and smelled of leather and straw, and Jennifer stared across the barn with eyes as wide as saucers.

The pony was grey with a velvet muzzle and a flowing mane, and Jennifer stood like a statue, her mouth dropping open in astonishment. Alan hung back as Susan led the awestruck child towards the pony.

'This is from Alan and me,' Susan said with a gentle smile, and still Jennifer could not find her voice.

Mary walked slowly forward and gave the pony a soft caress. 'What do you say?' she prompted, looking lovingly at her daughter.

Jennifer gazed up at Susan with a look that melted Susan's heart. 'Thank you,' she whispered.

'And what about Alan?' Mary said.

'Thank you.' Jennifer looked over her shoulder at Alan and he gave her his brightest smile.

'What will you call her?' he asked.

Jennifer walked slowly forward and laid a small hand on the pony's muzzle. 'Grey Lady,' she decided in a hushed voice, and Susan lifted her into the saddle.

January

Fox breathed in the sharp morning air and paused to admire a small cluster of snowdrops that had blossomed at the foot of an old gnarled elm, their pure white petals proclaiming new life in the lee of the tall tree's barren branches.

Fox pulled the door closed and checked the knot of his silk cravat before cutting a swathe through the dense bracken with his silver-tipped cane and emerging into the open field. A thin sliver of the moon hung low in the dark starless sky, its slight curve breaking fleetingly through the fast-rolling thunder-clouds.

'Rain tonight, I think,' Fox muttered to himself as he looked up at the swaying branches above the small copse. He broke into a gentle lope, moving svelte and silent through the cold night towards the dark shadow of Wixley Wood crouched on the horizon.

'Morning, old boy,' Fox greeted Weasel quietly as his companion stepped out from the edge of the quiet imposing wood, a lighted cigarette drooping from his bottom lip.

'Storm brewing, I think,' Weasel replied, folding the collar of his camel-hair coat up against the strengthening wind.

'I think you're right,' Fox agreed, passing an eye over the gathering clouds. 'Let's waste no time.'

Fox and Weasel hurried across the open ground, pausing momentarily at Dixon's Point to pass a wary eye over the coverless fields before moving on and scaling the drystone wall. Weasel led the way through the night until the pair came up against the flint wall that surrounded the farmyard. They peered around the edge of the wall, peeping between the crossbeams of the wide wooden gate, their gaze coming to rest on the dark and sleeping henhouse.

'What do you think?' Weasel whispered, his beady eyes fixed on the silent chicken run.

'Seems quiet enough,' Fox replied, his voice low.

The pair waited a moment longer, their slim figures unmoving in the darkness, until, satisfied that the cobbled yard was shielding no ambush, they hurried side by side through the yard towards the roosting chickens.

Weasel's paw fumbled in his pocket until he located the bent pin he required and then he inserted it into the open recess on the face of the lock. At the very same moment the first fork of glowing yellow lightning lit up the night and a loud commanding voice cut through the silent yard.

Weasel dropped the pin and the padlock fell back against the hasp with a loud clash. Fox spun on his heel, his cane held threateningly before him in the direction of the hailed challenge.

'Well, what are you up to?' the voice demanded a second time, and the first resounding crash of thunder boomed above the dark farmyard.

'Show yourself!' Fox snarled, his teeth flashing in the gloom.

'Why should I?' the voice queried. 'I'm not the one who is up to no good.'

Fox passed the cane slowly across his front as the ensuing silence descended into an uneasy stalemate. A second bolt of lightning lanced down from the blanket of heavy black clouds, illuminating for an instant the taut scene, and Fox caught a glimpse of his adversary.

'It's a cat,' he muttered to Weasel from the corner of his mouth.

'Yes, I am a cat,' the voice mocked.

Weasel glanced up at Fox from beneath the peak of his cap. 'A cat with good hearing,' he observed wryly.

'It's not his hearing I am concerned with,' Fox replied, his eyes riveted to the spot beside the barn door where he had sighted the cat. Another roll of thunder echoed through the night, followed by the first heavy drops of rain.

'We're going to get soaked.' Weasel winced up at the foreboding sky.

'Least of our worries,' Fox whispered. 'That cat looked enormous.'

Weasel looked slowly around the farmyard with wide staring eyes. 'I can't see a thing,' he murmured. The cat's high-pitched voice carried across the yard, full of confidence and loathing. 'Exactly!'

A third golden streak ripped apart the dark night, lighting up the yard like the flashbulb on a camera, and the huge figure of a ginger tom-cat in the peak of its condition sauntered out into the open.

'You must be joking!' Weasel croaked through his suddenly dry throat, and the ginger cat laughed and unsheathed the five sharp claws of its right paw like a razored scimitar drawn from the scabbard.

'Most impressive.' Fox passed a keen eye over his enemy's arsenal.

'It is rather, isn't it?' The cat smiled wickedly, before crouching into a supple and rippling pose, like a sprinter at the starting blocks.

'Are you a friend of Jennifer's?' Fox called suddenly, thinking fast.

'Jennifer?' the cat replied, and Fox detected the uncertainty in its voice.

'Yes, Jennifer Cobden.' Fox smiled, his mind racing. 'She's a friend of mine.' He watched, his body tense and the cane held before him, as the cat hesitated, its scorching onslaught checked.

'Is she now?' the cat said, its tone revealing its suspicion.

'Yes, we have lunch in Wixley Wood,' Fox said as amiably as he could.

'So I've heard,' the cat replied, the tension going out of its muscles as it sat upright. Fox lowered the cane and relaxed his posture slightly, ready to snatch up the cane again should the cat launch an attack.

'May I introduce myself?' Fox asked, a broad smile etched onto his face as he strode with a confidence he did not feel towards the powerful feline.

'I can see who you are,' the cat replied with a tone sharp and critical enough to bring Fox to a stop.

'And you are...?' Fox enquired mildly.

'Twinkle is the name,' the cat replied, looking Fox up and down with a disdainful eye.

At his spot beside the chicken run Weasel emitted a short snigger of derision. 'Twinkle!' he snorted through his whiskers.

Twinkle moved with a blur of speed, his elastic ginger form streaking across the cobbles, and Weasel found himself pinned up against the wire mesh, a huge ginger paw clamped tightly around his throat. 'Don't laugh at my name,' Twinkle hissed menacingly, his words accompanied by another roll of deep thunder.

'Sorry,' Weasel spluttered, his eyes bulging above his pink protruding tongue.

Fox stepped forward and laid a placatory paw on Twinkle's shoulder. 'I am sure he meant no offence.'

'It didn't sound like it to me,' Twinkle growled, holding Weasel so that only the tips of his toes touched the ground.

'I'm sure it will not happen again,' Fox promised, and Twinkle released his grip abruptly so that Weasel fell to his knees, clutching his windpipe and gasping for breath. Fox helped Weasel to his feet and slapped him robustly on the back, and Weasel coughed and spat.

'Better, old boy?' Fox asked. Weasel nodded, rubbing gently at his throat as the rain began to fall in thick curtains. 'Might I suggest we get in, out of the rain?' Fox raised his eyebrows questioningly at Twinkle.

'It's warm in the barn,' Twinkle replied, and the trio sprinted through the lashing rain and into the sanctuary of the large barn. Twinkle and Weasel shook themselves, spraying droplets of water onto the loose wisps of straw as Fox dabbed at his face with his cravat.

'That's better,' Fox observed. 'Much better to be friends, don't you think?'

'Nobody said we were friends,' Twinkle replied with a slight scowl.

'Well, I wish somebody would,' Weasel interrupted, his tone revealing his exasperation with the situation.

Fox stepped forward and offered his paw in a gentlemanly fashion. 'Pleased to meet you, old boy.' He smiled.

Twinkle grudgingly accepted the olive branch. 'And you,' he answered gruffly. He turned to Weasel with a trace of a smile on his lips. 'How's the throat?' he asked with a conciliatory inflection.

'Not so bad.' Weasel attempted a brave smile but only managed a tight grimace.

'Well, that's okay then.' Fox smiled. 'All's well that ends well.'

'Coffee?' Twinkle offered.

'Splendid,' Fox answered for them both, and Weasel nodded so that more droplets of rain fell from the peak of his cap.

Fox and Weasel sat opposite Twinkle and the three of them sipped at the hot beverage, listening to the sound of the rain pelting against the roof of the barn.

'Rather cosy,' Fox ventured, between the claps of thunder.

'Not a nice night to be abroad,' Twinkle agreed, the steam from the coffee moistening his whiskers.

'Tell me,' Fox began, 'what do you know of this motorway proposal?'

'Not much,' Twinkle replied. 'Nobody seems to know much about it, apart from it being laid through Wixley Wood and the outskirts of the village.'

'I would have thought that being so close to human beings, you would have been in a good spot to keep your ear to the ground, as it were.'

'True.' Twinkle nodded his ginger head. 'But they don't seem to know much themselves.'

'Do you think that if I gave you some photographs of the motorway plans you could put them in the right hands?' Fox asked softly.

'Photographs?' Twinkle repeated curiously.

'Yes, I have some in my possession, old boy.'

Twinkle sat pondering the question and Fox waited in respectful silence.

'Douglas Cobden is usually aware of what's going on.' Twinkle rubbed his chin with a slow paw.

'My thoughts precisely,' Fox murmured.

'I suppose so,' Twinkle nodded. 'It shouldn't be too difficult.'

'I shall bring them to you,' Fox decided, 'next week, probably.'

Douglas put a match to the paper. The blue flame danced across the kindling, licking up around the black coals, and the kitchen stove glowed. He transferred the match to the gas cooker and the fat sizzled and spat beneath the large rashers and the two fresh brown eggs.

He opened the back door and a cold draught ushered Twinkle into the kitchen. 'Morning, puss.' Douglas poured a little fresh milk from the fridge into the ginger tom's bowl, following it with a generous spoonful of wet meat.

The wood crackled and popped as the fire caught, and Douglas washed the bacon and eggs down with a large mug of tea before pulling a well-greased Barbour jacket on over a thick woollen jumper. He stepped out into the cold dark morning, his cap pulled down tightly on his thick black hair. A deep hoar frost carpeted the ground, rising up to nip at Douglas's nose and ears as he hurried across the murky farmyard, his breath clouding the icy air.

The barn was snug and cosy, warmed by the body heat of the animals. Douglas set to work, patting the broad rumps of the dairy cows and whispering softly to them as he set about chivvying the cattle out of the barn. He drove the small Friesian herd out of the barn and down the narrow track, guiding the slow-moving, steaming beasts between the sparse hedgerows and the lacy cobwebs that sparkled with frosted crystals, and through the silver field to the milking shed. The weak light from the pallid yellow sun illuminated the dark trees beyond the thin mist.

An hour later Douglas broke the thick ice on the cattle trough and walked slowly back up the track, the frozen ground crunching beneath his heavy boots. He leaned on the wooden gate to the front of the farmyard and took his time to roll a cigarette as he listened to the guttural ratchet of a cock pheasant punctuate the awakening countryside, before walking through the yard and creating a scattering of red hens.

'Morning, love,' Mary said, offering her cheek for his kiss as he entered the warm kitchen.

'Morning, all.' Douglas walked across the room and warmed his hands before the stove.

'Morning, Daddy,' Jennifer said around a mouthful of cornflakes.

Mary poured fresh tea into her husband's cup and ran a sharp bread knife the length of a well-filled bacon sandwich.

'Get that inside you.' She patted Douglas lightly on his back.

'I helped Mummy feed the chickens, Daddy,' Jennifer said, smiling up at her father with glowing eyes.

'Good girl.' Douglas patted his daughter's blonde curls fondly before taking a large bite of the sandwich.

'Come along, young lady,' Mary said, pulling off her apron. 'It's time you were getting ready for school.'

Jennifer was ready within minutes, throwing her coat and scarf on over her school uniform with boisterous haste. 'Bye bye, Daddy,' she said, standing on the tips of her toes and hugging Douglas's neck tightly as she kissed his cheek.

'Be a good girl.' Douglas returned the kiss.

Mary pecked Douglas's cheek. 'See you later.'

'I'll see if I can get a pheasant this morning,' Douglas replied as Mary turned for the door, 'so I may not be in when you get back.'

'Okay. I'll see you for lunch?'

'I'll be back no later than twelve.'

'Okay, bye,' and Mary ushered her daughter through the door and into the back of the estate.

The car drove away, leaving a cloud of hazy blue fumes in its wake. Douglas lifted the Purdey down from its place above the doorway. Piper immediately jumped up from his basket beside the stove and padded across the kitchen to sit at Douglas's feet.

'See if we can't bag ourselves a fat pheasant, eh boy?' Douglas patted the chestnut-coloured spaniel. He walked across the cobbled yard with the broken gun resting in the crook of his arm and Piper trotted dutifully at his side.

The coarse, rasping call of the pheasant pulled Douglas like a magnet across the hard, frozen earth towards the ragged collection of trees that stood naked beneath the bright winter sunshine. He stepped into the lee of a tall ash, its bare topmost branches clawing at the pale blue sky, and leaned his bulk on the damp, moss-green crossbeam of a wooden fence. He sent the cocker spaniel trotting forward, its breath coming in clouds of fog in the morning air.

Piper covered the open field to the trees in a straight, unwavering line and then began to quarter the ground, threading his way through the small quiet clump. Douglas pushed two fresh cartridges into the open barrels and waited patiently, confident of the dog's ability.

The hoarse, alarmed cock-call of the pheasant suddenly carried sharply across the cold farmland, and Douglas snapped the gun closed as the bird shot skywards out of the edge of the barren-looking copse, its resplendent plumage a splash of colour against the pale cobalt sky. Douglas heaved the gun to the shoulder and brought his sights to bear on the rapidly rising game bird. The pheasant hung suspended in mid-air, its wings held away from its body as it reached the summit of its rocketing trajectory, and Douglas placed the peak of his sights on the bird's fast-beating breast. He squeezed the trigger and the startled pheasant's graceful soaring glide disintegrated into an untidy spiralling tumble of reddish-brown feathers.

The blue gunsmoke drifted away into the slanting sunshine and Douglas rolled a cigarette as he waited for the spaniel to collect the fallen bird. Piper returned, brown and glossy against the sharp white frost, the golden-tinted pheasant held limply between his clamped jaws, its head swinging in time with his brisk scampering gait.

'Good boy.' Douglas lifted the bird from the dog's mouth, its feathers wet and sticky, and carried it by its neck between the two forefingers of his left hand as he strolled back across the frosted field with the broken gun cradled in his right elbow. Piper padded proudly at his side.

Douglas entered the farmyard to find a huge and magnificent Rolls-Royce parked on the cobbles, the driver wrapped in a black coat behind the wheel. Piper ran across to the unfamiliar car and passed his nose along its polished bodywork. The driver stepped from the car as Douglas approached.

'Mr Cobden?'

'That's right.' Douglas gave the man a puzzled nod.

'Lord Dembury is inside, sir,' the man stated.

'Lord Dembury?'

'Yes, sir. He would like to speak with you.'

'What about?' Douglas asked, frowning.

'Well, I shall leave that to His Lordship to tell you, sir.'

Douglas walked towards the kitchen door, a look of confused apprehension on his face, and called Piper to his side as he entered the warmth of the kitchen. Mary jumped up from the teacups on the bare table as the door opened, and the General rose, grave and distinguished.

'This is Lord Dembury, who has come to talk to you,' Mary introduced the General. 'My husband, Douglas.' Mary smiled.

'Lord Dembury.' Douglas laid the broken gun on the table beside the dead pheasant and offered his hand.

'How do you do, Mr Cobden.' The General accepted the large calloused palm with a firm matching grip. 'This is a fine-looking bird,' he complimented Douglas's bag.

'I presume you shoot, General? Quite well, I should think,' Douglas returned the compliment. 'Sit down, please. To what do I owe this unexpected pleasure?'

The pleasantries over, the General lowered himself onto the hard chair and ran a thoughtful finger along his bushy silver moustache.

'I assume you are only too aware of this motorway business,' the General asked, his voice grim.

'Ah yes, the motorway!' Douglas nodded, washing his hands at the deep enamel sink and feeling relieved that the subject was not fox-hunting. 'I don't think there can be anyone who isn't aware of it by now,' Douglas said, frowning as he dried his hands on a fluffy white towel.

'Well it would seem to me,' the General began, 'that we can all roll over and play dead and allow it all to happen anyway.' He paused. 'Or we can, all of us, join together and put a stop to it.'

Douglas sat down at the table and took a swallow of the hot tea which Mary had poured for him before replying. 'Why have you come to me?' Douglas saw a flicker of a smile cross the General's face.

'Let's just say I like the way you handle that gun,' and Douglas laughed aloud.

'What do you suggest?' he asked, and he opened a leather folder and extracted a cleaning brush and a collection of threaded rods.

'Organisation of the villagers,' the General replied as Douglas screwed the cleaning rods together. 'Demonstrations of solidarity.' Douglas smiled at the General's use of the word. 'Posters, picketing of Wixley Wood, that sort of thing.'

Douglas grinned broadly as he pushed the brush through the shotgun's barrels. 'You sound like a socialist.'

'God forbid!' The General said gruffly. 'And you need more oil on that brush.'

'And just how do I figure in all this?' Douglas asked, ignoring the General's instruction.

'You seem to me like the sort of chap who could rally the troops, as it were.'

Douglas peered through the shining black barrels before snapping the gun closed. 'Not me! I've got a farm to run.'

The General pursed his lips. 'Very well, as you wish.' He rose laboriously to his feet and offered his hand. 'Good day, Mr Cobden.'

'Goodbye.'

The two men shook hands. The General turned at the door. 'Thank you for the tea, Mrs Cobden.' He nodded perfunctorily.

'My pleasure.' Mary smiled wanly.

Douglas stood in the doorway as the General walked slowly towards Hodges, who stood holding open the rear door of the polished limousine.

The General turned at the door and looked Douglas square in the eye. 'If you still have a farm!' he said gravely.

The limousine rolled smoothly out of the yard, the hens running quickly out of its path. Douglas watched it disappear along the track, the General's words hanging heavily in the air.

He closed the door to find Mary already plucking the pheasant, her manner brusque and businesslike.

'We should leave that to hang for a week,' Douglas said, pulling up a chair, but Mary did not look up from her work. 'What's the matter?' Douglas asked with a heavy sigh, aware that his wife's furious plucking was more to do with him than the bird.

'You were rude!' Mary said without meeting her husband's eyes.

'I was not rude.'

'You were offhand, to say the least,' Mary snapped, pulling another handful of feathers from the bird's breast.

'Well, what do you expect?' Douglas defended himself. 'He's got a damned cheek, volunteering me for some sort of martyr.'

'Nobody expects you to be a martyr,' Mary flared. 'I was talking to him for about an hour before you came home and he had some very sensible ideas.

'Such as?' Douglas asked sarcastically.

'He is a lord!' Mary flung the bird down on the table. 'He can stand up in the House of Lords and make our voices heard.' Douglas said nothing, conceding the point. 'And he had a high regard for you,' Mary informed him, picking up the bird again.

'He doesn't even know me!'

'He knows you well enough.'

'Oh, does he now?' Douglas sneered.

'Yes, I think he does. He struck me as a good judge of men.'

Douglas got up abruptly from the table and placed the shotgun back in its place above the doorway. 'I'm not interested,' he said.

'Well, you should be. This might affect us more than anyone else.'

'Snow!' Jennifer shouted as she looked with wide eyes out of her bedroom window at the even carpet of virgin snow that had fallen during the night. She bounded down the stairs with the folds of her blue nightdress flapping around her ankles, to find her father pulling on a pair of Wellington boots.

'It's snowed,' she said, her voice full of wonder.

'So I noticed,' Douglas muttered.

Jennifer raced back up the stairs. She reappeared in the kitchen moments later, fully dressed and raring to go.

Mary brought her daughter down to earth. 'Not without some breakfast,' she said. 'You must have something hot inside you.' Jennifer's protests were silenced almost before they had begun as Douglas ordered her to do as she was told. She tried to wolf down her breakfast as fast as she could in order to be able to accompany her father on his rounds but Douglas was long gone before she was finished.

Mary knotted a woollen bonnet beneath her daughter's chin and Jennifer ran out into the yard. Douglas had left deep prints in the snow and Jennifer followed them into the barn. Douglas had forked fresh hay and oats into Grey Lady's stall and Jennifer patted the pony as it dipped its muzzle into the nosebag. She followed the footprints out of the barn and along the track towards the milking shed. The snow was deep in the track and bowed the hedgerows with its weight.

She shielded her eyes with a gloved hand from the glare of the snow. In the distance, only the arms of a stranded and long-forgotten scarecrow stood above the blanket of snow, its tattered red shirt offering the only splash of colour in the white landscape.

The silence was total, even the rooks had ceased their endless cawing. Jennifer dropped her hand to her side and the first snowball hit her firmly in the chest.

Fox laughed like a maniac from behind the hedge. 'Got you, old girl!' he crowed.

'Jennifer's eyes lit up and she scooped up a handful of snow and threw it at the grinning canine. Fox ducked easily out of sight and sneaked along the hedge before delivering another perfect hit on Jennifer's back. Jennifer squealed and fell over as Fox followed up with a veritable barrage of well-directed snowballs.

'Do you surrender?' he called.

Jennifer was laughing too much to be able to answer and Fox struggled through the snow and helped her to her feet.

'What are you doing here, Mr Fox?' Jennifer asked, once she had recovered her breath.

'I was caught out, my dear,' Fox replied. 'The snow came down so fast I couldn't see my paw in front of my face, so I holed up until the morning.'

'It is a long way home for you,' Jennifer observed.

'Indeed.' Fox nodded. 'But I've had a spot of breakfast so things shouldn't be too bad.'

'Are you going home now?'

'I certainly am. I shall see you again,' and with that Fox loped off across the fields, using his cane as a support through the snow.

Jennifer found her father in the milking shed. The shed was warm and her nose tingled. 'I've had a snowball fight with Mr Fox,' Jennifer told him.

'Who won?' Douglas smiled.

'I fell over,' Jennifer defended herself.

'I see, so Mr Fox won, did he?'

'It was a draw!'

Douglas chuckled to himself and gave Jennifer a pick-a-back ride across the fields. Fox watched their progress from the snow-capped boulder at Dixon's Point before turning and heading for Wixley Wood.

The door to Badger's sett supported a huge bank of snow and Fox had to dig most of it away before Badger would open the door. Fox kicked snow from his heels before stepping into the hallway. The sett was snug and Fox was soon warming himself in front of the log fire. Mrs Badger poured tea from a china pot and heaped two sugars into Fox's cup.

'Are the photographs ready?' Fox asked.

Badger glanced over the rim of his cup. 'They all came out splendidly,' he said.

'Excellent,' Fox rejoined.

'How will you get them to the girl?' Badger wanted to know. His voice was full of doubt.

'Well, obviously the cat is a non-starter.' Fox scratched his brow.

'That cat won't step outside in this weather,' Badger agreed.

'I shall have to get them to Jennifer personally,' Fox murmured.

'When will that be?'

'I shall go tonight,' Fox decided, and then he quickly corrected himself. 'No, early tomorrow morning when I can be sure she will be awake.'

Mrs Badger interrupted: 'In that case, you must stay here until then.'

'Mrs Badger,' Fox demurred, 'I could not possibly impose upon you.'

'Nonsense,' Mrs Badger cut him short. 'No point in making two journeys in this weather. You must stay here until tomorrow.'

Fox and Badger were right about one thing. Twinkle had no intention whatsoever of venturing outside. As far as he was concerned, the only place for any self-respecting cat to be at a time like this was curled up beside the kitchen stove.

Outside, Twinkle could hear Jennifer's squeals of delight as she and Mary completed the snowman. Twinkle stretched and sprang up onto the windowsill to inspect the finished article. The snowman was taller than Jennifer by a head and had coal for eyes and mouth, along with the obligatory carrot for a nose.

Very smart, Twinkle thought, and he jumped down from the sill and resumed his position beside the stove.

Twinkle did not know what he was missing.

Little Wixley took on a chocolate-box appearance that year as it sat silently in the grip of winter. For the most part, only the smoke rising from the chimney pots atop the snow-capped cottages betrayed any signs of life. The church in particular looked superb.

Alwyn Jones sprinkled breadcrumbs on the swept and salted path and felt rewarded when a pair of blue tits joined a robin for breakfast.

A grey squirrel sat watching from atop one of the snow-capped gravestones. Alwyn reached into his pocket and produced a handful of peanuts. Alwyn's relationship with the squirrels had improved during the winter as it became clear that without him the squirrels would have a very difficult time of it. He sprinkled the nuts onto the path and the squirrel was immediately joined by a second, and they scampered together across the snow.

Alwyn strolled along the path and paused beneath the gabled archway. The morning was quiet and still, the lane a causeway of snow. High in one of the bare branches of an elm a magpie chattered before disappearing across the white fields. Alwyn looked along the lane in the direction of the construction company compound and allowed himself a sly smile.

'This should slow things up no end,' he said to himself.

He hunched himself down into the folds of his duffel coat and tramped through the drifts and across the stone bridge. Mrs Buxton answered the door on his second knock and, within moments, Alwyn was enjoying tea and scones.

'Is there anything you need?' Alwyn asked.

'Young Susan next door has already done some shopping for me, thank you,' Mrs Buxton replied.

'Very good to have such considerate neighbours,' Alwyn said. 'You are most fortunate.'

Mrs Buxton smiled over her teacup and said nothing.

Fox hurried through the icy wood, the small package clamped tightly under his arm. His tread left deep tracks in the snow. He checked his watch against the face of the moon and the gold lid shone beneath the stars. He snapped the watch shut, satisfied with the progress he was making, and carried on through the eerie kaleidoscope of black on white.

The call of an owl, like the haunting cry of a lost soul, echoed through the stark trees as Fox exited the still wood and looked out across the bleak landscape. The blanket of snow lay deep and virginal across the fields, its icy grip quiet and complete beneath the full moon. Fox shivered against the cold and held a match to the tapered end of a Monte Cristo. He drew the rich flavour into his lungs and savoured its warming comfort before stepping out across the even snow.

The going was slow and tiring, the deep snow pulling at him with every step, so that the dawn was already breaking by the time he reached the white-capped drystone wall. Fox peered over the wall. Grey smoke was rising steadily from the farmhouse chimney and the windows glowed with yellow light.

Fox dropped over the wall and struggled through the snow until he stood in the shelter of the flint wall. He peeped around the gatepost, and saw Mary Cobden pass behind the kitchen window, a mug of hot tea in each hand.

Fox ducked quickly behind the wall as the barn door swung open. Douglas Cobden, wrapped against the winter in a duffel coat and thick scarf, stamped back through the pale dawn and into the kitchen.

Fox slipped through the gate and moved as quickly as he could across the snow and into the lee of the farmhouse. He followed the wall, keeping low beneath the level of the windows until he found himself beneath Jennifer's bedroom. He rolled a handful of snow into a tight ball and hurled it against the window, and the snowball disintegrated against the pane of glass.

The dark window became instantly bright as a light was switched on, and Jennifer's face appeared between the curtains.

'Mr Fox!' she cried, her voice full of surprise. She opened the window and looked down at Fox, his scarlet waistcoat dazzling against the white snow. 'What are you doing here, Mr Fox?'

Fox threw the brown package up to the window and Jennifer caught it and hugged it to her nightdress.

'Give that to your father,' Fox whispered, and without waiting for a reply, turned and headed back through the freshly falling snowflakes.

Mortimer pulled back the curtains in the lounge bar and looked out of the leaded windows. A fresh layer of snow carpeted the village and Mortimer could see the boy who delivered the newspapers struggling manfully across the green. Mortimer shivered involuntarily and rubbed his hands together before getting his day started.

The fire was crackling brightly by the time he dropped the bolts above the door, the pub warmed and comfortable. Max was first through the door, swapping his wellington boots for a pair of slippers before taking up his customary position at the end of the bar.

'Been to church?' Mortimer grinned as he cracked open a bottle of brown ale. Max was notorious for being about as God-fearing as Attila the Hun.

'Of course,' Max replied. 'Every Sunday there's a "Z" in the month.' He pulled on the match he held to his pipe before speaking again. 'That money jar is filling up nicely.' The jar was almost half-full.

'This weather will help, of course,' Mortimer agreed.

'Not much sign of life up at that compound,' Max muttered thoughtfully.

'Can't complain about that,' Mortimer said.

Max tapped at his teeth with the stem of his pipe. 'No Douglas this morning?'

'Difficult walk in this weather.' Mortimer looked out of the window as the snowflakes began falling again.

Douglas stood in the foyer of the long quiet entrance hall of Blackthorn House, waiting for the return of the butler. He fingered the knot of his tie for the hundredth time since entering the mansion, and again checked the shine of his shoes.

He looked up as Benton appeared in the hallway and began walking towards him across the plush carpet.

'His Lordship will see you now, sir,' Benton intoned, 'if you would care to step this way.'

Douglas walked along the hallway a step behind the immaculately dressed butler, taking in the large oil portraits which adorned the walls and the shimmering chandeliers which hung from the high white ceiling.

'Mr Cobden, M'Lord.' Benton held the brass and mahogany door to the drawing room open and Douglas stepped through.

The General stood dressed in a tweed jacket and a blue striped tie, warming his legs before the log fire, with two black Labradors slumbering at his feet.

'Mr Cobden.' He walked across the spacious room and offered his hand.

'Lord Dembury.' Douglas shook the leathery palm.

'May I introduce my wife?' Lady Dembury smiled sweetly at Douglas from the chesterfield beside the large fireplace. 'Mr Cobden.'

Douglas inclined his head politely. 'Lady Dembury, my

pleasure, ma'am.'

'Thank you, Mr Cobden.'

The General turned and made his way towards his leather buttoned armchair. 'Take a seat,' he said, indicating a similar chair adjacent to his own.

Douglas settled his large bulk into the deep, comfortable chair and looked up as the General held a box of cigars beneath his nose.

'Cigar?' the General enquired gruffly.

'Thank you, sir, no,' Douglas declined.

'A whiskey for me.' The General turned towards Liam Murphy as he selected a Havana. 'What's your poison, Mr Cobden?'

Douglas felt that two refusals would appear rude and so he accepted the offer and joined the General in a whiskey and water.

'A change of heart?' the General opened as he lowered himself into his chair.

'My wife convinced me.' Douglas smiled wanly. 'And my daughter.'

'Your daughter?'

'Yes.' Douglas placed his glass on the table beside the chair. 'She gave me these, which you may find interesting.' Douglas handed a large buff-coloured envolope to the General.

'What are these?' the General asked as he opened the envelope.

'Photographs,' Douglas replied. 'Photographs of the motorway plans, to be precise.'

The General flicked slowly through the photographs as the wood crackled in the fireplace. 'How on earth did your daughter get hold of these?' he asked softly, his brow creasing into a frown.

'That I don't know,' Douglas sighed. 'She says a fox gave them to her.'

'A fox?'

'I'm afraid so. She has a semi-tame fox in Wixley Wood that she feeds pieces of ham etc. to ....' Douglas spread his hands in a gesture of resignation. 'Apparently the fox gave them to her.'

Lady Dembury smiled. 'How sweet.'

'Well, no matter,' the General said. 'These could be very useful.'

'That's what I hoped,' Douglas replied, sipping at his whiskey. 'You could probably make more use of them that I could.'

'I certainly could!' the General growled suddenly, sitting upright in his chair with one of the photographs clutched in his bony hand.

The photograph was of a typewritten reply accepting an order for a consignment of concrete and one of the signatures at the bottom was decorative and pretentious.

'Bartholomew!'

Fox struggled through the snow, panting with every step as he sank in up to his knees.

'This is impossible,' he moaned. 'Weasel, old boy, I think you were right,' he said to himself.

Weasel was absent, having flatly refused to venture out again. The last expedition had provided nothing more than a road kill and they had chased away a pair of squabbling magpies before arguing themselves over how to divide the dead crow. Weasel had subsequently curled up beside his fire in the drystone wall and declared his intention to take up hibernating and stay there until the spring.

Fox paused to catch his breath. 'I'm bloody ravenous' he cursed.

He stared across the snowy fields. There was not a meal in sight.

Wrapped tightly against the winter, the General and Douglas strode side by side, the crisp snow crunching beneath their wellington boots.

The General had sent the beaters beyond the rambling wood which sat on the outer limits of his estate half an hour earlier, and now he and Douglas parted and stood divided by twenty yards with their loaded guns resting comfortably in their arms.

They waited for the first birds to break from cover and pass over the snow-covered track. Through the bare tees Douglas could hear the beaters begin their advance, calling and shouting to the quarry and thrashing at the dense bracken so that the brambles shook off the heavy snow in pretty white showers.

'They're off,' Douglas called.

'A pound the bag, we agreed on?'

'That we did.'

The two men snapped their guns closed and trained their eyes on the leaden sky, their breathing shallow and concentrated.

The tumultuous cries of the beaters drew nearer, their voices carrying clearly through the sharp cold, and the first cock pheasant broke from its sanctuary and soared above the trees on stiff wings.

The General brought his gun up in a high sweeping motion and the shot echoed above the sound of the toiling beaters. The bird plummeted from the sky.

'First blood, I think,' he called.

Douglas raised the Purdey as a brace of the streamlined birds rocketed out of the trees and over his head. The shotgun barked twice in quick succession and the pair of auburn hens tumbled to the snow.

'Have your pound ready, General,' Douglas countered.

The General closed his gun on a fresh cartridge with a steely determination, the other man's challenge coursing through his veins like molten lava, and a third pheasant, a large aristocratic cock, drummed the air with rapid wings. The General placed his sights on the exposed breast of the rising bird and the shot resounded through the cold morning. The pheasant cartwheeled from the sky.

'Not so soon.' The General threw the challenge back with a devilish grin.

The cold air swallowed up the gunsmoke and the sharp cordite, and the two men brought to earth the panicked birds as they screamed from the beaters' advance, until the gamekeeper blew the whistle and the volleys of gunfire ceased.

The spent cartridges sizzled in the snow and the blood of the fallen birds speckled the white landscape, their sightless eyes matching the glazed countryside. The General rested his weapon and offered Douglas the silver hip flask.

'I count eleven,' Douglas said, wiping his lips and allowing the strong brandy to heat his belly.

'I believe I had twelve,' the older man murmured, wiping the liquor from his moustache with the two scarred fingers of his left hand.

The gamekeeper walked forward through the snowy branches, a look of puzzled consternation on his face.

'What is it, Rutherford?' the General enquired.

The gamekeeper lifted the deerstalker from his head and ran a tentative finger along the smooth feathers which protruded from behind the badge of stags antlers that decorated it.

The General frowned. 'Well, man, spit it out!'

'We make it eleven each, M'Lord,' the gamekeeper said, avoiding the General's eye.

'Eleven!' the General said gruffly. 'I thought I counted twelve?'

'So did I, M'Lord,' Rutherford agreed, scratching his forehead with a puzzled finger as Douglas viewed the exchange with a light smile.

'Where is the twelfth then?' The General looked toward the beaters still searching the undulating banks of snow. 'It must be there somewhere.'

The gamekeeper joined his master in contemplating the puzzle, looking around the virgin snow with a confused eye. Douglas put a match to his cigarette before attempting to bring the potentially embarrassing situation to an end.

'Let's call it a draw, General. What do you say?'

The General looked critically around the field again, his frown dark and brooding. 'Don't understand it,' he grumbled, before his shoulders slumped in resignation. 'Very well, a draw it is.'

Fox leaned back in his chair and crossed his ankles on the dining table before lighting the cheroot.

'By God, but that was good,' he remarked with a satisfied sigh as he eyed the remains of the roast pheasant. 'His Lordship is a mighty fine shot.'

General Lord Dembury of Wixley sat in his chair, looking out of the French windows at the herd of fallow deer leaving tracks in the snow as they drifted across the oak-studded estate. Far in the distance, beyond the boundaries of Blackthorn, the bare winter branches of Wixley Wood scratched at the dull grey sky.

The General took a final draw on the Havana before throwing the butt into the fire with a gesture of contempt, and the yellow flames licked around the stub and devoured it. He had a strong head for drink and the glass he raised to his lips contained his fifth double whiskey. He downed the fiery liquid with one swallow so that all that remained were the reflective cubes of ice in the bottom of the glass.

'Bartholomew!' the General repeated for almost the hundredth time since Douglas had departed, and his voice had become more angry and loathing with each rendition. He snatched up the photographs and glared at them again, as though they were a tangible, living thing and he could attack them and beat them into submission.

The door to the sitting room opened and Lady Dembury entered, her expression serious and concerned. 'What do you think?' she asked, sitting down opposite her husband.

'It all depends on whether it's legal or not,' the General replied, dropping the photographs back onto the mahogany table as if they were repellent to the touch. 'I shall have to get some sound advice,' he continued. 'I know a few names, those who would know.'

He returned his gaze to the wood on the horizon, and the first drops of rain began to splash onto the wide-fronted windows, sending a shiver tiptoeing down his spine. He shook himself and reached down to place another log on the fire.

'Wixley Wood is centuries old,' he said softly, and one of the logs burnt through and crashed softly into the ashes. 'Laying a motorway through it is nothing short of criminal.'

The rain began to drum on the windows, blurring the view of

the distant wood and throwing the room into a murky gloom. Lady Dembury switched on one of the table lamps and the shadows receded.

'I shall fight this,' the General murmured. 'With all my heart I shall fight this.'

Chapter 6

February

Alwyn stepped back from the high wooden archway at the front of the churchyard and contemplated his handiwork. The poster was of bright orange with the words 'NO MOTORWAY' printed in large black ink.

Alwyn glanced down at the grey squirrel that had sat on the flint wall and watched as he had tacked the poster to the porch. 'What do you think?' He smiled at the small inquisitive animal. The squirrel bobbed up and down on its haunches, its long S-shaped tail twitching curiously. 'Was that a nod?' Alwyn enquired, enjoying the company as much as the game.

The squirrel turned and sprinted along the wall before leaping up onto a snow-laden overhanging branch and scampering expertly into the dark hole in the bole of the horse chestnut where it had made its home.

'And a good morning to you too,' Alwyn said, before hurrying along Church Walk as the first drops of rain began to fall on the narrow lane.

The rain was also beginning to fall across the river where Alan was doing his bit for neighbourly relations.

Alan swung the axe with both hands from high above his head and a multitude of sharp white chips flew from the large dry log. The wood split cleanly down its middle. Alan gathered up the collection of fist-sized logs, placing them one on top of the other in the crook of his elbow, and made his way around the cottage towards the front door of Mrs Buxton's home.

The old lady pulled back a net curtain as Alan walked up her pathway and motioned him with a wrinkled hand towards the rear of the cottage. She opened the back door as Alan approached and her lined face broke into a grateful smile.

'I've just made a pot of tea,' she said, looking up at the black clouds gathering beneath the dismal sky.

'I'll put these in your shed,' Alan announced. 'I think it's coming on to rain.'

Mrs Buxton poured the tea from a floral-patterned china pot and spooned sugar into the matching cups, and Alan accepted a slice of home-made lemon meringue pie.

'I've put one of your posters up in my window,' Mrs Buxton remarked, and Alan swallowed the sweet lemon before replying.

'So I noticed,' he answered. 'That's the spirit.'

'There are quite a lot of them springing up,' Mrs Buxton observed.

'The more the merrier,' Alan agreed, looking out of the window as the first drops of rain began to run down the glass.

'How is Susan?' Mrs Buxton enquired politely.

'She's fine,' Alan replied. 'She's out riding at the moment so I suppose she will come back soaking wet.'

'Oh dear,' Mrs Buxton sympathised. 'You will have to run her a nice hot bath.'

'I suppose so.' Alan smiled.

'And then get in with her.' Mrs Buxton chuckled, her eyes twinkling mischievously behind her horn-rimmed spectacles.

'Mrs Buxton!' Alan gasped, genuinely astonished, before breaking into a fit of laughter. 'I shall tell her you said that.' He laughed, still finding it difficult to believe that the old lady had really said it.

'Where has she gone riding?' Mrs Buxton asked over her teacup.

'Wixley Wood,' Alan answered, still smiling. 'I think she is going to put some posters up on her way.'

Alan looked up at the window a second time as a delicate tapping sound caught his attention. A cock robin, its red breast glowing against the darkening afternoon, stood perched on the snow-capped ledge, pecking urgently at the window pane.

'Ah, my robin.' Mrs Buxton smiled, rising from the kitchen table. 'He wants to come in out of the rain.' She opened the window and the robin hopped through and paused on the sill as it passed a wary eye over Alan, who sat quite still, enchanted by the proceedings.

'It's all right, he's a friend,' the old lady advised the small bird and, as if understanding her every word, the robin flitted down and hopped across the clean white tablecloth. Mrs Buxton broke off a small piece of the sweet meringue and placed it before the attentive bird. Alan watched with a sense of awe as the robin accepted the small crumb.

'I didn't know you had a pet robin,' Alan whispered, completely under the spell that the old woman and the small garden resident had woven.

'Lemon meringue is his favourite,' Mrs Buxton replied quietly.

The robin pecked quickly at the flaky pie as Alan and Mrs Buxton watched with silent and charmed interest, until the first resounding clap of thunder broke the spell. The delicate songbird lifted itself from the table and flew with a rapid beat of its wings out of the kitchen and disappeared into the hedges at the bottom of the garden.

'Fascinating.'

Mrs Buxton smiled. 'He often drops in for afternoon tea.'

'Well, I must be getting on.' Alan made his excuses. 'Thank you for the tea.'

'Thank you for chopping me some logs,' Mrs Buxton reciprocated.

'My pleasure.' Alan smiled as the old lady ushered him out of the door with a warning.

'If this storm keeps up, Tom Dixon will be out tonight,' she called.

Alan hurried through the rain at the same time as Susan, riding hard across the snowy fields, was trying to beat it. She pulled back on the reins and lowered herself into the saddle, and the glossy black gelding came to a high-stepping and whinnying halt. Susan patted Bucephalus's withers reassuringly as the gelding danced in a tight circle, until the powerful horse calmed and stood snorting through flared nostrils.

Susan jumped down from the saddle. She lifted the tan holdall from the pommel and extracted a single poster. The poster was a twin of the one she had given Alwyn at the vicarage thirty minutes earlier, and the words rang out against the lurid orange background.

Susan tacked the poster to the rough fence post with four

drawing pins and then vaulted back into the saddle and gathered up the reins before turning the gelding's head away from the fence and towards Wixley Wood. She put her heels into the horse's muscular flanks and Bucephalus broke into a canter.

She stood lightly in the stirrups and crouched forward over the horse's strong neck as her mount covered the open ground towards the wood with a flowing rhythm. She brought him up at the edge of the trees and tethered the reins to the thin trunk of an evergreen conifer before quickly proceeding to tack a series of posters along the tree-line.

The rain began to fall as she climbed back into the saddle and turned the collar of her Barbour up against it, giving Bucephalus his head and allowing him to gallop through the downpour, back across the open fields so that his hooves threw up great clods of wet earth. She reined in the blowing gelding at the gate to Douglas's yard and walked Bucephalus through to the barn, where she unsaddled and closed the stall door before removing her hard hat and allowing her damp hair to tumble down.

The door to the large barn opened and Douglas entered, shaking the rain from his coat and smiling ruefully.

'Hello, young lady. Come to get in out of the rain, have you?' he asked, hanging his dripping cap on a rusty nail.

'Well, you are closest, Uncle Douglas,' Susan replied, knowing how her bright smile always won her uncle over.

'Yes, I know,' Douglas observed. 'And it's no good giving me your "little girl lost" look either,' he said, knowing that he was lying as his niece never failed to win his favours. 'You must pop in and see your Aunty Mary. She hasn't seen you for a while,' Douglas continued. 'Ask her to put the kettle on as well. I'll be in as soon as I've finished here.'

Susan ran through the shallow puddles in the cobbled yard and burst in through the kitchen door, her face wet from the pelting rain. 'Hello, everybody,' she called, wiping raindrops from her cheeks.

Mary stood at the open door of the oven with a large home-made steak-and-kidney pie in her hands and her apron white with flour. 'Hello, Susan.' She smiled as she placed the pie in the heat of the oven.

Jennifer came running through the hallway to greet her elder cousin and promptly received her mother's admonishment not to run in the house.

'Hello, Jenny.' Susan grinned, lifting Jennifer up and settling her on her hip. 'You're getting too heavy for this,' Susan groaned, and she dropped Jennifer to the floor.

Mary filled the kettle with fresh water and the three of them sat at the table. 'To what do we owe this unexpected pleasure?' Mary enquired with a mildly mocking smile.

'I haven't seen you for a while, that's all,' Susan replied, and Jennifer snorted her derision.

'Fibber!' she said. 'You just got caught in the rain, that's all.'

'Unfair!' Susan defended herself against the seven-year-old's accusing glare. 'I really was coming to see you.'

'Fibber!' Jennifer repeated, and Susan knew when she was beaten.

'Oh, all right, I got caught in the rain,' she capitulated with an apologetic voice.

Twinkle appeared from beneath the table and promptly jumped up onto Susan's lap, purring and rubbing his ginger cheeks against her stomach. 'You're getting too big as well,' Susan observed, stroking the ginger tom affectionately.

'What have you been up to?' Mary asked as she rose to pour boiling water onto the tea.

'I've been putting up some of the posters that Alan had printed,' Susan replied with a mischievous grin. 'I even put one on the compound fence in Church Walk.'

'What posters?' Jennifer asked with a puzzled frown.

'The posters saying that we don't want a motorway,' Susan replied gently.

'That's right. Mr Fox says we don't need a motorway,' Jennifer confided with a serious voice.

The door opened and Douglas entered in a blast of rain and cold. 'How many valentines, young lady?' He grinned as he hung his dripping hat and coat on the hook on the back of the door.

'Only one,' Susan lied. She had received two, one from Alan and one from God knows who. She had not mentioned it to Alan. It was her secret and she loved it.

'How's Alan?' Douglas asked as he sat at the table and lifted a large mug of tea to his lips.

'He's fine, chopping some logs for old Mrs Buxton next door.'

'How is the poster campaign going?' Douglas asked, blowing onto the hot tea in an attempt to cool it.

'Most of the village is covered, and points towards Wixley Wood.'

'We shall have to have one for hereabouts,' Mary decided.

'Can I have one for Mr Fox?' Jennifer chimed in.

'Please!'

'Please,' Jennifer echoed, her eyes shining hopefully.

'Of course you can.' Susan smiled, her heart warmed by the happy smile which broke out on her young cousin's face.

Jennifer spent an almost sleepless night with the poster tucked beneath her pillow, after having secured her mother's promise that they would visit Wixley Wood the following day.

When the dawn arrived, it was grey and dismal and the morning soon turned to rain, fine drizzle that dampened not only the countryside but Mary's enthusiasm as well. Perhaps she could persuade Jennifer that mushroom picking on such a day was not a good idea.

The door to the kitchen opened and Jennifer skipped through, waving her wicker basket around the room.

'It's a bit miserable outside, Mummy,' she said, peering out of the rain spattered window at the wet cobbles.

'Perhaps it's a bit too miserable.' Mary seized the opportunity. 'Perhaps we should go another day.'

It was a brave attempt but one doomed to failure and Jennifer nailed it with a customary burst of exuberance. 'It's all right,' she declared, using her father's favourite phrase. 'It's only water.'

Mary sighed inwardly. She was of the opinion that the fact that it was water was as good a reason as any for spending the day indoors beside the fire. Jennifer, however, was already pulling on a pair of yellow rubber boots.

'Come on, slowcoach,' she said earnestly.

Mary began pulling on her waterproof clothing at a slower pace, so that Jennifer was already dressed and waiting impatiently beside the door long before her mother was ready.

The door opened and Douglas came in from the cold. Piper shook the rain from his coat before padding across to the stove. Douglas looked at the two women in his life as if they were both deranged.

'You must be mad!' he muttered, shaking his head disbelievingly. Mary had to agree. As far as she was concerned, it was Piper who had the right idea.

'Well, let's get going,' she said, finally giving in to the inevitable.

The fields towards Wixley Wood were covered with a low, thin mist, and Mary trudged through the rain and what was left of the snow. At the edge of the wood, hidden by the mist, Fox watched them approach.

'Well done, Mrs Cobden.' Fox raised a surprised eyebrow. He really had not expected to see either of them on such a day.

Fox retraced his steps through the damp wood and took shelter in the hollow of an old oak before lighting a cheroot and waiting for Jennifer to arrive. He did not have long to wait. Jennifer appeared in the clearing and for once she caught Fox by surprise. The smoke rising from Fox's Monte Cristo had betrayed his position and Jennifer crept up to the old oak and thrust her face into the hollow.

'Boo!'

Fox shot out of his hiding place as if the hounds of hell were snapping at his brush and was halfway across the clearing before he realised that he had been had. Jennifer was giggling fit to burst and Fox gave her a lopsided grin.

'Very clever, young lady,' he drawled affectionately.

Jennifer was bent double with laughter. 'You did look funny, Mr Fox.'

'I'm sure I did.' Fox indulged the child. He waited patiently for Jennifer's laughter to subside, and when it did her manner was suddenly earnest.

'I've brought you a poster,' Mr Fox, she said.

'A poster?'

Jennifer produced the poster that Susan had given her the previous day and Fox read it with delight.

'That's splendid,' he said.

'There are lots of them in the village,' Jennifer told him.

'I shall show this to the other animals,' Fox decided.

He was as good as his word. Within the hour he was in Badger's sitting room, drying himself beside the fire.

Badger glanced up from the poster. 'Can you get any more of these?'

'Possibly,' Fox replied. 'I shall have to see.'

'Did this child have any other news?' Badger asked.

Fox gave the brock a conspiratorial grin. 'Oh yes, her father is on the Defence Committee.'

'And?'

'The photographs we gave them have been a great help, something of a revelation apparently. The good General Dembury is most impressed.'

'Anything else?'

'They have nearly completed their petition,' Fox continued. 'Downing Street within a month, I should say.'

Badger pursed his lips and gave Fox an impressed nod. 'Things appear to be going well,' he said.

'My sentiments entirely, old boy.'

'We shall have to begin considering our next move.'

'Funny you should say that, old boy' – Fox adopted a lofty air – 'because I, with my renowned cunning, have been doing a little thinking.'

'Lord help us,' Badger sighed.

'Now, now, Badger,' Fox chided him, 'hear me out.'

Badger settled his bulk into his chair and gave the canine a look of undivided, if doubtful, attention. 'I'm listening,' he said.

'My idea is this,' Fox began, and five minutes later Badger had to agree that it was the best idea Fox had ever come up with.

General Dembury was in sombre mood. The gardener had put a match to the heap of old branches thirty minutes earlier and now the General stood before the bonfire staring thoughtfully into the flames.

He was unsure as to which plan of action he should adopt in the wake of the photographic revelations. He knew Bartholomew, knew him well. He was vain and boastful certainly, but he was not without influence and he was quite probably as slippery as the proverbial eel.

The General dragged his eyes from the yellow flames and stared out across Blackthorn Estate. The snow had lasted less than a fortnight and had now disappeared almost completely. Only the shadiest spots, those which the winter sun had only fleetingly kissed, were still white. The fallow deer were gathered together, a warm huddle in the midst of the cold day, and the woodsmoke drifted away from the crackling branches and towards the dull grey sky.

The General took a short, tapering branch from the fire and held the bright flame to the end of a Havana. He pulled on the cigar until it was drawing evenly and then threw the branch back into the flames. He turned from the fire and strolled back towards the house. Lady Dembury looked up from her magazine as her husband entered the sitting room.

'You're looking very pensive today, dear,' she said considerately.

The General settled himself into his chair and threw the cigar butt into the fire. 'I've been thinking,' he began. 'I shall have to telephone Cobden and arrange a meeting in the village, now that he has some form of committee in hand, to discuss what should be done with these photographs. I've been sitting on them for too long as it is.'

'It's unlike you to be unsure of what to do,' Lady Dembury said softly.

The General smiled wanly. 'Perhaps I'm getting old.'

'Nonsense. We all need advice at times.'

'You're quite right, my dear, as always.' He smiled affectionately at her.

Liam Murphy found Douglas Cobden's number and the

General waited patiently for the ringing to be answered. The conversation was short, brusque even, as was the General's fashion. He had no great affection for the telephone and had always steadfastly refused to say 'goodbye' once the conversation was over. 'Bloody nonsense thing to say,' he would scowl.

Lady Dembury looked enquiringly at her husband. 'Well?' she asked.

'He'll come over here. My suggestion. Hodges can drive us into Wixley. It will give me time to discuss it with him.'

The General glanced up sharply, a look of curious concern on his brow, as the blast of a shotgun echoed around the grounds. 'What's all that about?' he muttered.

He found Rutherford standing guard over the pheasant run, a broken shotgun cradled in the crook of his arm.

'A fox, M'Lord,' Rutherford answered his master's look of enquiry.

'Did you pot him?'

'Winged him, I think M'Lord.'

'Good man, Rutherford. Any birds taken?'

'No, M'Lord. I saw him coming. Ready for him, I was.'

The General passed a perfunctory eye over the run. He had never had trouble with foxes before and did not want any now. The birds were not cheap to rear and he could ill afford a fox running loose.

'Good work, Rutherford,' he said. 'Keep it up.'

Fox had been hungry. The recent snows had made everything very difficult. He would not usually have ventured out at such a time of day. He preferred the cover of night but he was desperately hungry.

He had used all his skill and cunning to avoid being spotted, using the hedgerows and dead ground instead of crossing the open fields, and he had felt sure that the area was deserted before approaching the pheasants.

The crash of the shotgun had come like the wrath of God and he had hobbled back the way he had come, resting to ease the pain only whenever he felt it safe to do so. Now he lay face down across Badger's kitchen table, a pillow supporting him, as Mrs Badger held his brush to one side and plucked the lead shot from his buttocks.

'They are only flesh wounds,' she told him. 'You were lucky, although you won't be able to sit down for a while.'

Mrs Badger sponged iodine across the wound and Fox let out a yelp.

'Stop it, cry-baby,' she admonished him. 'I don't know how this happened and I don't think I want to, but whatever it was, I should think this is the price you're paying.'

Badger scowled over his half-moon spectacles at the prostrate Fox. 'Thieving, no doubt,' he said coldly.

Fox had known that he would receive such an attitude from the Badgers when he had banged on their door, but he had been unable to go any further. He was prepared to suffer their frosty attitude in return for their help.

'It was all a dreadful misunderstanding,' he said weakly.

'As if it could have been anything else,' Badger said sarcastically.

Mrs Badger wiped her paws clean on a towel. 'All right, you'll do,' she said.

Fox struggled off the table. 'I really am most grateful, Mrs Badger,' he said. 'If there is anything I can do in return...'

Mrs Badger looked at Fox with a matronly eye. She had always had a soft spot for the canine, considering him to be something of a loveable rogue. 'Try keeping out of trouble,' she said.

Badger closed the door as Fox limped out. 'Fat chance!' he sneered.

Hedgehog unrolled himself and peered through his half-opened sleepy eyes at the bedside clock.

'February?' he mumbled.

The banging on the door which had roused him from his deep sleep had begun again, and Hedgehog yawned and stretched before climbing out of his bed.

'This had better be good,' he grumbled as he scratched at his spines. He padded through the hallway and paused before the door. 'Who is it?' he demanded.

'It's me, open up.'

'Who's me?' Hedgehog grumbled. 'I'm not psychic.'

'Hare.'

Hedgehog opened the door and Hare loped through.

'Morning, Hedgehog,' he said.

Hedgehog was unsure as to whether or not he was happy with Hare banging on his door. 'It's February,' he said darkly.

'I know,' Hare replied, with a confused frown.

'I'm hibernating!' Hedgehog growled.

'Well, it's nearly spring.'

'Nearly spring, my foot,' Hedgehog shouted. 'It's the middle of winter!'

'No, it is not, Hedgehog. It's March tomorrow, and besides, this is important.'

'It had better be!'

'It is. Badger has called a meeting.'

'To hell with Badger!' Hedgehog flared. He had never seen eye-to-eye with Badger.

'Now, now, Hedgehog,' Hare soothed. 'Badger isn't that bad. And everybody else will be there.'

'Exactly,' Hedgehog snapped. 'Fox as well, I suppose?'

Hare sighed as he nodded. Fox was another for whom Hedgehog had no time, although on that count he felt he had some sympathy. He did not trust Fox either.

'Yes,' Hedgehog sneered. 'I thought so.'

'Hedgehog,' Hare pleaded. 'You will be the only one not there. You must come. Everybody else is.'

Hedgehog was far from impressed and his voice oozed sarcasm. 'What is this meeting about that is so important?' he demanded.

'I don't know.'

'Oh, brilliant,' Hedgehog chortled derisively.

'Don't be so negative.' Hare sighed. 'I'll see you there.'

'Perhaps.' Hedgehog was not going to commit himself. 'I might go back to bed.'

'See you there,' Hare said with finality, and he loped his way out of the door and through the wood.

Hare paused at the edge of the wood and surveyed the open fields. The yellow sun hung low in the sky and the morning was still young, fresh and quiet. The fields were wet and heavy with dew and rabbits nibbled at the tussocks of grass. The trees were still without leaf and looked old and tired, and the only colour in the landscape was the occasional cluster of crocuses.

Never mind, Hare thought. March tomorrow.

March

Alan stared out of the window with a curious look on his face. Mrs Buxton was walking past his cottage with a steely glint in her eye and a fixed expression on her face. However, it was not that which had caught Alan's attention so much as the double-barrelled shotgun that the old lady was having difficulty carrying even though she was using both hands.

'That gun is almost as big as she is,' Alan muttered. He watched closely as Mrs Buxton made her way over the stone bridge and headed in the direction of Church Walk. 'What is she up to?'

Alan walked out of the cottage and followed the old lady along Church Walk, making sure that he kept at a distance. Mrs Buxton struggled on, past the vicarage, and passed out of sight around the bend at the top of the lane.

Alan drew level with the vicarage to find Alwyn Jones hurrying along the path.

'What's going on?' the Vicar asked.

'No idea.' Alan shrugged.

'Where on earth can she be going?' Alwyn was utterly bemused.

The two men walked quickly along the lane and only slowed their pace as they approached the bend in the road. Alan stretched himself to his full height and looked hard along the road.

'Good God! I don't believe it!' he exclaimed.

Alwyn's reaction was much the same, and the two men broke

into a sprint as they ran side by side along the road. Alan began to make ground the quicker, Alwyn being encumbered by his flowing black cassock, and was the first to arrive at the scene by a good ten yards.

Mrs Buxton was standing outside the fence which ringed the compound and the red brick building. Workmen had gathered beside two huge bulldozers and their faces were a picture of bewilderment and concern. Mrs Buxton stood with her feet planted firmly on the ground and the shotgun held at the shoulder, and the twin barrels swayed with the effort.

'You nasty, wicked men,' she said. 'Now I want you to pack everything up and leave. Now!'

Alwyn appeared at Alan's side. He was out of breath and his crucifix had swung over his shoulder and was hanging down between his shoulder blades.

'Mrs Buxton;' he panted, 'what are you doing?'

Mrs Buxton's gaze did not waver from the dumbstruck workmen as she spoke.

'What should have been done long ago,' she declared. 'This was my Harold's shotgun. He used to sit on the bridge every night during the war in case the German paratroopers landed. And I always had a pan of hot fat on the stove.'

'Mrs Buxton–' Alan attempted to interrupt.

'Never you mind, young man,' the old lady cut him short. 'We saw the Hun off and now we shall see these off.'

Alwyn took a tentative pace forward. 'My dear Mrs Buxton,' he said with a placatory tone.

'No sermons, thank you Vicar,' Mrs Buxton growled. 'My mind's made up. They're leaving!'

Alwyn's tone became more strident. 'Mrs Buxton! You can't threaten these people with a gun. It's illegal.'

'Minor detail,' Mrs Buxton snapped, and she adjusted her hold on the weapon so that she held the butt of the shotgun beneath her armpit.

Alan spotted the opening. 'Mrs Buxton, that gun is too heavy for you as it is,' he told her. 'If you pull the trigger the recoil will knock you for six.' Alan saw a flicker of doubt pass across the old woman's eyes. 'I really would advise against it,' he said.

Alwyn was nodding furiously. 'Very true, very true,' he said earnestly.

The barrels of the shotgun began to droop towards the ground as the old lady lost her strength.

One of the workmen, a teenager sporting a gold earring, decided his moment had come. 'Go home, you silly old bat,' he shouted.

Mrs Buxton's eyes flashed behind the horn-rimmed spectacles and one old gnarled finger tightened around the trigger.

Alan was later to relate that Mrs Buxton's false teeth, which shot out of her mouth and momentarily hung suspended in mid-air, had fallen to the ground long after the old lady had been thrown into the road by the recoil of the shotgun.

Mrs Buxton collapsed into a dishevelled heap as the gun clattered to the ground, and the workforce inside the compound stood frozen to the spot. Alwyn was the first to move. He sprinted across to the prostrate pensioner, cradled her in his arms and spoke to her in soothing tones.

Mrs Buxton, however, was far from finished. 'There's one more barrel,' she mumbled through her toothless gums. 'Let me have another go.'

Alwyn was going to do nothing of the sort. 'You just stay there,' he ordered.

Alan snatched up the shotgun and pointed it away before ejecting the unspent cartridge. Then he let out a sigh of relief. 'Rocksalt,' he said.

Alwyn was equally relieved. 'Mrs Buxton, you're a silly old lady,' he scolded, but his voice was full of sympathy.

Alwyn helped the bruised senior citizen back along the road and Alan soothed the fears and mounting anger of the workmen. After a few lewd comments and risqué jokes he actually had them laughing and, when he departed, all the tension had gone out of them.

That evening, in the lounge bar of the Three Pheasants, the old lady was the talk of the village. Mortimer's beard rippled with one burst of laughter after another and Max was talking of taking the gutsy old bird for his wife.

'You've already got a wife,' Susan reminded him.

'Yes, but after forty years I could do with a change,' Max joked.

The laughter was accompanied by a distant roll of thunder from beyond Poachers Hill.

'Another storm brewing,' Mortimer observed.

The thunder was booming above Little Wixley by the time Mortimer called last orders. 'If you hurry, ladies and gentlemen,' he advised, 'you may be home before the rain breaks.'

Max was the last to leave. He stood on the pavement and sucked the flame from a Swan Vesta into the bowl of his pipe. He shook the match dead and threw it into the gutter as the first drops of rain began to fall.

Across the village green he could hear hoofbeats clattering across the old stone bridge.

Badger sat at the top of the table with Fox seated to his right and Weasel to his left. The other animals sat the length of the table, looking at the old brock and waiting for him to tell them why he had called the meeting.

Badger shuffled the papers on the table in front of him and then looked over his half-moon spectacles at the assembled company. Otter was wearing his customary oilskins and, as usual, gave off a slight aroma of fish, which was why Badger had seated him at the far end of the table next to Polecat.

Woodmouse could only just see above the edge of the table, regardless of the extra cushions that Mrs Badger had provided, and was in much the same position as Dormouse and Rat. Hedgehog was not much better off as Mrs Badger had flatly refused to have her cushions ruined by his spines.

Rabbit was his usual nervous self, fidgeting constantly and obviously unhappy with being in such close proximity to Fox, and Mole was peering myopically through his thick spectacles. The Squirrels were as alert and attentive as ever but it was Hare that Badger was a little curious about.

There seemed to be something odd about Hare's behaviour. He seemed to Badger to have developed some sort of facial tic and his eyes were wide and staring. Badger decided to ignore Hare's strange demeanour and get on with the business in hand.

He began with his usual olde worlde manners: 'I should firstly like to thank you all for coming at such short notice,' he said. 'It was very good of you and I think you will find this meeting most interesting.'

Badger noted the looks of interest quicken around the table and paused to sip at a glass of water before continuing. He told them of the recent developments and showed them Jennifer's poster before coming to the crux of the matter.

'Fox has now come up with our next plan of action. As I am sure you are all aware, the construction company has driven marker pegs into the ground through the wood, marking their proposed route. Fox's plan is this – and it's quite simple. We move the pegs!'

Badger looked around the table at the raised eyebrows that had met his words. Only Hare seemed unaffected; his eyes seemed to be staring at some inner thought.

'Moving the pegs,' Badger continued, ' will confuse and –'

He progressed no further. Hare had suddenly leapt to his feet, his eyes were glazed over and his lips quivered as if he were suffering a fit.

'Five rounds rapid fire!' Hare shrieked, before leaping up onto the table. 'I've never chased a wild goose!' he shrieked again, his voice strangulated, the white foam flying from his lips.

Badger stared at Hare aghast and his shock was matched by the other animals. Only Fox seemed unsurprised by the performance.

Hare ran along the table in a jerky, spastic fashion, like a demented witchdoctor, his arms and legs flying out in all directions so that he sent Woodmouse tumbling from his cushions, and caused Hedgehog to immediately roll himself into a defensive ball.

'My father was the Duke of York!' he screeched, his voice rising an octave with each word.

Badger dragged his eyes from the cavorting Hare and looked with wide eyes at the unconcerned Fox.

'The Duke of York?' he mouthed.

Fox raised a weary eyebrow. 'Same thing happens every year, old boy,' he sighed, as Hare broke into a shrill rendition of "Abide with Me"'. 'The very same thing every year,' Fox said again. 'Every March, to be precise. Goes completely off his trolley.'

Badger stared in bewilderment as Hare attempted a swallow dive into Weasel's glass of water. 'I thought that was a myth,' he said.

'No such luck, old boy,' Fox replied. 'You'll get no sense out of him for the rest of the month.'

Hare suddenly bolted for the door, pausing on his way to plant a huge and sloppy wet kiss on the tip of Otter's nose before disappearing out of the sett. A shocked silence descended upon the room as Weasel shook water from his coat and Rat helped Woodmouse back to his chair.

Otter sat transfixed. He had never been kissed by a hare before. 'He kissed me!' he squeaked. Nobody said anything. There was not much they could say.

Fox gave Hedgehog a friendly tap with his cane. 'Out you come, old boy,' he drawled.

Hedgehog uncurled himself and peered around the room. 'What happened?' he queried.

'He kissed me!' Otter told him, his voice full of astonishment.

Weasel was another who was far from impressed. 'Long eared lunatic,' he sneered through his wet whiskers. 'Needs locking up.'

Badger decided that things had gone far enough.

'All right, everyone,' he ordered. 'Let's settle down and get back to business.'

The assembled company settled themselves into their chairs and returned their attention to Badger.

'As I was saying,' he continued heavily. 'Moving the pegs will confuse the road planners and may well even put back their schedule by some considerable length of time.'

'Hear, hear,' Fox chimed in.

'Therefore, every time any of us sees a peg, we move it. Agreed?'

A chorus of agreement met his words and he decided to bring

the meeting to a quick end.

'Very well, gentlemen, that's all. Thank you very much.'

Otter was the first out of the door, still muttering under his breath about the indignity of being kissed by a hare, and Fox was the last. 'Goodnight, old boy, splendid fun,' he grinned.

Badger pulled a face. 'A fat lot of good the hares will be to us for a while,' he observed.

'Can't be helped, I'm afraid,' Fox replied, and with Weasel at his side he melted into the wood.

'Where to, Foxy?' Weasel asked.

'I have a pheasant hanging. Come round for dinner?'

'Most decent of you, old boy,' Weasel imitated Fox's clipped tones.

Fox laughed. 'Any more of that and you can have eggs on toast.'

Fox roasted the pheasant to perfection and they washed it down with a few glasses of wine. Now he and Weasel lounged in the sitting room, each of them nursing another large Scotch as Fox held forth on his favourite topic.

'The thing about vixens, old boy, is that you have to let them think they are having their own way.'

'It's the same with weasels,' Weasel stated through the smoke rising from his cigarette.

'I don't doubt it.' Fox nodded, and he drew on his cheroot before continuing. 'It makes for an easy life because the moment the female does not believe she's getting her own way, then watch out!'

'First the charm offensive,' Weasel declared.

'And if that does not work?' Fox asked rhetorically.

'Hell hath no fury!'

'Precisely.'

'Stamp foot, throw things, tantrum.'

'Quite. And nobody wants that because you cannot win. You stand accused of being a bully. Indulge them.'

'To tell you the truth,' Weasel said, 'I can't be bothered half the time.'

'Oh, Weasel, old boy, you must.'

'Why? If the tantrum doesn't work they just slip into the

"I'm-not-talking-to-you" sulk.'

'Because for all their faults, they are still lovely creatures.'

'Rubbish!'

'Weasel, you're a misogynist.'

'What's one of those?'

'A chauvinist, only worse.'

'Sounds about right.'

Fox laughed aloud and replenished their glasses from the crystal decanter. 'I'm afraid this is almost empty. Most unfortunate,' he observed with a critically raised eyebrow.

Weasel winked up at his friend and reached inside his coat.

'Weasel, old boy, you're an absolute marvel!' Fox cheered as Weasel produced an unopened bottle of Scotch.

'Got to have something to go with Badger's water,' Weasel remarked with a hint of sarcasm.

'Very wise,' Fox agreed, nodding sympathetically.

The bottle was empty by the time the dawn began to break and they had both long since passed the point where their words made any sense.

'Foxy, I've got to go,' Weasel slurred around his cigarette.

'Time for my bed as well,' Fox decided, and he drained his glass of its last mouthful.

Weasel tottered across the room and Fox held the door open so that the cold morning air rushed in and the pale sunlight revealed the hazy smoke and the whiskey fumes. Weasel blinked his eyes rapidly in a vain attempt to focus them before pulling his cap down firmly onto his head.

'Cheerio, mate,' he said, and then his legs gave up the fight. With a resounding thud he fell flat on his face.

'Weasel, old chap,' Fox giggled drunkenly. 'Do get up, eh?'

Weasel was beyond being capable of responding and his snores reverberated against the carpet. Fox lifted his unconscious friend from the floor and the two of them swayed through the room like a couple of war-wounded soldiers before Fox unceremoniously dumped Weasel onto the settee.

'Sleep well,' Fox mumbled, and then he staggered through to his own room and was asleep before his head hit the pillow.

Hodges opened the rear door of the sleek, imperious Rolls-Royce and General Lord Dembury of Wixley ushered Douglas in before himself with a sweep of his hand. The car rolled away across the white stone chip forecourt, skirting the spartan sycamores, and picked up speed as it glided smoothly along the lengthy driveway.

The tall oaks reached toward the pale grey sky with bare, skeletal branches, reaching out for the sun and an end to winter's icy clutch, as if knowing that the beds of yellow and purple crocuses at their feet were a beginning to that end.

'Stop, Hodges,' the General suddenly barked from the comfort of the calf-leather seat. Hodges brought the saloon to a controlled stop and the General let himself out of the car and walked around to the rear, a flinty glint in his eye.

'What's going on?' Douglas whispered conspiratorially.

Hodges leaned back in his seat and nodded the peak of his cap in the direction of the wide, landscaped lawns. 'His Lordship doesn't like daffodils,' he confided in hushed tones.

'Daffodils?' Douglas queried, as he saw in the reflection of the rear-view mirror the General lift a double-barrelled shotgun from the boot of the car and ram two fresh cartridges into its shiny black barrels. He watched with mounting amazement as the General snapped the gun closed and trained his sights on a single daffodil standing brave and alone across the even lawns.

The shotgun rang out in the cold evening, sending a rabble of strident crows cawing out of the topmost branches of the trees, and the luminous head of the solitary flower exploded in a fluttering shower of yellow petals.

The General ambled back to the car and Douglas raised his eyebrows in wonderment at the 'seen it all before' look in Hodges eyes. The General climbed ponderously into the car and nodded perfunctorily at Hodges and the car pulled away.

'Now then,' the General began as if the entire episode had never taken place, 'as I was saying, with these photographs we can actually pre-empt their plans. Gives us something of an ace in the hole, wouldn't you agree?'

'Yes, I would.' Douglas nodded, a little vacantly, having not quite recovered his senses.

'What we must do at this meeting,' the General continued, 'is to persuade the others that some form of direct action is required, yes?'

'Yes.'

'What I shall propose is that we publish extracts from these photos, piecemeal as it were, so that they begin to worry that we might know more than they realise, without being entirely sure, yes?'

'Yes.'

'Splendid.' The General settled himself into the comfort of the chair as the expensive motor car passed through the open gates of the estate and onto the country road. It cruised at a sedate pace, Hodges dutifully observing the speed limit, until Douglas could contain himself no longer.

'May I ask you something, sir?' he asked tentatively.

'Most certainly,' the General replied.

'Why did you shoot that daffodil?' Douglas asked in a bewildered tone.

'Cannot abide the bloody things!' the General answered gruffly. 'Insipid, weak, whining... bloody things!'

Douglas looked out of the window at the banks of daffodils adorning the grass verges and reflected that the General must loathe this time of the year.

'Did you see that, old boy,' Fox asked, both his eyebrows raised in surprise.

'What did he do that for?' Weasel answered obliquely as they watched General Dembury put the shotgun back into the boot of the car.

'Beats me.' Fox shrugged. 'perhaps they've declared an open season for daffodils.'

The limousine cruised away and Fox and Weasel turned together and headed in the opposite direction.

'What's the plan, Foxy?' Weasel asked. 'We could take a look in the bins at the back of Dembury's house.'

Fox sniffed disdainfully. 'I do not rummage around in dustbins,' he said.

'There could be some rich pickings,' Weasel persisted.

'No!' Fox closed the subject.

'Well, what do you suggest then?' Weasel queried.

Fox gave his cane a confident twirl. 'I was thinking of popping into the village. We did rather well the last time, if you remember.'

Weasel could remember only to well and he ran a suddenly salivating tongue across his sharp teeth as he recalled the four white rabbits they had taken from the back of the butcher's delivery van on their last foray into Little Wixley.

'Good idea,' he said with a hungry nod.

The moon was hidden by heavy cloud and the streets were wet from the constant drizzle by the time Fox and Weasel reached Busjibber Lane.

'Four-thirty,' Fox commented, looking at the gold hunter.

Weasel used his long white scarf to wipe a droplet of rainwater from his nose and then he sniffed loudly. 'We are a bit early,' he observed, and he hawked and spat into the gutter.

'I wish you wouldn't do that.' Fox frowned, 'It's so undignified.'

'Go howl at the moon, Foxy old boy,' Weasel said amiably, and he crouched in the shelter of a wall and began rolling a cigarette. He cupped the lighted cigarette in his paw and the pair crossed the stone bridge at a fast, agile pace.

Fox led the way along the main street and into a narrow alley which separated the butcher's shop from the greengrocer. The alley was dark and silent and Fox and Weasel sheltered from the fine rain behind a collection of dustbins. They waited in silence for the hour to pass.

The sound of a motor engine preceded the twin beams of yellow light which lit up the wet road in front of the butcher's shop, and Fox checked his watch as the engine died.

'Six o'clock exactly,' he murmured. 'Right on timc.'

Fox and Weasel listened intently to the driver's footsteps slapping through the rain and the sound of the rear doors of the delivery van being eased open. The bell above the shop door tinkled and the two men exchanged greetings. Fox and Weasel tiptoed along the alley and Fox peered around the corner.

The delivery man was entering the shop with the pale carcass of a pig balanced on his shoulder, the shop door being held open for him by the butcher.

Fox knew the routine. The shopkeeper would open a further door, the one to the back room, and then perhaps the cold storage room, which gave Fox at the very most forty five seconds.

'Come on, old boy,' he whispered, and Weasel sprinted behind as Fox raced out into the street and then leapt into the back of the van. The interior was dark and murky and Fox snatched the corpses of two white rabbits from the hooks which suspended them from the ceiling, and threw them out of the open doors. Weasel caught them with a safe pair of paws and then sped off along the street. Fox reached up a second time and pulled a third rabbit from its hook before tugging at a fourth. He pulled at the rabbit ineffectively as the sharp hook dug deeper.

'Oh, do come along, dammit,' he cursed under his breath, and his ears pricked to the sound of a soft footfall. Fox released the hanging rabbit and spun on his heel, and came face to face with the most dishevelled-looking character he had ever seen.

The newcomer stood in the van, framed by the open doors. The scarlet waistcoat was faded and threadbare with the top button missing, and the silk cravat was soiled and unkempt. A thin scar ran from the top lip and up the left side of the face, revealing a yellowing canine tooth and setting the mouth into a permanent sneer.

Fox's tone was sharp. 'Who are you?' he demanded, and the answer came in a voice loaded with menace.

'Urban Fox. And this is my patch!'

Fox relaxed, letting the tension go out of his body, and then he adopted his most nonchalant pose, resting his weight on his cane and taking his time in selecting a Monte Cristo. He struck a match off the wall of the van and held it to the end of the cheroot before flicking it out of the back of the van in a dismissive fashion.

'Is it now?' he drawled, a mocking smile playing on his lips.

'Yes it is,' Urban Fox said, with low threatening whisper, and the blade of the flick knife opened with a deadly snick.

Fox looked from the blade back to urban Fox's glaring eyes and then he drew deeply on the Monte Cristo and blew a perfect smoke ring which floated slowly through the ether and burst on the end of urban Fox's snout.

Urban Fox gave no warning and the cold blade flashed through the dark, hissing like an enraged adder. Fox stifled a yelp at the stinging heat as the flick knife cut open his left shoulder. He jumped nimbly backwards, staying on his toes, as Urban Fox lunged with the bright blade kept low, the point of the knife weaving back and forth across Fox's belly.

Fox levelled the cane, holding it like a fencer, as his left arm began to grow numb. 'That, my friend,' he said evenly, 'was a colossal error of judgment.'

Urban Fox feinted to his left and then brought the knife back with a sweeping motion, stabbing for Fox's ribcage. Fox parried the thrust and then drove the weighted silver tip into his adversary's stomach. Urban Fox blew out hard as his stomach muscles contracted, and he slashed at Fox's chest with an angry swipe.

'Temper, temper,' Fox said smoothly, and he blocked the blow with the haft of his cane before bringing the silver tip down onto his foe's wrist. Urban Fox shrieked as the bones in his wrist cracked, and the flick knife clattered to the floor. Fox swung the cane like polo player driving for goal and the silver tip caught Urban Fox on the underside of his chin. Urban Fox's head snapped backwards and he slid unconsciously down the side of the van and lay in a heap in the corner.

Fox leant against the side of the van and dabbed with his cravat at the deep red blood welling up from his shoulder.

'Rather nasty,' he muttered, touching at the burning wound, and the bell above the shop door tinkled. Fox snatched up his cane and flung himself out of the van. He sprinted along the street with the excited cries of the two men reverberating in his ears.

Weasel was waiting impatiently for him at the far end of Busjibber Lane. 'What kept you?' he whispered, and his eyes alighted on the long cut. 'What the hell happened?' he gasped, and Fox crumpled into his arms.

General Lord Dembury of Wixley sat at the head of the long oak table in the Three Pheasants with Douglas on his right and Alan on his left. Max sat further along the table and Mortimer listened intently from behind the crowded bar as the General detailed the developments.

'The photographs which have come into our possession,' he was saying, 'deal with the planned route of the motorway and the companies and persons involved, and, as far as we know, those parties are not aware that we have this information.' He paused to allow the information to be digested by the committee and took the opportunity to sip at his whiskey. 'It is my proposal,' he continued, 'that we write to those persons and companies outlining our objection to these intentions and their involvement in them.'

The General looked around the table for any sign of agreement and was met by a series of thoughtful nods.

'I think that perhaps I should write these letters. Headed notepaper can work wonders,' the General suggested with a wry smile. 'Is there anything else to discuss?' he asked, and Alan cleared his throat.

'The extra posters I wanted have been printed. They should be delivered shortly,' he said.

'Very good,' the General complimented him and he made the necessary entry in the log. 'Anything further?' he enquired.

Max lifted his pipe from between his teeth and stared into the bowl. 'I have six thousand signatures on the petition so far,' he declared. 'I don't know that there will be many more. It might be time to deliver it.'

General Dembury looked around the table and asked for a show of hands in favour of presenting the petition. 'Carried,' he intoned. 'When would you like to deliver it?'

'Any time this week,' Max replied.

'I can drive you down,' Alan cut in. 'I can pick up those posters on the way.'

'Splendid,' the General commented. 'Two of you are better than one.'

'I will let the papers know,' Alan said with a conspiratorial air.

'Anything else?' the General asked, and he allowed a polite pause to pass before bringing the meeting to a close.

Alan cornered Max at the bar as the room began to empty. 'Is Wednesday alright with you?' he asked.

Max grunted over his pipe as he drew on a fresh match.

'I'll pick you up at eight o'clock?'

'Fine,' Max replied.

Susan sidled up to the bar and took Alan's arm. 'Can I come?' she asked.

'Of course.' Alan smiled, and looked at Max for confirmation.

Max nodded. 'You can help me carry all those papers.'

Alan finished his drink and turned for the door with Susan on his arm. He said his goodbyes to those remaining. Mortimer rang the bell and announced last orders as Alan and Susan stepped out into the rain. The street was dark and wet from the fine drizzle and they hurried through it and into the warmth of the cottage.

The fire in the sitting room was still bright and Alan shovelled black coals into the flames as Susan made the coffee.

'Where am I?' Fox whispered huskily.

Vixen lifted the damp flannel from Fox's brow and dabbed at his rheumy eyes. 'You're in my bed. Now just relax. You've lost a lot of blood and you need rest.'

'How did I get here?' Fox asked, looking up at his nurse.

'Your friend Weasel carried you here. Now that's enough talking. Try to get some sleep.'

The tiredness returned and Fox closed his eyes as the sleep overtook him. Vixen lifted the bowl of lukewarm water and walked quietly out of the bedroom. Weasel stood up from the hallway chair, a look of concern etched into his features. 'How is he,' he asked softly.

'He'll be all right but he needs rest. It's a nasty wound.'

Weasel nodded his understanding. 'Thank you, Vixen,' he said.

Vixen smiled. 'I'll let you know how he does.'

Weasel pulled his cap onto his head and crept out of the

house. The dusk was already falling and he felt the exhaustion of the past twenty four hours catching up on him as he headed towards the sunset.

Night had fallen by the time Weasel opened the door to his house in the drystone wall that ringed Douglas Cobden's land, and he fell onto the bed and slept the sleep of a dead weasel.

Hare pushed upon his hind legs and raised himself to his full height. He lifted his nose into the air and held his front paws in front of his chest in the classic stance of the pugilist, and the black tufts of his ears stood tall and erect, shouting his challenge to all comers like the war bonnet of a Sioux chieftain.

His challenge was answered immediately, his rival in combat rising up an inch taller, his face a mask of scorn. Hare sprang forward, his powerful rear legs launching his body at his opponent, and his first punch landed on hard bone.

His opponent's head spun sideways and hare followed up with a rapid left and right combination, each punch scoring as he danced around the brown hare who began reeling on the spring grass.

It was over almost before it had begun, the defeated hare turning and bounding away across the field, his ears held flat across his neck. Hare stood upright, masculine and triumphant. The madness coursed through his veins as he thrust out the barrel of his chest, and the force of the lead pellets snapped his breastbone before the report of the shotgun reached his ears.

Douglas Cobden ejected the spent cartridge and rested the broken Purdey in the lee of his elbow before strolling forward and picking up the dead hare. He wrapped twine around the hare's ankles and hung it head down from the hook on his belt.

April

'It went splendidly,' Max said around the stem of his pipe.

'Did you get to see the Prime Minister?' Mortimer asked as he placed a pint of Guinness at Max's elbow.

'No, you don't actually get to see the PM,' Max replied. 'Some dogsbody or other just comes to the door and collects the thing.'

Mortimer gave his white beard a thoughtful stroke. 'So we don't know if the powers that be will actually see it?' he ventured, looking from Max to Alan enquiringly.

Alan was certain that they would. 'They will see it,' he assured the landlord.

Max held the same opinion. 'It's too big to miss,' he said.

'I hope you're right,' Mortimer rejoined. 'It would be a shame if it went to waste.'

Alan finished his drink and turned to leave. 'Don't worry, it won't go to waste. Now I've got to get along. I promised General Dembury that I would let him know how we got on.'

He drove at speed through the deserted lane and the tyres crunched across the white stonechip forecourt just as the night began to close in. Benton already had the oakwood doors open and Alan mounted the steps two at a time.

'Good evening, sir. His Lordship is expecting you.'

Alan followed the butler through the long hallway, taking in the rich opulence of his surroundings, and waited politely for Benton to announce him before entering the General's study. The room was spacious with a high ceiling and oak-panelled walls. It smelled of cigars and brandy and the two black Labradors snoozed on the carpet; everything in it echoed to the trappings of masculinity.

The desk was bound with green leather and upon it stood a hussar at the gallop, the intoxication of the charge captured in solid silver. The walls were decorated with oil paintings of Balaclava and Waterloo interspaced with wall plaques of regiments past and present, and a glass case displayed a collection of mint-condition coins from the four corners of the British Empire.

In the corner of the room stood a gun rack which boasted a fine and well cared for collection of shotguns, but it was that which lay upon the floor that captivated Alan's attention.

The General noted Alan's look of fascination. 'My father shot that,' he began, 'in India at the turn of the century. Man-eater, you see.'

Alan stared at the tiger skin, entranced by the beauty of its sheen and appalled at the ugliness of its life and its untimely death.

'Can I offer you a drink?' the General enquired, breaking the spell. He poured brandy into two balloon glasses and Alan accepted a cigar.

'Well?' the General asked as he held a match to the end of his Havana.

'It went well, General,' Alan replied. 'The television crews were there and the petition was accepted into Number Ten.'

'Splendid. Local news, I should imagine, is the best we can hope for.'

Alan gave the General a wry smile. 'Things may have gone a little further than that,' he said, leaving the General hanging onto his next words. 'It might be an idea, General, to watch the next news bulletin.'

'What happened?' the General asked slowly.

'My girlfriend, Susan,' Alan was beginning to grin.

'Yes?' the General's suspicions rocketed to a peak.

'She may well have captured the front pages tomorrow at least.'

'You still haven't told me what happened.'

'Let's watch the news, General. I don't see why I should be the only one to be surprised.'

The General and Alan settled themselves in the rear sitting room and waited patiently for what the General described as 'another brain-rotting soap' to finish and for the news to begin. When it did the old General's mouth fell open.

'By God, but she has some front!' he said, and immediately regretted his choice of words.

Alan was grinning like the proverbial Cheshire cat as he watched the presentation of the petition follow the main headline of the day.

The General was riveted to the screen. 'She certainly knows how to attract attention,' he said.

'Media event, General. It will go national now,' Alan told him.

'Indeed,' the General replied, his tone still one of astonishment.

The General was not the only one who was shocked. At Violets Farm, in the Cobden household, Douglas sat watching the screen as if he could hardly believe his eyes. There, as large as life, was his favourite niece at the door of No. 10 Downing Street, waving her top above her head so that the whole world could see everything she had.

Douglas was speechless. Susan had used bright red lipstick to emblazon the word 'NO' across her breasts and was managing to sidestep the desperate policemen's every lunge. In the background, Max was studiously attempting to ignore the commotion as he handed the petition through the door, and Alan was laughing like a drain.

'I don't believe it!' Douglas croaked.

The following morning the newspapers were just as Alan had predicted. The tabloids had a field day, using endless puns to link the photographs of Susan with the state of the nation.

'You're a star.' Alan grinned across the breakfast table.

'I don't know what all the fuss is about,' Susan said dismissively. 'It's only a pair of boobs!'

'Yes, but what a pair.' Alan leered in a jocular fashion and Susan threw a napkin at him.

'I might end up in court,' Susan said.

'Ten years, M'Lud!'

'It's not funny.'

'Don't worry,' Alan assured her. 'If it does come to that it will probably only be a small fine and I'll pick that up.' He decided to let the matter rest by changing the subject. 'What time do you want to go to the stables?' he asked.

'About ten okay?'

'Fine. I can drop you before I collect Douglas,' and Alan paused, his head tilted to one side. 'Listen,' he said.

Susan could hear it as well. 'Spring,' she said.

The sound could also be heard in Church Walk, where Alwyn stood in the study of the small seventeenth-century vicarage with his breath held and his ear cocked towards the open leaded window. He was sure he had heard it. The announcement had carried quite clearly through the fresh spring morning.

Alwyn stood still, afraid that the slightest movement would break the spell, and his patience was rewarded by another call, like that of an old friend, as the herald of spring sounded the end of winter's chill grip.

His features split into a wide smile and he sat down at the polished bureau and snatched up an unspoiled sheet of paper and his blue fountain pen.

21 April *The Reverend A. Jones MM*
The Vicarage
Church Walk
Little Wixley

Sir,

This morning I had the pleasure of hearing what I believe to be the first cuckoo of spring.

Yours sincerely
A. Jones

Alwyn sealed the white envelope and addressed it to *The Times* before slapping the palm of his hand onto the moistened first-class stamp. He hurried down the path between the small neat lawns and along Church Walk, managing to reach the postbox set deeply in the ivy-dressed flint wall moments before the postal van appeared at the bottom of the lane.

'Just in time.' Alwyn smiled as he dropped the envelope into the box's wide mouth. He nodded a greeting to the driver of the van before turning and ambling back along the narrow scented lane with a happy lift in his step.

Alan stood at the window of the small kitchen waiting for the kettle to boil and delighting in the change coming over the garden. Glorious colours of red and yellow blazed beneath the lustrous spring sunshine and the twin sycamores at the foot of the lawn were already heavy with fresh green leaf. The long, even lawn shone neat and trim between the bursting hedgerows and the tinkling of the pond's waters carried purely through the calm morning.

He looked skywards, leaning forward against the enamel sink as the pair of kestrels which were making their home in the lofty branches of the tallest pine soared in on silently spread wings and settled artfully on a long horizontal branch.

Alan lifted the whistling kettle from the gas and waited while the tea brewed before carrying the tray upstairs, pausing on the way to pick up the morning paper. Alan drew the bedroom curtains back and the splendid sunshine poured unchecked over the pine bed, and Susan pulled the eiderdown up over her tousled hair.

'Wakey, wakey.' Alan tugged at the thick quilt. 'Cup of tea time.'

Susan stretched and groaned beneath the covers before peering out and blinking up at the new day. 'What time is it?' she asked, stretching her arms above her head.

'Cover yourself up, you wicked wench,' Alan admonished her playfully.

Susan made a moue and pulled the quilt up to her chin before rolling over and accepting the offered mug. 'Nine o'clock,' she said dourly. 'It's still the middle of the night!'

'You shouldn't go out boogying all night,' Alan replied, scanning the front page of the newspaper.

'It was your idea,' Susan protested coyly, sipping at the tea.

Alan flicked through the paper until he reached the financial section and passed a critical eye the length of its columns.

'Are you going fishing today?' Susan interrupted his close scrutiny of the dealings of the financial world.

'Yes, about eleven,' Alan answered distractedly.

'Fish for tea, is it?' Susan grinned, digging at Alan's appalling track record with regard to actually catching anything.

Alan folded the newspaper with exaggerated care and slowly placed it upon the pine bedside table. Then he snatched the mug from Susan's cupped hands.

'And you for breakfast, cheeky wench!' he growled, ripping the duvet back.

A solitary heron stood at the edge of the quiet reeded lake with its head drawn in onto his hunched shoulders, silent and watchful, as Douglas cast the delicate and brightly coloured fly across the still waters.

Alan stood on the bank beneath the new leaves of a tall silver birch, shading himself from the dazzling spring sunshine.

'Looks like we could be in for a good summer,' he observed, looking up at the clear blue sky.

Douglas did not reply, his attention focused on the artful fly resting lightly on the clear water. He lifted the tapered rod back above his head and the long line arced through the hot morning air, whipping back sharply, and he cast forward again, bringing the fly to rest gently on the lake's calm surface.

Alan poured himself a cup of hot coffee from the large flask at his feet before inspecting his own line, passing a critical eye over the lurid purple and red feathers bound tightly to the small, sharp hook.

'Not having much luck with this,' he grumbled, looking down at the empty keep net lying partially submerged at the water's edge.

'Neither's that heron,' Douglas replied, casting the fly again with a powerful practised arm.

'He hasn't moved all morning,' Alan agreed, eyeing the grey frock-coated bird. Douglas played the line out, feeling for its travel with his left hand as the fly floated across the tranquil waters. 'Not much doing, is there?' he sighed, and the long cane rod bucked in his hands as the fly disappeared in a sudden commotion of sparkling, splashing water.

'Talk of the devil,' Alan said, looking up sharply as the tip of the rod bent forward beneath the pressure of the taut line.

'That's more like it,' Douglas agreed, as the radiant rainbow colours of a silvery trout broke above the stirring waters and created a foaming shimmer of diamond blue waters.

He played the fish as it leapt and dived in its furious attempt at escape, guiding it away from the deep sanctuary of the thick reeds.

'Come on, my beauty,' Douglas coaxed, and he caressed the line with the gentle touch of a lover.

'It's a big one,' Alan said encouragingly.

Douglas played the fighting rainbow trout towards himself, lifting and dipping the rod as he smoothly worked the reel. He dipped the edge of the triangular landing net beneath the rippling surface and drew the tired and beaten fish over it with the tip of the rod held high.

'Three pounds, I'd say.' Douglas beamed as he waded towards the grassy bank. The fish kicked and twisted as Douglas lifted it onto the scales and Alan held the scales steady until the trout had calmed, before reading the weight.

'A little better than that,' he said. 'Three pounds eight ounces – a good fish.'

'First this year.' Douglas smiled as he lifted the fish from the scales and held it up for appraisal. 'Nice fish,' he concluded, taking in the brilliant tinted stripe above the flashing silver belly before dropping the fish into the captivity of the keep net.

Along the water's edge the artful heron unwound its tight neck and its long sharp beak broke the water's surface with a blur of speed before drawing back in a jerky movement and holding aloft the twinkling prize of a smaller rainbow trout.

'Must be my turn,' Alan commented wryly before picking up his own rod and, holding it clear of the pond's waters, he waded in up to his waist. His turn was not long in coming, the rod bucking in his hand with his fourth cast.

'Play it!' Douglas advised earnestly. 'Don't fight it, play it.'

Alan eased the pressure slightly and the trout took up the sudden slack and leapt high above the pond's surface, twisting and turning against the sharp hook.

'Let it wear itself out,' Douglas encouraged. 'Let the fish do most of the work.'

The long, bowing rod kicked and jerked in Alan's hand as the silver fish tugged violently and angrily at the end of the line. 'When do I start reeling him in?' Alan asked, his voice full of excitement.

'When the leaping stops you'll know he's tired,' Douglas answered, his eyes fixed on the turbulent water as the resplendent tints of the rainbow broke the surface again.

'He's got a lot of fight in him,' Alan observed, and the fish dived deeply, the line slicing through the rippling surface like a hot cheese wire.

'Now?' Alan asked, and suddenly the taut line slackened. 'Oh, no!' Alan cried. 'Not again,' and all the fight evaporated from the slender rod.

'Reel in quickly,' Douglas shouted from the bank. 'He's running in. Quickly now.'

Alan turned the reel with a determined fury and the slack line cut through the still waters. 'I can't find him,' he cried again. The line came up sharply and the long rod bucked and doubled over, the taut line singing with the pressure.

'Easy now,' Douglas warned, as the sparkling fish rose and thrashed on the water's surface.

Alan wound the reel, dipping the rod periodically as Douglas had shown him and the trout gleamed just beneath the clear surface, its open pink mouth revealing the lure as the line pulled it towards the net. He lifted the pole from the water and the defeated fish lay tired and beaten in the belly of the triangular net. He strode through the deep water with the net held aloft and a beaming smile on his face.

'Well done,' Douglas congratulated the younger man as they read the scales. 'Seven pounds exactly,' he said, his tone one of a man well impressed.

'Let's get another.' Alan grinned, full of enthusiasm and bursting with joy. Douglas chuckled as he remembered the tingle he had felt on landing his first fish.

That evening Alan stood framed in the kitchen doorway with an enormous smile on his face and his chest thrust out, bursting with triumph and pride.

'Well?' he enquired with a victorious grin.

Susan folded her arms across her black blouse and leaned back against the edge of the pine table as she passed a keen eye over the rainbow trout. 'Not bad,' she decided, a mischievous twinkle in her green eyes.

'Not bad!' Alan repeated. 'What do you mean, "not bad"? It's terrific,' he declared stoutly.

'I know,' Susan chided him as she placed a light kiss on his unshaven cheek. 'I was only joking.'

Alan crinkled his eyes at her, unsure whether to believe her or not.

'It is good,' Susan insisted, with an apologetic ring in her voice.

'We shall have it for tea, eh?' Alan grinned, his pride restored.

'Give it here and I'll clean it,' Susan offered. She cleaned the fish with a deft skill born of years of the practice of country life, while Alan showered upstairs.

'Are we going to the quiz tonight?' Alan appeared in the kitchen wearing a clean pair of jeans and a freshly laundered white shirt.

'Yes, it could be fun,' Susan replied as she dressed the fish with almonds and lemon.

'I've a few things to do first,' Alan declared. 'What time's tea?' he enquired, placing a light hand on Susan's waist as she placed the fresh fish under the grill.

'Half an hour,' she answered, pecking his cheek. 'Now you get out from under my feet and let me get on.'

'Yes, ma'am.' Alan threw up a parody of a salute and retreated to the living room, where he immersed himself in a sea of papers.

Susan walked in with the trout grilled to a turn and garnished with new potatoes and green beans, and Alan pulled the cork on a bottle of burgundy.

'Delicious,' he declared after they had finished the meal. 'My first fish.' He raised his glass to himself. 'And cooked to perfection.' He smiled, bowing his head to Susan, who rested her chin on her interlocked fingers.

'Thank you, kind sir,' she responded, accepting the compliment in the manner it was given, lightly but from the heart.

Susan dealt with the clearing of the table and Alan allowed himself a large cigar as he sat in the deep armchair, a picture of satisfied contentment.

'Three Pheasants, then?' Susan asked, entering the sitting room and running a brush through her long auburn hair so that it sparkled against the shafts of evening sunlight lancing through the windows.

They walked along Busjibber Lane, their jackets buttoned against the falling temperature. 'Evening all,' Alan called as he entered the pub and held the door open for Susan.

'How's the master fisherman?' Mortimer enquired as he poured Alan a fresh pint.

'Don't ask!' Susan interjected. 'His head is big enough as it is.'

'It was a beautiful fish,' Alan defended himself. 'I'm entitled to gloat.'

'Gloating is one thing.' Susan winked at Mortimer as she lifted her glass of wine. 'Booking the entire front page of the *Wixley Herald* is another!'

Alan had to join in the laughter himself. The only person at the bar who did not laugh was Liam Murphy. He had not wanted to spend his evening in the Three Pheasants but it was either that or go to the White Horse, and that would have meant having to put up with His Lordship's son. Liam had quite enough of Timothy during the day without spending his evenings in his company as well.

Liam's expression was not lost on Susan. 'Hello, Liam,' she said, fixing her eyes on his, and Liam felt the same flush come to his cheeks again. 'Why don't you join us for the quiz?'

'Sorry.' Liam made an excuse. 'I'm up early tomorrow.' He finished his drink and walked out.

Fox sat up in bed supported by two huge white pillows, with his left paw held in a sling across his chest. The door to the bedroom opened and Vixen stepped through. Fox's eyes sparkled.

'Good morning, you beautiful creature,' he said with a rakish smile.

'Not much wrong with you obviously,' Vixen observed. 'And you have a visitor.'

Weasel slipped through the door with a brown paper bag clutched in his paw. 'Morning, Foxy.' He smiled with true affection.

'Weasel, old man, how good to see you.' Fox returned the warm smile.

Weasel sat beside the bed. Vixen ordered no smoking and then left them to it.

'What's in the bag?' Fox enquired, a merry twinkle in his eyes.

Weasel immediately looked a little guilty. 'Well, they were grapes,' he began hesitantly, 'but I got a little carried away.'

Fox laughed aloud as Weasel produced the paltry remains of the bunch of grapes from the bag for his inspection. 'Never mind, old boy. It's the thought that counts.'

Weasel turned quickly to other matters. 'When will you be up and about?' he asked.

'Only a couple more days,' Fox replied, and he grinned enigmatically. 'Pity, I'm beginning to enjoy it.'

'Don't get too comfortable,' Weasel warned. 'I need my partner back.'

'Never fear, old boy, I'll be back. In fact, I was thinking of taking a trip into the village.'

Weasel frowned darkly. 'I don't think that would be such a good idea,' he commented, and Fox grinned mischievously. 'I gave Vixen both of the rabbits, by the way,' Weasel remarked.

'Don't I know it.' Fox sighed. 'I've been virtually force-fed rabbit broth for the past fortnight.'

'It's good for you,' Weasel observed with a wry smile.

A long silence then ensued as Fox tried to find the words he needed, and when he spoke his voice was full of sincerity.

'I owe you my thanks, old boy,' he said softly. 'I could well have died if it hadn't been for you.'

Weasel waved a dismissive paw to hide the embarrassment he felt. 'You wouldn't have died,' he said.

'That's not the case, and you know it.' And Fox offered his paw. Weasel and Fox grasped each other's paws in a firm, masculine embrace and Weasel nodded perfunctorily.

'I've got to be going,' he declared. 'I'll be back when you're up and about,' and he turned and left the room.

Weasel returned two days later to find Fox fully recovered and on his feet. 'Fit and well?' he asked.

'Never felt better,' Fox replied. 'Time to be going home.'

'I'll come with you,' Weasel said.

‘Thanks, old boy, but I can manage.’

Vixen gave Fox a matronly look. ‘No, you can’t,’ she said. ‘You have a long journey to make. Weasel can go with you.’

‘It’s not a long journey,’ Fox protested.

‘No arguments.’ Vixen cut him short before turning to Weasel. ‘Keep an eye on him, and no rough stuff,’ she ordered.

Weasel waited outside as Fox said his goodbyes. ‘Thanks, old girl.’ Fox took Vixen’s paws in his own. ‘You’ve been marvellous.’

‘Yes, I know. Now go on with you,’ Vixen replied, aware that she would not see him again for some time. She knew him too well.

‘Come to dinner,’ Fox said, and Vixen’s eyes lit up. ‘I mean it,’ Fox said. ‘Tomorrow. I owe it to you.’

‘You don’t owe me anything,’ Vixen stated, feeling a little hurt.

‘I want you to,’ Fox said softly, and he looked deeply into Vixen’s eyes.

‘What time?’ Vixen asked guardedly.

‘Seven?’ Fox suggested, and Vixen adopted a contemplative air. ‘Seven-thirty?’ Fox queried, and Vixen looked at the ceiling. ‘Eight?’ Fox persisted.

‘Yes, okay, eight o’clock,’ Vixen accepted, and Fox kissed her lightly on her cheek.

Weasel was waiting with a lit cigarette between his lips. ‘Another broken heart?’ he mocked.

‘Not this time, my friend,’ Fox replied, ‘not this time.’

‘Sounds serious,’ Weasel remarked, and Fox gave him a lopsided smile.

‘Who knows,’ he replied.

It took two hours at a slow pace for the pair to reach the small spinney, and Fox cracked open a bottle of champagne which he had been saving.

‘This is as good a time as any,’ he stated, and the two toasted each other’s health. Fox sipped delicately at his glass as Weasel quaffed his in one quick swallow.

‘That is no way to drink champers, old boy,’ Fox admonished him light-heartedly. Weasel replenished his glass and flopped down onto the sofa.

'So, when are you seeing the lovely Vixen again?' he asked with a broad grin.

'Tomorrow night,' Fox replied, 'although I haven't the foggiest idea with what I am going to feed the poor girl. The cupboard is bare.'

'Rabbit?' Weasel laughed.

'Rabbit is definitely off the menu,' Fox stressed.

Weasel grinned craftily. 'Chicken?' he said.

'Cobden, you mean?'

'Where else?'

'Twinkle wouldn't have it.' Fox shook his head. 'No, it will have to be somewhere else.'

'That's just it,' Weasel said with an air of exasperation. 'We are running out of places.'

Fox sipped at his champagne thoughtfully. 'Dembury's pheasants perhaps?' he suggested.

'Too far.' Weasel dismissed the idea. 'You're not up to it yet.'

'I don't feel up to much, to be quite honest,' Fox admitted.

'I'll see what I can do,' Weasel said, getting up from the sofa. 'Right now I'm off home.'

'Take care, old boy, and thanks.'

'You're welcome.'

Rupert Bartholomew's eyes widened and the manicured fingers holding the letter trembled. His mind raced. How could these photographs have come about? How could anybody have possibly known?

Lord Bartholomew looked down again at the bold signature at the foot of the page. It was a signature as uncompromising as the headed paper itself. This was no joke, that much was sure.

Charles Dembury had never been noted for his sense of humour. Rupert Bartholomew snatched up the telephone with a suddenly sweating palm and began dialling as if his very soul depended on it.

Fox answered the knock at the door to find Weasel looking very pleased with himself.

'Morning, Foxy.'

'What are you looking so happy about?' Fox asked as he held the door open for his friend. Weasel stepped through the door and produced a quail from each of his coat pockets.

'One for you,' he said, ' and one for the lovely Vixen.'

'Where on earth did you get those?' Fox asked, his tone that of a fox who was well impressed.

'Ask me no questions...' Weasel grinned enigmatically.

'I am most grateful, old boy,' Fox said as he accepted the two birds. 'Drink?' he offered.

'Good idea.' Weasel nodded his head vigorously. 'It was a little chilly last night.'

Fox led the way into the sitting room and Weasel made himself comfortable as Fox poured a generous measure of Scotch into a clean glass. 'Good health,' Fox toasted his friend.

'I was over at Cobden's place last night,' Weasel began. 'I had a word with Twinkle. It seems the villagers have presented a petition to Downing Street, a list of signatures against the motorway.'

'Good news,' Fox agreed.

'Apparently it was on the news, local TV channel and radio.'

'Excellent.' Fox nodded. 'That means it will turn up in the newspapers. We shall have to get a copy.'

'That's what I thought,' Weasel stated, and then he drained the glass of the fiery liquid and pulled the peak of his cap down over his eyes before lying back on the sofa. Within moments he was snoring loudly. Fox gave Weasel a fatherly look and then tiptoed from the room.

The quails took two hours of Fox's time to prepare and then he crept through to the bedroom, taking care not to disturb the sleeping Weasel, and snuggled himself into the folds of the quilt.

In the sitting room, Weasel listened intently to the sound of Fox taking to his bed and then he rose from the sofa and crept stealthily across the carpet and lifted the decanter of whiskey to his lips. Weasel's Adam's apple bounced behind the white scarf as the spirit poured unchecked down his gullet. When he replaced the decanter in its position on the sideboard it stood half empty. Weasel smacked his lips appreciatively and wiped his whiskers across his sleeve before creeping out of the den.

The copse was bathed in bright spring sunshine and Weasel blinked against the sudden glare. He then headed at a nimble pace towards the long drystone wall that followed the contours of the rolling fields.

He covered the ground to the wall in good time and then sat on its top and admired the fresh spring farmland as he rolled a cigarette. The pungent odour of the cattle grazing in the adjacent field reached his nostrils and a swallow skimmed the grass in search of young flies. Weasel lit the thinly rolled cigarette and disappeared into the dark confines of his home.

Chapter 7

May

The first swallow, tired after its long journey from Africa, landed gratefully on the high telephone wire which crossed the cobbled yard at the same time as Douglas began herding the cattle along the track towards the new day's pastures.

Douglas closed the gate behind the grazing cows and paused beneath the brightening sky to roll a cigarette and enjoy the early peace. He leant on the wooden gate, rested one booted foot on its bottom rail and watched a fox cub padding quickly along the wooded edge of the field, a large black rat clamped between its jaws. The cattle moved slowly through the dew.

Douglas crushed the cigarette beneath his heel and strolled back along the track. The hedges were plump and full of chattering sparrows and the distant song of a cuckoo carried clearly across the spring fields above the coarse fractured cry of a hidden pheasant. He walked across the yard and the weary swallow was joined by another equally tired traveller, and Douglas nodded the peak of his cap in greeting as he passed beneath them.

Mary stood on the red brick kitchen step with her hair tousled and her blue dressing gown tied at the waist. 'Another lovely day.' She smiled as her husband kissed her cheek.

'Almost as gorgeous as you, my sweet,' Douglas answered, giving her bottom a playful pinch, and Mary slapped him lightly on the arm.

Jennifer, a smaller version of her mother, sat at the bare wooden table and rubbed the sleep from her eyes.

'You're up bright and early, young lady.' Douglas said as he crossed to wash his hands at the sink.

'Susan and Alan and me are going for a picnic in Wixley Wood,' Jennifer said, as if amazed that her father would have forgotten.

'Oh yes, that's right.' Douglas nodded, thinking that the first week of May was a little early in the year for a picnic.

'We are going in Alan's car,' Jennifer continued. 'It's a BMW,' she said earnestly, and Douglas and Mary exchanged indulgent glances.

'I think you'll have a nice day for it,' Douglas remarked as Mary served his breakfast plate of gammon and eggs. 'What time are you going?' he asked, after taking a swallow of hot tea.

'Nine o'clock, two hours' time,' Jennifer replied, looking up at the clock above the door, ' and I'm going to bring Mummy some flowers as well.'

Mary sat at the table and scrutinised her daughter with a keen eye. 'Not until you've had a wash, grubby little urchin,' she said, pulling a distasteful face as if genuinely appalled at her daughter's appearance, and Jennifer instantly protested. 'No complaints,' Mary cut her short. 'Off you go now.'

Jennifer rose from the table with a grumpy look on her face and stamped as loudly as she could up the stairs.

'And don't forget to have a shave,' Douglas called after her with a short chuckle, but Jennifer did not answer and Mary looked sternly at him from the corner of her eye. 'So we have the place to ourselves today, eh?' Douglas said with a conspiratorial tone and a rakish smile.

'Huh!' Mary pulled a face. 'I've far too much to do.'

'I'll have you in that bed by five-past nine,' Douglas whispered, his smile becoming wicked.

'Nonsense.' Mary dismissed the idea as she got up from the table. 'Now I'm going for a bath.'

'Good. I like you smelling sweet,' Douglas drawled.

Mary raised her eyes to the ceiling and made her way upstairs. Douglas could hear her run the bath water as he dropped his plate into the sink.

The sun had warmed the yard and Douglas sat on the steps with Piper at his side as Alan brought the car to a stop at the farmyard gate. Susan jumped from the passenger seat and ran across the cobbles, leaving Alan to follow at a more leisurely pace.

'Hello, Uncle Doug,' Susan said, stopping to peck her uncle's cheek, and Douglas grabbed her by the waist and pulled her down onto his lap.

'And how is my favourite niece?' he asked with a wide grin.

'Your only niece!' Susan replied, placing her arms around Douglas's neck.

Alan sauntered slowly across the yard with an amused smile on his tanned face. 'Morning, Uncle Doug,' he said. The two men roared with laughter and Susan slapped her uncle's shoulder playfully. She pushed herself up from his lap as Jennifer appeared in the doorway.

'Ready?' Susan asked as Mary stepped into the doorway.

'Yes, ready.' Jennifer nodded her blonde curls. 'Hello, Alan.'

'Hello, Jennifer. How are you?' Alan smiled, his white teeth gleaming beneath his dark hair.

'Very well, thank you,' Jennifer replied politely. She took Susan's hand and Alan led the way to the bright red car.

'Have a nice time,' Mary called.

'And be a good girl,' Douglas finished the sentence.

'I will,' Jennifer called back, and Douglas watched the BMW purr away and disappear from the lane before rising from the step and entering the kitchen.

Mary turned from the step to find her husband eyeing her with a look in his eye of which the most mischievous imp would have been proud.

'Oh, don't be ridiculous.' Mary waved the back of her hand at him. 'I've far too much to be doing today without...' and her words disintegrated into a squeal as Douglas lifted her up with one muscular arm and threw her over his shoulder. 'Douglas!' Mary squealed again. Her husband gave her ample bottom a hearty slap. 'Put me down!' she demanded, but her voice tailed off into a girlish plea and Douglas knew she did not mean it.

'Less of it, my girl,' he said gruffly.

Mary stopped struggling and went limp over his back and Douglas trotted up the staircase with ease.

Jennifer ran ahead and Alan and Susan walked hand in hand behind, following the track between the tall trees.

'Don't go too far,' Susan called lightly.

'I won't,' Jennifer called back without looking around.

'Sweet child,' Alan observed.

'Very well brought up,' Susan agreed, her attention suddenly caught by a pair of roe-deer sprinting away into the trees.

'Did you see those deer?' Jennifer stopped and looked back at the two adults.

'They were lovely, weren't they?' Susan replied with a bright smile.

Jennifer ran on, her wicker basket swinging wildly from her arm and the rays from the sun which penetrated the leafy branches lighting up her yellow dress and her bouncing blonde curls.

'Would you like children?' Alan asked.

'What? Now, you mean?' Susan giggled, and to Alan her laughter sounded like tinkling water.

'If you like,' he replied, grinning. 'But what would Jenny say?' and they laughed together.

Jennifer came bounding back along the beaten track. 'I've found where we can have a picnic,' she said. 'It's along here.' She sprinted away again and Alan and Susan walked along to where the child had vanished into the trees.

'Where are you?' Susan called as they stepped off the track. 'Jenny,' she called again. 'Jennifer?' Susan called a third time, her voice an octave higher, but only the silence of the trees answered her call.

Alan released Susan's hand and walked forward to the edge of a small sunlit clearing.

'Jennifer,' he called, his voice a little earnest, 'where are you?'

He looked slowly around the clearing and cupped his hands to his mouth.

'Jennifer?' he shouted, his voice echoing through the wood, but the only reply he received was the kiss of the gentle breeze against his cheek.

He glanced over his shoulder at Susan, who stood with her arms folded defensively across her chest and a waxen look on her face.

'It's all right,' Alan soothed. 'She's around somewhere.'

Susan did not reply, her eyes betraying her worry and Alan called again, his tone sharp.

'Jennifer, don't play games. Now answer me. Where are you?' And then he saw the wicker basket lying in the tall grass at the far edge of the glade.

Alan walked across the clearing, a frown of concern on his brow, and stopped short of the small basket. The basket was upturned and its contents had spilled on to the grass. Alan felt a pang of panic and anger. 'Jennifer!' he shouted, his eyes darting wildly from the desecrated basket to the trees and back again. He looked over his shoulder. Susan had the white knuckles of her right hand between her teeth and a single tear was running down her cheek.

Mary lay with her head resting on Douglas's bare chest and her arm wrapped around his waist. She looked up at him from beneath her long lashes.

'Animal, that wasn't fair,' she purred.

Douglas smiled without showing his teeth or opening his eyes and pulled his wife closer against his body. Mary snuggled against him.

'Now this is the way to spend a Sunday,' Douglas said, and the telephone rang from the hallway. 'Ignore it!' he ordered.

'It might be important,' Mary said in a sleepy voice.

'And then again it might not.' Douglas closed the subject.

The telephone's ringing became more insistent and Mary eased herself from Douglas's arm. 'I'll see who it is,' she said, and Douglas let out a slow sigh.

Mary tiptoed naked down the stairs and Douglas listened with barely concealed irritation at the disturbance as Mary spoke into the mouthpiece. He opened his eyes as an unnaturally long silence ensued. Mary called to him from the hallway and her voice was thin and hesitant.

'What is it?' Douglas queried, his annoyance replaced by a concerned frown.

'Can you come here?' Mary replied, her tone tremulous and weak.

Douglas jumped from the bed and took the stairs two at a time. Mary stood with the handset held towards him and a worried look in her eye.

'Who is it?' Douglas asked briskly.

'Susan.'

'Susan?' Douglas said into the mouthpiece. He listened in silence to the frightened voice at the other end. 'All right,' Douglas soothed. 'Let's not panic. I'm on my way. I'll see you there,' and he put the receiver down without waiting for a reply.

'I'm coming with you,' Mary told him.

Douglas drove the estate out of the yard with his foot to the floor and the gearstick flew through the gears. The car shot through the winding country lane.

'She's just wandered off, that's all,' Douglas said, without taking his eyes from the road, but Mary made no reply.

Wixley Wood grew larger as Douglas drove beyond the speed limit until he parked in a cloud of dust beside the red BMW. Susan stood beside the car, her eyes red and wet.

'I'm sorry,' she said as Douglas and Mary stepped from the estate, and her shoulders shook with another welling sob.

'All right, it's not your fault,' Mary comforted, hugging her tightly.

Douglas ran through the trees, calling loudly to Alan, and Alan's reply echoed through the wood. Douglas found him searching vainly through the trees, his mouth set in a grim line.

'I've looked all around here. Nothing, not a thing,' Alan said as Douglas looked in all directions.

'Where's the basket?' Douglas demanded.

The two men hurried back to the glade and stood staring down at the jumbled contents of the fallen basket with silent eyes. Douglas dragged his eyes from the basket and took a deep, thoughtful breath.

'She was only out of sight for a matter of seconds,' Alan said disbelievingly. Mary and Susan stood hand in hand at the edge of the clearing, their faces pale and worried.

Douglas made his decision. 'Mary, use Alan's phone and inform the police. She's probably got lost, is all, but it will take more than us to find her.'

The two women hurried back along the earthen track and Douglas and Alan separated and began combing the wood, their eyes darting into every fold in the ground and behind every tree.

The first patrol car pulled to a controlled stop and a tall policeman in white shirtsleeves stepped from the passenger seat. Mary and Susan burst into a cacophony of explanations.

'Calm down, ladies,' Constable David Hollis said mildly. 'One at a time, please.'

Mary nodded in deference and Susan spoke in a faltering voice. PC Hollis listened without interrupting. 'Can you show me where the basket is?' he asked. The two women led him and his colleague to the quiet clearing.

PC Hollis crouched down and passed a professional eye over the upturned basket before looking up at his partner. 'Get onto the station, Chris. Possible abduction. Full description and search required.' And the words placed a cold, icy clutch on Mary's heart.

Fox pulled the door quietly closed and stretched his tired limbs. The Vixen had been splendid company, he reflected, but it really was time to be going home.

He looked up at the slow twilight and then to the evening shadows that darkened the rolling English fields, before stepping off at a brisk pace through the quiet dusk. He kept to the hedgerows dividing the green pastures as the small spinney fell away behind him, until he paused at a narrow country lane which lay like a sleeping snake in a sunny meadow, peaceful but deadly.

Fox peered through the gloom, both left and right, and pricked his ears towards the bend in the road. The lane remained quiet and still, without the sudden glare from the headlights of a speeding car, and Fox hurried across and into the sanctuary of another field of tussocky grass and wild flowers.

He carried on through the undulating valleys and over the small hillocks, keeping the rising moon to his left and his face towards the cool breeze. He ignored the sign that warned the traveller that he was entering private property and broke into a trot, passing quickly and quietly between the tall oaks of Blackthorn Estate and over the narrow wooden bridge which spanned a fast-running length of the Wix.

The lights from the large house twinkled in the distant darkness and Fox trotted on in silence before pausing on a rocky knoll which afforded him a view of Wixley Wood, which sat, darker than the encroaching night, on the far horizon. He checked his watch and held a flame to the end of a cheroot.

He passed a sharp eye over the cool farmland. Rabbits had begun to appear, nibbling their way across the short grass, their cottontails flashing like semaphore through the darkness. Fox drew deeply on the mild cigar and allowed the smoke to drift lazily from his nostrils.

The stillness was broken by the sudden chopping of a helicopter passing overhead, its spotlight trained on the ground, a bright eye that chased the rabbits to their warrens. Fox watched the helicopter disappear over the brow of Wixley Wood before grinding out his cheroot on a jagged rock. Then he set off at an adjacent angle to the wood, away from the distant cut of the helicopter's blades.

The afternoon sun had passed over the searching policemen and the tireless troops in their camouflaged uniforms and now began to sink beyond the earth's curve, and a blackbird sounded the onset of dusk. The beams of the flashlights lanced through the darkening wood and the silence crackled to the sound of the police radios.

Douglas tramped through the thick wood, his voice hoarse from shouting his daughter's name. Mortimer laid a comforting hand on his shoulder.

'We'll find her,' he said softly, but Douglas made no reply. 'And if somebody else finds her, then Mary and Susan are at home.'

Douglas did not lift his eyes from his search but his voice betrayed his darkest fears. 'That's if somebody hasn't found her already,' he said grimly before carrying on between the trees.

An authoritative, military voice reverberated through the wood, demanding instant attention. Douglas ran through the trees, ignoring the whiplash of the low branches. A tall soldier with the double stripes of a corporal sewn on his sleeve stood beside a large bush of brambles. The light from his torch shone on a torn patch of yellow cloth.

Fox trotted quickly through the dark night, looking forward to the warmth of his bed against the falling temperature. The half-moon hung high in the starless sky, buffeted by the heavy dark clouds which the strengthening wind harried across its face, and Fox decided he wanted to be home before the clouds turned to rain.

He passed between a pair of tall beech trees and paused in the darkness of a thick hedgerow. He peered through the night along the dark country road. The road lay quiet and Fox stepped gingerly out onto the tarmac. The tarmac was cold to the touch and Fox trotted quickly across. He made the hedgerow on the far side just as two broad shining beams punctured the darkness and a pair of headlights ushered a black Rolls-Royce through the night.

Fox stood quite still, hidden in the folds of the hedge, and the limousine glided quietly past and disappeared along the winding contours of the murky lane. Fox stepped through the hedge into a wide undulating field and looked across to a spot which the passing headlights had fleetingly illuminated. He strained his eyes against the darkness, trying to decipher the shape of the object. A low bleating reached his ears. The ewe had found its way into a deep gully as protection against the prevailing wind but had subsequently lost the company of the rest of the flock and its pathetic bleating would no doubt carry on until the dawn.

He turned from the sorry sight and headed towards the grey area where the horizon began. Then the thought struck him that there were no sheep in the area. He looked back over his shoulder and the wind carried the low keening across the field to his pricked ears. He trotted cautiously back, a curious frown on his brow, and circled the gully until he came up downwind of the bleating ewe, and he peered through the darkness.

The sheep had a very bright, even unusual, wool and was huddled on the ground, its legs drawn up beneath itself. Fox crept forward, his breathing as quiet as his tread. He had never encountered anything like it before and his eyes reflected a mixture of curiosity and superstitious dread. He stopped short, his heart in his mouth, as the sheep suddenly rose up on its legs.

Fox turned to flee but then a familiar voice cried out to him. He turned back, his face a picture of amazement, his eyes wide and his mouth open.

'Jennifer!'

General Lord Dembury of Wixley drained the glass of its whiskey and extinguished his half-smoked Havana. The leather buttoned armchair squeaked as he lifted his weight from it and the portraits hanging on the wall followed him with silent eyes as he walked out of the sitting room.

The General collected his hat and coat and the commissionaire bade him a good afternoon as he exited the Wellington Club and made his way along the warm London street. Hodges held the door of the limousine open and the General eased himself into the rear of the car. He relaxed as he enjoyed the sights and sounds of London in the early summer as Hodges negotiated the Rolls-Royce through the busy city roads. The car broke free of the rash of red traffic cones blighting the North Circular Road and throttled out of the bustling city and into the heart of the English countryside.

The General lifted a buff-coloured envelope with an already broken seal from inside his jacket and began again to read its contents.

The limousine cruised along the network of A roads, through the shires and counties of England, and the General raised his eyes from the papers and stared out of the window with a thoughtful expression. The furrows creasing his brow and the thin line of his mouth revealed his disappointment with the revelations of the papers but the steely glare in his grey eyes declared his determination. The General folded the papers and pushed the envelope back into his jacket pocket. He settled his body into the seat and admired the passing scenery.

The Rolls-Royce swung off onto a B road just as the glowing orange sun began to give way to the moon's reign, and motored gracefully through the leafy winding lanes, passing between the tall trees and the darkening shadows. Hodges flicked on the headlights and two broad beams lanced through the closing dusk, chasing shadows from the car's path. He drove the limousine on through the quiet roads, changing down the gears with a smooth dexterity as he negotiated the tight bends. The bright lamps illuminated the rabbits grazing by the roadside and sent a solitary fox scampering for the cover of the night.

The sleek motor car covered the last few miles to Blackthorn Estate without interruption or passing another traveller, and Hodges drove at a sedate pace up the long straight driveway. The lights in the house twinkled a warm welcome.

Hodges suddenly slammed his foot onto the brake pedal and the car came to a sharp stop, its tyres screeching its protest at the violent application of the brakes. The General lurched forward in his seat and steadied himself with outstretched arms that thudded into the back of the driver's seat. Hodges gripped the wheel with white knuckles.

At the entrance to the stonechip forecourt a red fox had suddenly leapt out from behind one of the tall sycamores and now stood prancing in the pool of light from the car's headlamps.

'Beg your pardon, M'Lord,' Hodges apologised. 'Frightened the life out of me.'

The fox started to howl, its head thrown back, and the piercing cries echoed through the night.

'What on earth...?' The General's voice tailed off as he watched the excited fox throw himself back and forth in front of the car.

Hodges leant on the car's horn and the hooter blared out into the darkness. The fox paid no attention, its howls like a banshee shrieking into the night. Lady Dembury appeared on the mansion steps, the open door throwing light out onto the forecourt.

The General climbed from the limousine and looked down amazed at the frantically howling fox.

'What on earth is going on, Charles?' Lady Dembury asked as she approached the unusual scene.

The General's eyes fixed on a strip of yellow cloth tied around the fox's neck. The cloth had a ragged, uneven edge and was tied with a large granny knot.

'I think perhaps it's choking,' the General answered as his wife stepped beside him.

Lady Dembury stared at the cavorting fox for a long moment and then clutched at her husband's elbow. 'Charles, I think it's Jennifer's fox,' she said, without taking her eyes from the fox.

The General looked at his wife with a curious frown. 'What are you talking about?' he asked.

Lady Dembury's face registered a look of anxiety and concern. 'There was a policeman here today,' she began falteringly. 'Apparently Mrs Cobden's daughter, Jennifer I think her name is, has gone missing.'

'Missing?'

'From Wixley Wood this morning. The policeman asked if I had seen her.'

'What has all this got to do with this fox?' the General asked in a bewildered tone.

'Jennifer is wearing a yellow dress, apparently, and that fox is ...' Lady Dembury tailed off as her husband held up a perfunctory hand.

'Catherine,' he said a little patronisingly, 'it's a fox that's caught its head in a noose, that's all. It's not something out of "Lassie, Come Home".'

Lady Dembury replied with a tone that matched her husband's and her smile was deceptively sweet. 'Then why is it leaping about here, in front of us? Most unfoxlike, I would have thought.'

The General looked down again at the howling fox. 'It's probably demented,' he said, dismissing this wife's opinion with a wave of his hand.

The prancing fox suddenly leapt forward and threw itself against the General's legs before turning and sprinting towards the rolling fields that made up the majority of the estate's grounds. The General stood transfixed as the fox turned and came hurtling back. His mouth fell open in awe as the fox again rebounded against his legs before speeding off towards the fields.

'What's it doing now?' he asked, as the fox howled at him from beyond the forecourt.

'He wants you to follow him, of course!' Lady Dembury said earnestly.

The General rounded on his wife with a furious glare.

'Don't be ridiculous, Catherine,' he shouted. 'It's a fox, not a collie!'

Lady Dembury turned from her husband and ran into the house, reappearing moments later wearing a jacket and a pair of sensible shoes.

'What are you doing?' the General asked, his voice full of astonishment.

Lady Dembury walked past her husband and towards the howling fox with a determined stride. 'If you won't go, then I shall,' she declared in ringing tones.

The General looked aghast at his wife. 'Don't be ridiculous. You can't go gallivanting around the countryside after some half-crazed fox in the middle of the night,' he cried.

'Just watch me.' Lady Dembury threw the words over her shoulder.

'Oh, good Lord,' the General sighed despairingly. He looked at Hodges still sitting behind the purring engine. 'Well, don't just sit there,' he growled. 'Switch that damn thing off and follow me.'

'Jennifer!'

Fox could scarcely believe his eyes, eyes which suddenly shone as bright and as wide as the moon.

'What the dickens are you doing here?' he asked in astonishment as he ran towards the shivering child.

Jennifer's eyes were red from crying and her cheeks were still wet from the falling tears. Her knees and elbows were grazed and sore. Fox knew without further questioning what had happened and what had to be done.

'Stay here,' he ordered, and he ripped a length of cloth from the hem of Jennifer's skirt and knotted it beneath his chin. 'Stay here, Jenny,' he repeated in gentle tones. 'I'll get some help.'

Jennifer responded with another burst of tears which poured unchecked down her face and she rubbed her eyes with her small bunched fists.

'It's all right,' Fox comforted her. 'I'll be back shortly. Stay here and wait for me.' Jennifer nodded weakly. 'Promise?' Fox asked quietly.

'I promise,' Jennifer sniffed.

Fox turned from the child and sprinted away, back through the hedge and across the road without bothering to check for oncoming traffic. He raced across the fields, his stride lengthening with each elastic bound until he came up onto the brow of a small hillock.

The lights from Blackthorn House shone like a beacon and the headlamps guiding the Rolls-Royce through the darkness cruised towards them along the estate's driveway. Fox sprinted down the grassy bank and headed towards the mansion, his heart pounding in his chest and his breath panting over his lolling tongue. He reached the white stonechips fifty yards ahead of the black limousine and paused in the shelter of a leafy sycamore to catch his breath.

The car turned into the forecourt and Fox leapt out into the glare of the headlamps. He prayed silently that the car would stop in time. Stonechips flew into the night as the car screeched to an abrupt halt, and Fox filled his lungs and bellowed at the top of his voice.

The General turned and set off in pursuit of his hurrying wife without waiting for Hodges to join him.

'Catherine, wait for me, damn it!' he called irritably.

Lady Dembury made no reply but instead quickened her pace so that she gained ground on the hysterical fox.

'For God's sake, Catherine!' he called again as Hodges appeared at his side.

Lady Dembury turned on her heel and gave her husband a

steely glare. 'Well, get a move on then,' she ordered tartly.

'Catherine, this is ridiculous,' the General panted as he drew level with his wife. Lady Dembury ignored her husband and turned away, moving off again at a brisk pace. The General rolled his eyes at Hodges before hurrying after her.

The fox started to howl again and the General let out an exasperated sigh as Lady Dembury called to the animal that she was coming as quickly as she could.

'Madness,' he muttered.

The fox bounded away, stopping only when it was on the point of being swallowed up by the darkness, to turn and begin again to howl like a demon.

The General came up short and looked back at the receding lights of Blackthorn House. 'Catherine, we must have gone over a mile by now,' he shouted, his voice carrying a pleading tone.

Lady Dembury strode on, oblivious to her husband's complaints, until she arrived at the thick hawthorn hedge which marked the boundary of the estate. The fox had vanished, its lithe frame having disappeared once it had reached the hedge, and Lady Dembury stood looking out across the narrow country lane that bordered it. The General came struggling up to stand beside his wife.

'There! You see?' he said, following his wife's gaze. 'A wild-goose chase.'

The urgent howling erupted again from the low field on the far side of the road.

'Oh, no, not again!' the General despaired as his wife began searching along the hedgerow for a suitable opening. 'Catherine, please,' he begged as Lady Dembury found a gap in the hedge and began to fight her way through it.

'Stop whingeing,' Lady Dembury barked, and she strode across the lane.

Hodges held the hawthorn apart as His Lordship pushed his way through, and then followed, his expression thoroughly bemused beneath the peak of his cap.

Lady Dembury struggled through the second hedge and headed for the spot where the fox was cavorting and howling. The General and Hodges clambered through the hedge and followed behind. Lady Dembury paused at the lip of a deep gully and the two men joined her. The fox stopped its howling and sped off into the night.

'Well, that's that!' the General stated. 'Now perhaps we can all get home before this wind brings some rain with it.'

Lady Dembury took a slow step forward and looked around the collection of gorse bushes which nestled in the gully. The General turned to Hodges and raised his eyebrows in resignation at his wife's intransigence.

'Torch, Hodges,' he demanded.

Hodges looked at His Lordship with amazed eyes. 'I don't have one, M'Lord,' he murmured.

'Why the hell not?' The General flared. Hodges assumed a look somewhere between apology and complete bewilderment.

Lady Dembury came to the hapless driver's rescue. 'It's quite all right, I have a torch.' She shone the expanding beam around the gully, picking out the darkest corners behind the thick bushes, and the light settled on the frightened and shivering child.

'Good God!' the General gasped.

'Yes,' Lady Dembury replied softly, 'I rather imagine he is,' and she stepped down and gathered the crying child into her arms.

The news flashed through the police radio net and Douglas Cobden crashed to his knees, his face buried in his hands. Max rested himself on his cane and laid an old hand on his friend's shoulder as the sobs convulsed the big man's body.

Mary and Susan cried into each other's arms and the patient policewoman waited until there were no more tears to cry before driving the two women to Blackthorn Estate.

Douglas was already there. The hug he gave his daughter caused the General to turn away to hide the embarrassment he felt at having witnessed it. Jennifer ran into her mother's arms when she entered.

Douglas sipped at a brandy that the General had poured for the child, only to be told by his wife that this was a seven-year-old and not a Coldsteam Guard. Douglas listened to how Hodges had carried Jennifer back to the mansion after wrapping her in his jacket.

And the fox! Douglas could not quite believe it himself.

Lady Dembury sat modestly accepting the laurels that were showered upon her, and the nurse declared there was no reason why Jennifer could not go home, as long as she stayed in bed for a day or two. 'And no more chasing any foxes!'

Tom Peterson looked out of the window at the motley collection of protesters who had gathered outside the compound. The double gates were padlocked and a security guard stood with his arms folded across his chest and an indifferent look in his eye.

Tom could pick out one or two of the more familiar faces. That old lady with the shotgun was there. So too was the landlord from the local pub. About a dozen in all.

Susan Hamilton could see Tom looking out of his window, and his face appearing through the glass made her shout even louder. 'No motorway.' She waved her placard above her head as she shouted.

Liam Murphy did his best to shout even louder, at the same time as making his voice sound deeper and more masculine. He barely looked at the compound. He could not take his eyes away from Susan.

Chapter 8

June

The sett was illuminated by a single lamp which highlighted the wispy smoke drifting from Weasel's cigarette and the burning cheroot clamped between Fox's teeth.

Badger sat hunched over his cards, his broad shoulders shielding his hand from prying eyes. Badger placed two of his cards face down on the table and Fox flicked two from the deck to replace them.

Fox's eyes swivelled to Weasel, who sat repeatedly opening and closing his hand like an oriental fan. Weasel squinted through the acrid smoke rising from his cigarette and dropped three cards onto the table.

Fox skimmed three cards across the green baize before turning to his own cards. He thumbed the hand open and the three aces peeked out from behind the pair of kings. He closed the hand and placed it face down on the table before tossing a pound coin into the pot.

Badger stared over his cards at the canine. Fox lounged in his hard-backed chair, one paw hanging nonchalantly over the arm of the chair and the other resting easily on the baize.

'Are you in, old boy?' Fox raised a patronising eyebrow.

The pile of coins and notes in front of him testified to his skill at the game and his air of easy confidence had grown during the evening. Vixen stood at Fox's shoulder, her eyes shining with undisguised adoration at her champion as he brushed an imaginary speck of dust from his waistcoat.

Badger replied by dropping three pound coins into the pot. Weasel sneered beneath the peak of his cap and threw his hand onto the table in disgust.

Fox smiled lazily and flicked ash from the Monte Cristo before raising the stakes by a further six pounds. Badger grunted and his hand followed Weasel's.

'My game, eh?' Fox smiled.

'Again!' Badger said heavily.

'Come, come, Badger.' Fox's eyes twinkled above the pearl white teeth. 'Let's not have any bad losers.'

Badger's heavy black eyebrows knitted into a tight frown. 'You haven't lost a hand since you got the deal,' he said darkly.

Fox's smile did not waver but the twinkle in his eyes vanished, extinguished like embers in a flash flood. 'Are you implying something, old boy,' he whispered, the rhythm of the shuffling of the cards beneath his fingers unbroken.

Vixen caught the change in mood. 'No fighting now,' she interrupted them.

'Deal the cards,' Badger ordered gruffly.

Fox placed the shuffled deck on the baize and Badger cut them in a boorish fashion. Fox began dealing the cards with his usual customary opening flourish when a sharp double rap on the door stilled his paw.

Badger checked his pocket watch. 'Callers at this time of night?' he muttered.

Vixen crossed to the door and eased it open, and the fur on the back of Fox's neck rose and his eyes turned to ice.

'What's the name of this game?' Urban Fox demanded as he swaggered into the room.

'What's it to you?' Weasel sneered.

'Heard there was a game on. But if my money is too rich for you...?' Urban Fox let the challenge hang in the air.

Fox's eyes took on a calculating look and he forced himself to relax, drawing his paw away from the silver-topped cane. 'Pull up a chair,' he said evenly.

Urban Fox dragged a chair across the floor and rested his elbows on the table before lifting a pawful of crumpled banknotes from his pocket.

'A tidy sum,' Fox commented.

Urban Fox detected the trace of sarcasm in Fox's tone, and the long scar on his face shone bone-white against the flush on his cheeks. 'Can you match it?' he snapped.

Fox reached into the pocket of his waistcoat and produced two tight rolls of brand new twenty pound notes.

'Let's play,' Badger ordered.

Fox placed the shuffled deck in front of Urban Fox. 'Cut,' he said, his voice full of challenge and loathing.

Urban Fox matched Fox by dividing the deck with an air of nonchalant disinterest. Fox dealt. The cards fanned and clicked and the pot rustled and chinked. Urban Fox won easily, displaying a keen eye and hidden instinct for the right play. The pile of notes in front of him grew as he turned the game his way. Fox sat and watched as his earlier gained winnings steadily shrank.

'My luck must be in,' Urban Fox gloated as he drew another large pot towards his chair.

'So it would seem,' Fox answered. He had no intention of allowing the newcomer to ruffle him.

Weasel dealt and Fox opened a hand that made his heart jump. He froze his features, forcing himself to appear neutral. Badger was tentatively exchanging one card, obviously looking for the one to complete a run or a full house. Weasel refused to even enter the game, throwing his cards face down and proceeding instead to roll a cigarette. Fox swivelled his eyes towards his main antagonist, only to find himself the subject of study.

'Good hand?' Urban Fox smiled cunningly.

Fox kept his features neutral. 'You'll have to find out,' he countered.

Badger opened the pot with two pound coins, his lips pursed into a thin line, and then capitulated as Urban Fox covered his bet with a ten-pound note. 'Too rich for my blood,' he muttered.

Fox cocked an eyebrow at his adversary and Urban Fox's scarred top lip curled into a sneer. 'Too rich for you as well?' Urban Fox challenged.

Fox drew a heavy breath, as if dealing with a particularly dim-witted student, and then carefully placed a crisp twenty-pound note into the kitty. 'Rich?' he queried, feigning confusion.

Urban Fox hesitated for only a fraction of a second and then he doubled the stake. 'Forty pounds.'

The tension in the small room became as taut as a bowstring

as the two canines eyes locked across the table. The ash from Weasel's cigarette fell unnoticed into his lap. Vixen stood like a statue at Fox's shoulder, her whiskers twitching nervously. Badger's eyes stared at the growing pile of money.

'Let battle commence,' Fox said, with the trace of a smile. 'One hundred pounds.'

Vixen went pale as her paw flew to her mouth. Weasel pinched the cigarette from his lips.

'It's supposed to be a friendly game, lads,' he cautioned. 'A bit of fun, that's all.'

Urban Fox smiled lazily. 'I couldn't be having more fun if I tried,' he said. 'Two hundred pounds.'

Badger hardly dared breathe. Weasel leant forward, his attention riveted on the play the aloof Fox would make.

Fox slipped the rubber band from the second roll of twenties and peeled off a sheaf of notes. He struck a Swan Vesta on the edge of the table and held the flame to the end of a fresh Monte Cristo. He stared at his rival's money over the end of the cheroot as he fanned the match dead, and then dropped four hundred pounds into the kitty.

Vixen's mouth fell open.

So did Weasel's.

Urban Fox glanced up at the waxen Vixen. 'I think you are going to disappoint the lady' he murmured.

'I never have yet.'

'First time for everything,' Urban Fox murmured again, and he dipped his paw into his waistcoat pocket.

Fifty-pound notes. Ten of them.

'Wonderful finding money in old pockets.' Urban Fox grinned wickedly. 'Five hundred!'

Fox glanced down at his own money. He had tried to frighten the newcomer into throwing in the towel but, as he quickly counted his funds, he knew the reverse had happened. He could not cover the bet. Fox stared hard into Urban Fox's pale yellow eyes, holding the look as he tapped ash into the ashtray.

'It would appear I am short,' he began. 'I'll wager the vixen to see your hand.'

Vixen looked at Fox for one long moment and then she

collapsed into a heap at his feet. Badger and Weasel stared at Fox with eyes like dinner plates.

'Done,' said Urban Fox, and he spread his cards onto the baize.

Badger and Weasel looked from the cards to Fox. Fox swallowed, his throat felt like parchment.

'A good hand,' he complimented his opponent.

Urban Fox spread his paws in a gesture of supreme confidence. 'The best,' he smiled.

General Dembury sat comfortably in the folds of an oxblood leather armchair with a copy of the *Evening Standard* held before him. The Wellington Club was silent save for Sir Montague's customary snoring.

He glanced over the top of the paper towards the figure at the far end of the room. Lord Bartholomew instantly looked away from the General's cold glare.

The General allowed himself a secret smile. He was sure the other man was sweating.

Urban Fox spread his paws in a gesture of supreme confidence. 'The best,' he smiled.

Fox smiled back lazily. The cards his opponent had spread upon the baize were the reason why Urban Fox was so bold.

A royal flush. Spades. The ace seemed to leer up at Fox from the table, the death card laughing at his demise.

Fox opened his hand and studied the cards. 'The best, you say.' He looked into Urban Fox's pale yellow eyes.

'The best,' Urban Fox repeated wickedly.

'I was under the impression,' Fox drawled, 'that a royal flush in hearts was the best, as you call it?'

'Have you got it?' Urban Fox sneered.

'As a matter of fact,' Fox spread his hand upon the baize, 'Yes, I have.'

Weasel let out a whoop of delight and Badger breathed out heavily.

Fox stared hard into his rival's cold eyes. 'Now get out,

guttersnipe,' he snapped, 'and don't ever come back. I shouldn't want to have to give you a third lesson.'

Tom Peterson stood back from the theodolite and stared over the tripod into the trees. He pushed his cap to the back of his head and scratched at his brow before pressing his eye to the instrument for a third time. At his side, his foreman was becoming impatient.

'It's like I told you,' he said. 'Somebody is moving the pegs.'

Tom stood straight and stretched his back muscles. 'Looks like it,' he agreed.

The foreman began to grow ever more excited now he had his boss on his side. 'See, I told you,' he raved. 'It's that bloody old woman- what's her name? – Buckshot!'

'Buxton,' Tom corrected him.

'That's the one, interfering old goat!'

'George, don't get carried away,' Tom chided his foreman. 'That old woman is past the age where she could come out here and do this.'

'Not if she came by broomstick!' George Reynolds snapped.

'And the posters?' Tom queried. 'She did that as well, I suppose? No, this is the work of more than one person. Those photographs were proof of that.'

Tom Peterson looked around the wood at his men working beyond the trees.

'I think,' he said, a cruel edge to his voice, 'we have a mole!'

The fourth teacup shattered against the wall and Fox dived for cover behind the settee.

'Bastard!' Vixen shrieked. 'You dare wager me!'

Fox raised his head above the settee. 'Listen, old girl,' he pleaded, before ducking beneath the settee for a second time as the fifth teacup sailed between his ears.

'Don't you "old girl" me,' Vixen shouted as she snatched up another missile. 'You keep your bloody canine neck down or I'll break the bloody thing!'

Fox peeked above the settee. 'May I remind you, my dear, that you also have a canine neck.'

The sixth teacup parted his hair. 'Canine it may be,' Vixen snarled. 'At least it's not as brassy as yours!'

Fox vaulted the settee at the same time as Vixen delved into the cupboards in search of a fresh arsenal. He grabbed her by the wrists and shook a dinner plate from her paws before pinning her against the wall.

'Now steady on, old girl,' he soothed. 'I couldn't have lost you. I had an unbeatable hand.'

'HA!' Vixen sneered, all twitching brush and flashing teeth.

'Really, darling, it was only a ploy.'

'So that's it,' Vixen barked, 'I'm just a ploy now, am I!'

Fox cut short another tirade by crushing Vixen's lips in a fierce kiss. She struggled against his grip until the fight went out of her and she melted against him.

'Better?' Fox asked.

'I hate you,' Vixen whispered.

'I know you do.'

'Bastard,' she hissed, and Fox crushed her lips again.

Douglas opened another of the hundreds of letters of support that had been flooding in since April. This one was much the same as all the others, words of encouragement followed by a small donation. He had been genuinely touched by some of the letters. One had been from a ten-year-old girl who had sent her pocket money for the week.

'It's a good job,' he said to Mary, 'that we don't have to reply to all of these.'

Mary sighed a little. 'I hope it won't all be for nothing.'

'We have right on our side, my dear,' he replied. 'Be confident.'

George Reynolds held the door open with the toe of his boot and stood framed in the open doorway.

'It's one of you,' he seethed, wagging a trembling finger at the confused regulars sitting the length of the bar. 'It's criminal, that's what it is,' he shouted. 'Criminal bloody damage.'

Max pulled his pipe from between his teeth. 'What are you talking about?'

'You know. You know full well,' George Reynolds shouted. 'Well, you won't get away with it. I can assure you of that!' He stormed out into the street and the door slammed behind him.

'What was all that about?' Timothy Dembury mumbled.

'Won't get away with what?' was Alan's question.

'Who was he anyway?' Max wanted to know.

Mortimer had the answer. 'Village idiot probably.'

Fox watched with interest as Mole disappeared beneath the ground, leaving behind a growing mound of soil. Two minutes later Mole stuck his head out of the hole and peered through his thick spectacles at the canine.

'You pull and I'll push,' he ordered.

Fox rested his cane against a towering beech and took hold of the marker peg with both paws. 'Ready when you are, old boy.'

Mole vanished into the hole and a moment later Fox stood with the peg free of the ground.

'Well done, old boy,' he congratulated Mole.

'That's the easy part,' Mole opined. 'Getting it back in the ground will be the tough part.'

'We are equal to the task,' Fox said with an air of confidence. Fox and Mole carried the peg through the trees and Fox selected a spot in the lee of an ancient oak. 'This should do,' he decided.

Mole set to work and Fox did not have long to wait before Mole had excavated a hole he thought deep enough to accommodate the peg. Fox held the peg upright in the hole and Mole began to push the mound of soil back to support it.

'There you are,' Fox declared as the two of them surveyed their handiwork. 'Easy,' and the peg promptly fell to the ground.

Mole looked up as the smile slipped from Fox's face. 'You were saying?'

'Minor setback,' Fox defended himself. 'If at first you don't succeed, old boy.' He inspected the fallen peg before delivering his opinion of what the problem was. 'The hole's not deep enough,' he declared.

'There's nothing wrong with my hole!' Mole bridled.

'Moley, old boy, don't take it so personally. I am merely pointing out that, as splendid as the hole may be, it simply is not deep enough.'

'I notice you're doing no digging,' Mole grumbled.

'Oh Moley, don't be absurd. You are a far better digger than I, and you know it.'

Mole crawled back into the hole, complaining that he was being fed a lot of soft soap, and began to dig deeper. Moments later he reappeared and his manner was intense.

'Fox. I've found something,' he said.

'Something?'

'It's metal, I think.'

'Never mind that, Moley,' Fox said impatiently. 'What about the peg!'

'To hell with the peg,' Mole replied with a look of urgency. 'If this is what I think it is, there won't be any more pegs.'

'Do explain, will you?' Fox asked irritably. He had never been one for riddles.

'Fox! Get me Badger. And quickly! He can dig as well and faster than me,' and Mole vanished into the hole before Fox had time to argue.

Fox returned with Badger within thirty minutes, both of them grumbling about Mole having probably lost his senses, but equally intensely curious as to what Mole could have discovered.

'Moley,' Fox called, and Mole appeared from beneath the ground.

'Ah, Badger.' Mole smiled. 'Start digging here, will you?'

'What's going on?' Badger asked.

'I'm not entirely sure,' Mole replied, 'but if I'm right, this should put paid to all our problems.' And with that Mole dived back into the hole.

Fox and Badger exchanged sidelong glances before Badger shrugged his shoulders and began to enlarge the hole Mole had begun. Fox watched closely as Badger made short work of the task, and soon Mole's voice carried to them from just beneath the surface.

'Steady now, Badger,' he ordered. 'We are almost there.'

'How much further?' Badger queried.

'Just a few inches,' Mole's voice came back.

Badger scraped away at the moist earth until Mole's snout appeared, followed closely by his thick spectacles.

'Dig lengthways,' Mole instructed, and Badger began to dig a long furrow, throwing the dirt behind him into a growing hill, until his claws scratched at hard metal.

Mole and Badger brushed away the last handfuls of soil and the evening sunlight shone for the first time in over a thousand years on the dull metal.

'I was right,' Mole gloated.

The three of them stared at the long-buried relic in silence until Badger put into words what they were all thinking, and his voice was almost a whisper. 'SPQR. It's Roman. If there are more of these, they will never be allowed to lay a motorway through here.'

'Precisely,' Mole agreed.

Fox dragged his eyes from the ancient standard and looked at Badger. 'I will let Jennifer know,' he said. 'This is a godsend.'

Badger had to agree. 'Well done, Mole,' he said, and Mole glowed with pride.

'Yes.' Fox joined in the congratulations. 'Jolly well done, Moley.'

'Wonderful.' Mole beamed. 'Just wonderful.'

The flashbulbs popped and the cameramen called, 'Face this way, please.'

Douglas helped Jennifer to hold the ancient standard upright as she sat on his lap and grinned at the cameras. Her smile had a gap from where two of her milk teeth had fallen out and it gave her an impish appearance.

'The Tooth Fairy left fifty pee,' she told the journalists, something which she felt sure was of much more importance.

The *Daily Mail* wanted to know how Jennifer had found the standard.

'Mr Fox showed me,' she told them, and the siege was over without a shot being fired.

Jennifer's toothy smile was all over the papers the following day, and within the week Fox had shown a copy to Badger.

'I think we are going to win this one,' Badger decided confidently.

Lord Dembury of Wixley, General Charles Randolph Tobias Dembury, MC, rose from the red leather benches and drew himself to his full height before passing his gaze around their assembled lordships, and his eyes resembled the twin barrels of one of his favourite shotguns as they came to rest on the corpulent figure of Lord Bartholomew seated on the opposite side of the House.

Lord Dembury waited, judging the moment when he would have the House's undivided attention and their lordships hanging onto his every word; and when he judged the time to be right, his voice was low and dignified. The archaeological excavations at Wixley Wood were daily revealing new finds of undoubted historical value, he told them, and how even as he spoke some of the nation's foremost historians were acclaiming the discovery as the greatest find concerning Roman Britain for centuries.

Lord Dembury carried on, his voice gathering speed, until his eyes burned like hot coals and his silver whiskers bristled as he swung into the peroration.

'The identity of a nation, its very soul, is encapsulated in its history. The passing down from generation to generation of its triumphs and achievements, of its progress and advancement towards it present civilisation, is its lifeblood. I use the word progress because I am in favour of progress, of advancement. However, not at the expense of great historical value.'

Across the room Rupert Bartholomew began to look like a man who knew when he was beaten. His shoulders slumped and his chins rested on his chest as he listened to the General drawing to his inevitable conclusion.

'The proposed laying of a motorway through Wixley Wood

would undoubtedly destroy for ever a site of national interest and importance, a record of this island's history and a testimony to the development of our people. My Lords, there must be no motorway through Wixley Wood.'

Fox sat hidden behind the rotting bark of a fallen log and watched the devoted labouring of the archaeologists as they probed carefully amongst the artefacts that were being gradually drawn from the depths of history.

The excavations already measured a hundred yards square and the area was cordoned off with red and white tape which hung motionless in the sweltering noonday heat. Fox dabbed the sweat from his brow as the bare-chested archaeologists toiled in the deepening pit.

A small crowd of onlookers had gathered at the far side of the excavations, and Fox picked Jennifer and her mother out from amongst them. He raised himself above the log and lifted his cane above his head, and the silver tip caught the sunlight. He watched as Jennifer detached herself from her mother's side and made her way around the red and white tape and headed in his direction.

Jennifer sat on the log and gave Fox her brightest smile. Fox winked up at her in return.

'Any news, Jenny?' he asked.

'Lots and lots, Mr Fox.'

'Do tell, my dear.'

'Daddy says that there isn't going to be a motorway after all because Susan was on the telly meeting the Queen,' Jennifer replied, letting her imagination run away with her. 'And Mr. Lord Dembury went to London and he said No as well, and so your home will be all right.'

Fox smiled. 'That's splendid news, Jenny.'

'Will you tell your friends?'

'I shall tell them all,' Fox replied. 'Badger will be most impressed.' Fox peeped over the log as Mary Cobden approached. 'I had best be going,' he decided, but Jennifer had other ideas.

'My mummy can be your friend as well, Mr Fox,' she said. 'She wants to meet you.'

'I am not so sure, my dear,' Fox answered tentatively.

'She's very nice, Mr Fox. She won't hurt you,' and Jennifer's almost pleading tone struck a chord in Fox's heart.

'Very well, but only for a short while,' he said, and he waited nervously for Mary to cover the short distance to where he sat.

Mary's shadow fell across the log and Fox's courage almost deserted him, so that he flinched and turned as if to flee, but Jennifer's soft whisper stayed his flight.

'Mummy, this is Mr Fox,' and Fox looked up at Mary Cobden.

Mary said nothing, enchanted as she was by the magic of the moment, until she was prompted by her daughter.

'Say hello, Mummy.'

Mary stood quite still and her voice came in a low whisper calculated not to frighten the fox. 'Hello, Mr Fox,' she said.

Fox stood equally still, not trusting himself to speak, and then Jennifer reached out a small hand and stroked his brow with a gentle palm.

'It's all right, Mr Fox,' she assured him. 'Mummy won't hurt you.'

Mary could hardly believe what she was seeing as the fox nuzzled her daughter's hand and then raised its right paw.

'Shake,' Jennifer said as she took the fox's paw in her hand, and then the fox turned and trotted away into the wood.

'He's lovely, isn't he?' Mary smiled.

Jennifer nodded. 'He's my friend.'

Mary lifted her daughter into the saddle and held the bridle as Jennifer rode Grey Lady back across the fields.

Douglas waved to them from beneath the flock of seagulls that were following the tractor, and Susan came at the canter from the direction of Little Wixley. She was in buoyant mood.

'Isn't it wonderful?' she greeted them. 'It's all over now.'

Mary shielded her eyes from the dazzling sun as she smiled up at her niece. 'That's what Mr Fox says as well,' she said, and Jennifer laughed so hard she almost fell from the saddle.

Epilogue

November

The chimes of Big Ben rang solemnly out over the heads of the quiet crowds lining the route the long parade would take.

General Dembury stood with his chin held high and his back straight, his body in total harmony with his mood. The General glanced down over his groomed moustache and the row of medals sparkled against the chill winter's morning.

Reveille rang out, bright and full of life, like a new dawn, and the General heard again the words of Winston Churchill echo through his memory.

'We shall fight in France...'

Her Majesty stepped forward and laid the nation's tribute, the blood red of the poppies respectful against the cold grey of the proud monument.

'We shall fight on the seas and oceans...'

The flags hung motionless as the wreath was followed by more of the same.

'We shall defend our island, whatever the cost may be...'

Dark clouds rolled low and sombre over the hushed London streets.

'We shall fight on the beaches...'

'We shall fight in Wixley as well.' The General allowed himself a tight smile.

The band played, mournful and serene.

'We shall fight on the landing grounds...'

And the first sharp pain lanced through the General's heart. 'What on earth!...'

The officer's salute was as sharp as a skinner's knife.

'We shall fight in the fields and in the streets...'

A band of steel tightened around the old General's chest. 'Good God, Dembury, brace up!...'

The guardsmen stood, silent and sentinel.

'We shall fight in the hills...'

The furled umbrella slipped from the tired General's nerveless grip.

A file of black coats bowed their heads in reverence.

'We shall never surrender...'

And the cold hard ground rushed towards the General's dimming vision.

Heavy rain drummed against a sea of black umbrellas on the day Alwyn led the sorrowful cortège slowly out of the ancient church and between the headstones towards the freshly dug grave.

Lady Dembury leaned on her son's arm, her black veil hiding her reddened eyes, and the rain poured a thousand tears down the smooth polished sides of her husband's oaken coffin.

Max stood beneath a wide umbrella, its bone handle held in his cold, sad hand, and the coffin was lowered into the wet earth.

Alwyn sprinkled dirt onto the coffin from the edge of the grave. 'Ashes to ashes, dust to dust.'

Douglas bowed his head, his lips clamped into a tight, grieving line.

Nobody noticed the damp fox beyond the flint wall pad quietly away.

June

'I pronounce you man and wife.' Alwyn's face broke into a beaming smile and Alan lifted the long fresh veil and placed a deep kiss on Susan's full red lips.

Jennifer sat on the top of her father's shoulders and threw handfuls of confetti into the dazzling sunshine, and the ornate coach swayed as Alan lifted his wife up onto the bright red upholstery.

The liveried coachman shook up the reins and the white pony cantered away, its hooves clattering on the winding road, leaving behind the joyfully called wishes of the small country village.

August

Liam Murphy had packed all his worldly possessions into a single duffel bag, left his room in a tidy fashion, and crept out of the house as the first grey streaks of dawn had spread across Blackthorn Estate.

It was an hour before the driver of the lorry pulled over and asked him where he was going.

'Thought I'd try my luck in London.'

'You're in luck,' the driver replied. 'Jump in.'

The driver put the vehicle into gear and the long articulated lorry pulled away. From the raised cab Liam could see the first lights coming on in Blackthorn House.

December

The storm. Always the storm. Black clouds, heavy with the coming rain, blocked out the weak light from the late December moon, and a wind with an edge like a knife lifted the mist from the river and blew it through the dark and silent streets of Little Wixley.

Tom Dixon spurred his mount across the village green, and the wind whipped the tricorn from his head.

He used the reins to lash at the stallion's withers, and the hoofbeats clattered across the old stone bridge and echoed from the cottage walls. The hoofbeats, as always, had faded to nothing before they reached the end of Busjibber Lane.